The McLoughlin Correspondents

With great affection: Letters between a brother and sister during the fur trade era

For Mr. Yale who inherited the future these people lived in a past era

The McLoughlin Correspondents

With great affection: Letters between a brother and sister during the fur trade era

Betty Donaldson

ATHENA PRESS
LONDON

ISBN 1 84401 749 4

First Published 2006 by
ATHENA PRESS
Queen's House, 2 Holly Road
Twickenham TW1 4EG
United Kingdom

Printed for Athena Press

*Dedicated to all who contributed
to the development of this book. Their interests, enthusiasms,
and talents enriched the dialogue. Thank you.*

Mary McLoughlin.
Courtesy of le Monastère des Ursulines de Québec.

John McLoughlin.
Courtesy of Glenbow Museum.

An introduction to Dr. John McLoughlin and Sr. St. Henri

One morning in the late 1930s, a woman opened an old secretary desk while cleaning a house her father had inherited. Inside she discovered a packet of old letters. They had been written nearly a century earlier by members of her family. Standing in the manor house built on a seigneury estate that had been in her family since the 1760s, this Quebec matron recognized their importance. They were not just family history. They were fragments of the life and times of people who had played important roles during the fur trade era when British colonial Canada and the United States were defining boundaries and Europe was recovering from the Napoleonic Wars. Written during a span of many years and sent across the continent, these fragile documents were proofs of enduring family bonds and shared adult interests.

About fifteen years later, an old leather-bound letter book was purchased from a sheep rancher in Michigan. Some of the hand-copied letters were duplicated in the archives of the Hudson's Bay Company (HBC) in Winnipeg, but others were not. They provided fascinating glimpses into the daily management of an international corporation, one of the first to transcend oceans and continents. More recently, the undelivered letters of fur trade employees stored in the archives have been published. They reveal a daily life quite different from the gentlemen officers and directors of the company.

Letters were frequently lost or destroyed. It took two years for a cycle of letters to be exchanged because the annual canoe brigade went east during the mid Summer and returned west the following Spring. Thus, personal letters usually were written throughout the Fall and Winter and sent during the Spring–Summer cycles. Concerns and congratulations were responded to during the next Fall and Winter but, at intense times, exchanges overlapped or were lost. Letters were, therefore, cherished mementos, read and reread many times, excerpts shared with others, and, in part, they were essays about life itself. Business letters might be sent with various groups of Indians who moved between posts and sometimes by horse or ship but the cycle of personal letters was a more slow rotation unless carrying news of a crisis. Such private and public letters help reclaim a shared human heritage because they are markers salvaged from what has been lost.

The following letters are fictional, but based upon many exchanges between a brother and sister during his years in the fur trade of Canada and her years as an Ursuline nun in the convent at Quebec City. This is the story of Dr. John McLoughlin, Chief Factor of the Hudson Bay Company and his sister, Mary McLoughlin, Mère St. Henri of the Ursuline Order of Sisters. As adults, this brother and sister wrote letters to each other for more than forty years. Completely bilingual, they often inserted common French, English or Latin phrases into their communications. Eventually the brother and sister evolved distinguished careers. He became known as the "Father of Oregon" and she was venerated as the most admired Mother Superior since Marie de l'Incarnation founded the *Ville de Quebec* convent in the 1600s. Early years are often formative ones and decisions made during that period become the foundation for decisions in later life. Their background included life in the early days of newly acquired British colonies that became the nation of Canada. Both were well educated for their times and they also had good social connections in a colony that did not yet have representative government. Thus, their interests included religion, politics, governance of their own establishments, family, and their own affairs. Their discussions reflect these diverse interests and talents.

Most of the time, daily life moved at a pace quite distanced from international affairs although issues might be debated extensively during long evenings. The annual fur trade rendez-vous meeting included a business agenda at which important decisions were made and individual employment contracts signed. It also provided a social reunion during which marriages and alliances were formed or terminated. The annual cycle of the

Ursuline convent was regulated by religious observances, the school year, and events in the colony that surrounded it. The cadence and rhythm of lives were shaped by the emergence of modern society just as ours are being forged by postmodern pressures. Messages from the past remind us that under a triumphant banner of progress, much that we value may get trampled.

Skilled trackers reconstruct an entire narrative from footprints, bent branches, and dropped spore. The following letters are fiction; the people and events are not. These letters have been organized into three major sections: The early years; evolving challenges, and the final cycle. A prologue and an epilogue provide background information about the family, and the preceding and successive generations. A glossary of italicized French terms and an appendix of research resources put into context some phrases and sources for interested readers.

John McLoughlin's geographic and cultural worlds from birth near Riviere du-Loup, 1784, to death at Oregon City (near Ft. Vancouver) 1857

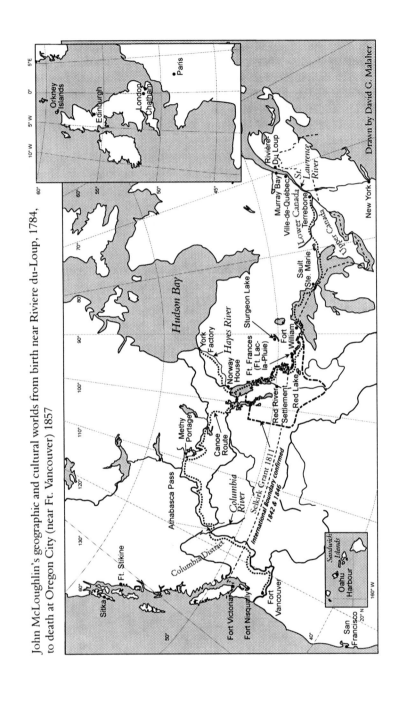

Drawn by David G. Malaher

Exterior view of the Ursuline Convent, Québec City. Courtesy of le Monastère des Ursulines de Québec.

Contents

I: The Early Years, 1803–1816

During the early years of his career, John McLoughlin moved between trading forts not far from Lake Superior in territory beyond colonial Canada, while Sister St. Henri was cloistered within convent walls in the rapidly growing *Ville de Quebec*. This time period, 1803–1816, included momentous events that eventually affected this brother and sister profoundly. Napoleon was fighting for his empire; Victoria, future Empress of the British Empire, was a newborn princess. France had just lost control of a continent and American republicans were extending their ambitions beyond the borders of the original states of the Union.

The fur trade was an ascendant profitable business. Montreal-based North Westerners (NWC) won local battles with the Hudson's Bay Company (HBC) in the *pays d'en haut*, but lost the war for dominance of the Indian Territories. By the end of this period, the continent had been traversed by Alexander MacKenzie and surveyed by David Thompson. The Pacific coasts were contested international waterways with Russian, Spanish, English and American ships seeking ports in the region, interacting with skilled Indian navigators in canoes.

West of Lake Superior, there were no missionaries and no magistrates except for businessmen appointed by distant British authorities. White women were absent, thus social life at a fur trading fort comprised the gentlemen officers of the companies, their *voyageur* crews and laborers, aboriginal trapping families, and Indian or half-breed women who became country wives of the white men. From this melange, the *Metis* emerged, mixed-blood descendants who claimed nationhood for their people.

Glimpses of these dramatic events are portrayed in the letters that Dr. John McLoughlin and his sister, Marie Louise, Sister Saint Henri exchanged during the first thirteen years of their careers as they passed through their second decade of life to the third.

1804/5, Written from the High Country during the Winter, for mailing Spring/Summer of 1805 to Quebec

My beloved sister,

Your letter arrived with the Summer brigade from Montreal and I have carried it with me to my remote trading cabin. It is a welcome voice from a more civilized world than mine. Both of us have chosen paths of intense commitment but the destinations are very different. Although I hope to yet escape from this vast wintry imprisonment, each day, each month, is dedicated to the God of Mammon. Sheltered behind the tidy stone walls of your religious community, your daily routines are marked more by tinkling bells calling you to prayer than by the changing seasons. As you study the Spring green of the shady trees in your cloistered garden, think of me, tramping along muddy traplines in rolling hills far from home. After we have collected the pelts, we paddle and trek to Fort Kaministiquia for the Summer *régale*.

I become more doctor than trader clerk during this great rendezvous. Everyone who comes to the fort seems to have some medical problem for which I provide some advice before we all scatter again to our distant traplines and hibernate like the animals. By August, our celebrations and meetings are all concluded because Mother Nature has forces greater than any colonial power. We must be safely tucked into our cabins with traps set in their waterway hiding spots before the deep frosts come. In a few weeks, this letter will travel with the loaded canoes going East after the rendezvous. I imagine you sitting and reading it in your lovely large convent home surrounded by blazing red leaves.

We have a sort of maple tree here but it is different from Murray Bay, Riviére-du-Loup, and *Ville de Quebec*. Salt water is very far off. Here at the edges of the Great Lakes we have fresh water with few large meadows that could be cultivated as easily as those along the St. Lawrence. I do not think you could understand how very big are some of the lakes that we traverse. *Lac Supérieure* is more wide in the center than the breadth of the salty Saint Lawrence near grandfather's manor. Men do not light fires on *levées* to signal messages across watery expanses here. No, the long and dark months are a silent sleeping time. We read during the brief daylight hours. We repair equipment. Some visit with the Indians and form relations with their women. I do not think it is more cold than Quebec, just more lonely. At home, travel a few days and one finds companionship. Here, travel a few weeks in any direction, whether by snowshoe or canoe, and your companions remain the dog, the rabbit, the beaver family, and other such wild animals like the deer. We do not yet know the boundaries of this unknown continent. Although the Pacific Ocean is on the other side of the Rocky Mountains, some rivers begin to flow southward not far from where we trap. Our preferred routes take us north because the furs are better.

When the breezes whisper of Spring promises, the curtain lifts on a great drama. By middle April, the lakes shake off their icy mantles. In one day if the wind is in the right direction, bustards arrive in great flocks, forming dark fast-moving clouds in an otherwise blue sky. Fresh trout and pickerel are very tasty after a diet of dried-out supplies. In Summer the blueberries are much larger than at home. In September, native women harvest *ma-no-mum*, a dark rice growing in shallow lakes where the bottoms are sandy and muddy.

This is the stage on which I have a small part! It is Act One for us – who knows whether there will be Act Two, or Act Three. Within your smaller setting, you take a larger role, nurturing a shimmering soul. I scarcely know the geographical horizons of my world but I fear that my soul will wither. The most vicious animals I confront are the other escapees from the civilized world. They bring with them, as did I, all the unfinished turmoils of their past. We clash and butt like stags in heat. Animals fight for natural procreation rights. We do it for money. There is no law but what we brought with us, and since we are mostly Scots, French, English and *sauvage,* with a few Europeans to spice the mix, there is little order except that of monetary wealth, physical strength, and presentation with wit. Then there is the new species: the American, who purports to have thrown off all the shackles of civilization while freeing the ideals. These individuals, and individual they are, are not so enlightened as they are adventurous. There is a raw courage that ebbs out. Like iron, it is hard and somewhat brittle, but the strength has a force not to be ignored.

Those of us born here, like the Canadians, wonder which shall prove the greater threat. Is it the British merchants who enter the fur trade from Hudson's Bay in the North or the shrewd Republican Yankee traders who negotiated the Louisiana territory from Napoleon for $27 million? I know it is not our French or Irish forebears whose blood flows in our veins, nor even the *nouveaux riche* Scots of Upper and Lower Canada. They are hardy but too few in number.

Arterial blood is red; venous blood is blue. The heart cleanses each and beats out the rhythm of life. What songs do our hearts beat, dearest sister? You say your daily office in the French tongue but are just as proficient in English, with an Irish infusion, of course. I do my daily chores using English and Scottish, French and some Chipweyan and Latin, for medical problems. Your faithful heart is quickened by Catholic anointment. Mine is unshriven.

What would our family mentors tell us? Grandfather Malcolm Fraser's voice would not hesitate. Loyalty to the clan is first, foremost and fairest. Our motto: "*Je suis preste*." Father's Irish lilt would advocate for self-control and virtue. Mother would have a quieter caution – to love and to be civil. As for the uncles, well I need not imagine one of them. I can hear Uncle Alexander shout from where I write: "Live the moment well. Take a country wife rather than suffer a cold bed and lonely days. Do not do all the daily labor yourself. Her presence may save your life as well as soften it." In fact, that is exactly what he has done, so we three sinners live argumentatively in a little cabin in the quiet woods. I understand better now what our mother meant when she advised us to Summer with the Scots, for they relish the grand out-of-doors, but Winter with the Irish because their stories and songs make any warm hearth more lively. Eat French style and, when disputing, use English law.

In this *pays d'en haut* we eat dried pemmican prepared by Indians. We drink Scots whisky or rum so watered it barely flames in the fire. We fight like the Irish; that is to say, to exhaustion but not to victory. We party and repent like the jolly French, engage our wits in duels with British competitors and wonder whether we would be better off as Republican free traders. Our lakeside trading post will soon belong to America anyway because it is too far south.

In Summer, I doctor, there being no other except a drunkard for thousands of miles although illnesses travel rather well wherever human bodies are to be found. In Winter, I am an apprentice clerk for the Montrealers, making rich men more prosperous. Uncle Simon Fraser sits in Terrebonne, among wealthy merchants while I labor like an indentured servant to keep those *bourgeois* in the style to which they have become accustomed. I long to be riding beside you in a *calèche* on our way to a grand *soirée*. It is small comfort to realize that the path you freely chose denies you those pleasures also.

I ask for verification of how the promises Mssrs. McTavish, Frobisher & Co. made to me by Simon McTavish, the recently deceased "Marquis," will be kept. If I Winter next at Kaministiquia where William McGillivray is expanding the fort, perhaps he will honor oral promises made to me by his uncle from whom he inherited the mantle of leadership. Sister, listen to powerful men talk, observe their actions as signs of character, but watch most closely what they commit to paper. While I have mastered many new skills, this is the primary lesson I now have learned as apprentice clerk in the fur trade.

My best wishes to you, to our father, mother, and sisters, to *notre* seigneur Colonel Fraser, and any others who might remember this wandering soul.

With great affection,

Yr brother, John McLoughlin

Fort William 27 July 1807

My Dear Father and Mother —

It was with a good deal of Disappointment that at the return of the [?] I received no letters from You, I rather think that they have miscarried than that you should forget me so soon nor am I conscious of saying any thing in Mine that could force you to act so towards me —

I pass'd a dull Winter of it last Year — but hope It will be better this Year I am astonish'd to find that my Sister is Married In Your Last You only said that such thing might happen — although she can [?] she has not done it Yes — How does my Grand father, my Uncles John and Cornelius come on I hope they are very Well Is my Uncle Alexander making great Improvements at Rivière du Loup — When does Mr Stewart Leave before As I have no News of Importance to mention To You so must remain wishing You a Pleasant Winter and good health In the mean time I remain

Honor'd Father and Mother
Your Affectionate Son
John McLoughlin

A letter from John McLoughlin to his parents.

Mon Cher papa et ma Chere Maman.

J'ai reçu votre lettre daté du 18 fevrier qui m'a fait beaucoup
de plaisir, qui m'apprand que vous vous porté bien, ainsi que
Maman, et mon Cher Grand pere, et mes Cheres Grandes mieres,
et toûte la famille, pour moi je me porte fort bien et je goute
avec plaisire mon bonheur, je n'ai point pris l'halit le 21 comme
je devois, la mort de la mere St Augustin en a été la cause
je suis remis pour le 27 du mois, ainsi je ne puis vous dire ancore
le nom que je porterai, le retour de ma grand mere me procurera
j'espure une occasion favorable pour lcrire, et vous serez j'une
flatte persuadé de la tendre affection que j'ai et que j'aurai toujour,
croiez moi avec les Sentimets les plus sinceres pénétré d'un profond
Respect avec lequel je suis

Des Ursulines de Quebec
ce 24 Fevrier; 1798.

Votre tres humble et tres
Obeissante fille et Servante.
Marie McLoughlin,
Postulante.

Jean et David se porté bien il trouve le voiage de ma Grande mere
un peut trop long, et moi en mon particulier j'en pense quil serais long
tems quelle fut de retour

A letter from Mary McLoughlin to her parents.
Courtesy of le Monastère des Ursulines de Québec.

*1805, From the Ursuline Convent, Quebec, in the Fall
season, for carrying by canoe brigade in May 1806 to the West*

Beloved bro. Jean,

Your letter has been opened, read, folded, reopened and reread so
very many times. It is like conversing with you, a joy that I much
miss. Little did David, you, and I dream, during those sunny
childhood days at Mount Murray, that a time would come when
we would not see each other for months, years, possibly never
again. We now all seem destined for quite different futures. Jean,
you are so very far away. Further than the *coureur de bois* of the old
regime. For them, their adventures didn't go much further than
what are now settled farms. It takes weeks of hard paddling to
reach your cabin – if the weather is favorable. You visit unmapped
landscapes, making them more familiar, bringing some
civilization with you, although your purpose is the trading of furs
for household supplies and trinkets.

   Our brother David visited me regularly this Winter. He does
well in his medical apprenticeship, but misses your protective
mantle. An older brother provides wisdom and support. David
dreams of traveling to Scotland for further study as a surgeon
because there is no training available here excepting Dr. Fisher's
medical office. I suspect David also wants opportunity to visit the
Lord Lovat estates that Grandfather's stories have so immortalized
in our minds. Dr. Fisher asks after you, his other apprentice, and
wonders what type of Summer practice you have established. He
and David both think you will have memorized your entire
library by now. We are certain that your employer will provide
you with all necessary supplies but the lack of consultation with
others who have diagnostic experience must make some decisions
difficult. Dr. Fisher requests that you write and tell him what you
think is cause and what is effect of the diseases you observe. Do

remember that God will be listening to your questions and He also hears our prayers asking Him to guide you.

Mother and the wee sisters are well. Honorée is still in school but the others are courting. Uncle Joseph is the senior family member but Father does the real work of managing the seigneuries at Rivière du Loup. He brings regular news of our family when he comes for Catholic Mass followed, of course, by an Irish evening of song at the tavern. Grandpa Fraser spends the Winter in the *Ville de Quebec* and Summers at Mount Murray Manor.

I am not certain Grandfather will ever be reconciled to the idea that the majority of his descendants will be of the Catholic faith because it is the majority faith of women here. He lost a grand battle within the family when I made my profession of faith within the Holy Catholic Church. I had the fine example of our own mother's profession of faith after she attended our Ursuline school for girls. Our mother had the good example of her mother who was born into the faith, there being no alternative during the French regime. Religious teaching is absorbed with the milk seeping from a mother's breast, just as Christ Himself was suckled at His Mother's breast.

Grandfather Malcolm seems more concerned about protecting the properties he has acquired than about the daily cultivation of his soul. The English have taken legal ownership of all Jesuit property and the land titles to our Ursuline House of Nouvelle France properties will be reviewed. Grandfather is registered as a Presbyterian on all official records, even though it is considered a dissenting Protestant religion among the British. He joins the fight to have a kirk established very near our Convent. The new Church of England cathedral will be built directly across from our house to reinforce its favored position in society. Grandfather is active in other disputes as well. As Colonel, he maintains regimental loyalties, claiming he is ready to fight again should the occasion warrant and is more soldier than seigneur, unlike his bosom friend, Mr. Nairne. The English language becomes linked to Protestantism doctrine and the French language to the Roman Catholic faith. I do not think it need be so, but that is how the battlements are being drawn up in the capital of Lower Canada.

We live our daily lives within a French land usage tradition and an English system of law and order, all managed by Scots. The highest positions of governance are, of course, held by English gentlemen from across the ocean. There is a possibility for evolving a society that represents the best of all these cultures but civilized men seldom demonstrate only their best possible qualities. Their character is all too often an unfortunate chaos of best and worst traits. Younger brother, do not neglect your spiritual life, regardless of any vast fur trader domain. Reflect upon the wilderness that is within your soul for surely it holds possibilities for cultivating and reaping the greatest harvest of all.

Our Scots-Irish-French blood beats through my body and makes me strong. However, neither the anger of Grandfather Fraser nor the power of British law could thwart the union I feel with God. This mystic connection is the essential difference between Catholic and Protestant. As a seventeen-year-old novitiate, when I took the veil, I was preparing to take final vows of service to God if I were worthy. My vows have married me to Christ. I strive to feel His Presence daily so that my own life is more enlightened. Protestants have a more pragmatic Christian faith. In remembrance of His holy example, they demonstrate their beliefs by positive actions toward those less advantaged. Regardless of whether a life radiates from a Holy Light within or whether charitable attitudes lighten the lives of the unfortunate, it is love that illuminates our souls. I know, as do you, of many whose lives are not so very ennobled. But the interior darkness of so many souls makes my daily duties more necessary.

Indians living in these lands when the first colonists arrived share a luminous understanding of the Holy Spirit. Nearly two hundred years ago illustrious founder Mère Marie de l'Incarnation came from France to serve in a remote setting, surely not very different from the *pays d'en haut* in which you now wander. *En songe*, Mère Marie envisioned a vast mountainous land in which she was to establish a school for girls, including the *filles sauvages* (a much less harsh phrase in French than in English). In France, among the students in the convent at Tours, she had already met a Micmac child so she had an example of what might be possible in this new world. In her letters to our Mother House,

Mère Marie wrote about her eager students: "*Elles sont si souples*. They so easily adapt to our lessons. They sing, they sew, they read and write, in their own languages as well as French." Most important of all, they returned to their villages as very good Christians who influenced their husbands and communities through their inner spiritual life, their wise advice, and their demeanor. Mère Marie wrote a sacred history and prepared catechisms and prayers for her students. She observed that these girls did not survive well when enclosed permanently with us, but they could maintain divine communication with God when they had their customary freedom and some support. It is not just men who have mentors. The writings of Marie de l'Incarnation still inspire us to make the world more civilized through study and prayer.

As a consequence of such sustained devotion, in spite of the British victory, our religious community has grown to thirty *religieuses professes* although none are Indian. All nuns take the three vows of chastity, poverty, and obedience. The fourth vow that Ursuline Sisters make is to educate young girls. We now board young girls as full-time *pensionnaires* and they come from many backgrounds, including fur traders' daughters. A few are day students, *les externes*. As we enlarge their minds, we elevate their souls. During the early centuries, Ursuline nuns eventually impressed dangerous Iroquois and therefore we now hope to influence the even more dangerous English.

Elisabeth Dougherty (*Soeur St. Augustine*) and I have become the first English-language instructors in our school, thereby satisfying the new law that commands all schools to have such type of language instruction. Although our Community might absorb some English, it will never become Protestant, in spite of the politics of Anglican Bishop Mountain. For the past five years, my dear friend Monsignor Plessis has been permitted to be the *Surintendant de l'église romaine* but he is not anointed as Bishop of Quebec. I doubt the English will ever relinquish any senior appointment or legal jurisdiction that affects religion; nevertheless the French will hold to their language, and thereby their souls. In Quebec we do not have religious peace but Ursuline sisters sustain the religious sentiment. My life commitment to the

Catholic faith, and that of our own mother, testify the power of the divine Spirit.

I think I am more deeply married to my God of Love than you are to your God of Mammon! As a Catholic nun, I experience the mystical body of Christ. I feel his presence as strongly as I sometimes can see your face. There is a difference in this passion. His is unchanging and eternal, so much greater than the brief span of a single human life. When next we meet, dear brother, you will note changes in my face and demeanor and I in yours. But the visage of God never ages – He is for all time, all ages. Like you and me, Christ was in his twenties when he began to apply his talents. Unlike you and me, two sinners who must work for salvation, His sacrificial work was finished when He was but a young man. Our souls are not so pure and elevated but our contributions will be evidence of faithful service. May you serve God more industriously than your employers for His contract with you is for eternity.

Marie-Louise, *Soeur Saint Henri*, o.s.u.

1806, Written at the Lac La Pluie depot during Winter for delivery East the following Summer

Ma chère soeur,

This Winter I am posted to Rainy Lake, having acquired some reputation for administration during the building of Fort William. Perhaps our childhood Summers in the seigneuries of Quebec were a deeper form of apprenticeship than the years I spent with Dr. Fisher. Like Dr. Munro, my predecessor in this Godless country, I have become more acquainted with the subtleties of the fur trade than the new discoveries of medicine. One obvious lesson is that the numbers of patients is worth less than the numbers of furs to the company. Also, the numbers of furs benefit the NWC senior partners much more than those contracted to clerk as traders with the Indians in the Wintering meeting places. I long to leave this desolate place but fear my prospects are even more limited in Lower Canada.

Kaministiquia is renamed Fort William in honor of William McGillivray, newly appointed Director of the North West Company. McGillivray was the first senior trading partner to live a full year in the outer regions, he is *un homme du Nord,* like all who Winter here. Now that my assignment takes me to Lac La Pluie beyond the Great Lakes, so am I. *Je suis un homme du nord* is entry to an exclusive fraternity of which I now am a member. Of course our northmen joust with the canoemen who paddle the eastern routes, calling them *mangeurs du lard* because their routes are shorter and closer to tables of good food. Their fistfights and skill contests improve performance in ways that assist profits, and sometimes keep me busy as doctor. Little restrains the *voyageur* except his pride. The freedom of spirit resulting from a Winter sojourn influences traders and partners as well. If men who live in this territory a long time can return to Lower Canada and enjoy such success, perhaps it is possible for me also to prosper in this trade.

Lac La Pluie is near where the continental waterways divide North and South. The post also marks a division in how the Trade is organized. Some brigades go to the western interior and far North with the canoe convoy, becoming smaller and smaller as each outfit spins off into various trading forts in the Indian Territories. The larger brigade going East traverses a well-known return route from Fort William to the settlements of the Canadas, quick strokes pushing loaded canoes that return them to civilization. Therefore, the brigade guides going West have devised a ceremony that has much the same purpose as the one at Ste. Anne's shrine near Montreal but with less obeisance to God and more commitment to our wild brotherhood. At a high dividing point of land, the senior guide sharpens his knife, cuts a bough from a tree, dips it in the water, and *blessés* the kneeling novice. Whether gentleman trader or hardy *voyageur*, the newcomer then swears allegiance to his companions in the Trade and he promises to never kiss a wife without her permission. It is a raw form of knighthood. Although I could tell you many stories of questionable behavior related to business, this vow is not violated. As a consequence, native women have some protection and fighting is reduced between comrades, although not between rivals. Perhaps the original intent of Christian charity is thus more honored than in more civilized society where priests and lawyers are kept busy sorting out what is good behavior and what is not.

The main building of the establishment at Fort William has a gracious balcony sixty feet long and houses the agents and senior partners. Inside is a central Great Hall, sixty by thirty feet. It seats two hundred at a banquet and we eat well. Crystal and silver complement each successive course. Surrounding the Hall, we have buildings to repair canoes, to build kegs and warehouses to store furs and goods for trade. The doctor's little house is near the main gate, not far from the *cantine salop* and the jail, so I am well situated for visitors. Summer *régales* are outside as much as indoors. We dance the reels, merrily jigging with Indian women as our partners, the senior agents always getting first choice, of course. A large bust of Simon McTavish, early winner of the trade war with Sir Alexander MacKenzie, but early loser of the greater fight for longevity, has been positioned to remind us of our mortal brevity.

Nor'Wester agents and traders have five banquet toasts: To the Mother of All Saints; to the King; to the Fur Trade in all its branches; to *voyageurs*, wives and children; to absent members. At the business meeting this July, we considered the report prepared by Mr. Alexander Henry last year. "Report of the Northwest Population" claimed 368 women and 569 children living with 1,090 employees in the fifteen departments of the NWC Company. Among the *engagées,* several families live in a house and most of the clerks and traders, having a larger house, also take a woman, with children soon arriving. Because the total number of dependents is nearly equal to the numbers of employees, the Council took action. We voted to fine men who take full-blooded Indian women as wives *au façon du pays.* The fine is £100, a year's wage. Men must support their wives and children with their own monies because the increasing numbers of families negatively affect Company profits. However, country marriages with the half-breed daughters of white men are not a violation of this resolve. These families will be supported as usual.

In a land where there is no colonial government nor Christian priest or preacher, the policy begins to protect children resulting from our unions. These outcomes of our residence in the high country may be classified in many ways. Since the days of the French, Canadians call them *bois brulées.* If English-bred, they are called half-breeds or mixed-bloods. Among those who begin to settle near the Red River, their name for themselves is *Metis.*

The voyage to the West is still an unknown frontier that takes more than seventy-five days of hard paddling and good weather to reach our furthest outpost. Even then the Pacific Ocean is nowhere nearby. The terrain and Indians are different from the ones we know at home. The only other white men we might see are wary competitors, sometimes friends.

William McGillivray, nephew of our deceased Director and his successor, made an early peace with MacKenzie's XY Company but now is caught in a vise between the HBC to the North and the American traders in the South. British law of 1803 is supposed to prevent trading abuses in the Indian Territories such as arson, theft, kidnapping, destruction of property and excessive use of liquor, but it is not much enacted here because who would be the enforcer? Chief Trader Duncan McGillivray was fined £500 under the new law two years ago because he slashed a trader's tent pitched too near Fort William, but that example of British justice has not stopped the harassments.

Our Company cannot permit competition from free traders in the Territories so it is quite inventive to find ways that make them less successful. One good story we all are enjoying I can share with you. This Fall on the trail near Sault Ste. Marie, Alexander McKay, a Wintering partner of the NWC, met de Lorme from Montreal who was trying to sneak around Fort William to trade north of Lake Superior. Mr. McKay devised a good method of deterrence. The NWC crew felled trees across the streams so the free traders' loaded canoes caught in branches and could not pass but could tip or get wet. At Fort William, the Nor'West Company, gentlemen traders all, purchased de Lorme's remaining trading goods, at Montreal prices of course. A slow route to China indeed, so the free traders decided to return East with empty pockets. McKay should get a bonus for this clever strategy but fur trade profits are not shared as equitably as hardships.

At Lac la Pluie we are building a supply depot so the men might move goods more quickly. It is like two gigantic circles, one turning to the West and back again, and the other goes clockwise to the East. There are other circles as well. From the North, the Hudson's Bay Company moves quickly into the North West and establishes posts directly opposite ours. This competition is not free trade but a monopoly sanctioned by the London governors, who present a formidable challenge. Presbyterian Scots traders and Catholic French *voyageurs* may have center stage in the poorly mapped waterways of this continent but titled Anglican merchants in London will influence the outcome of this drama. The forces of change that sweep Europe with Nelson currently facing Napoleon might end on a bloody battlefield there. Ripples from that clash of powerful European empires become whirlpools that could submerge all of us, even here at Rainy Lake. As always we have the example of Wolfe and

Montcalm, whose personal fates were decided at the Battle on Abraham's Plain but the final outcome for the colonies of England and France remain less certain even now.

I am reading Mr. Alexander MacKenzie's book, *Voyages from Montreal, on the River St. Lawrence, through the Continent of North America, to the Frozen and Pacific Oceans in the Years 1789 and 1793; with a preliminary account of the Rise, Progress, and Present State of the Fur Trade of that Country.* It has been translated into French so Napoleon could study it. This effort didn't do him much good because the great Emperor has been humbled by a greater force, the Mississippi River, which has swamps more challenging than anything his armies face in Europe.

It is perhaps fortuitous that I am in charge of Rainy Lake this Winter because I also am at a fork in my life. Next Spring my contract term is completed. Uncle Simon Fraser, absorbed in the European War, may take a commission in the military. His Terrebonne seigneury would then need a good manager. After my experiences at Fort William and here, I am well qualified. As to medicine, I think my recent experiences in the woodlands makes me less qualified. I am a physician who has learned some surgery but would hesitate to apply these skills now in civilized society.

I am the only trained practicing doctor anywhere in the Great Lakes area and should be paid for my services because they are additional to apprentice clerk. I was promised £100 additional if I were to support Dr. Munro during my first five years. Dr. Munro's contract was for £100 per year whereas mine was £100 for five years. But I did not negotiate this part of my contract in writing with Simon McTavish, so sadly now prematurely passed on. Inspired by profits and a lack of senior men in the field, Dr. Munro moved into trading furs during my first year here. Thus, I have been physician as well as apprentice clerk since then.

"Act in haste, repent in leisure." I left *Ville de Quebec* in great haste. The British officer whom I dumped so precipitously in the mud when he insulted my lady companion might have returned to a lordly home in England but his military friends still live in *votre grande ville*. A lesson has been taught but the learning has a long apprenticeship indeed. Control of my great temper is to be forged in the cauldron of regret but my conscience is clear. I defended my lady and addressed insufferable arrogance. Nevertheless I wish I might have done so with more elegance and less brute strength.

What chance do I have to begin again at a proper level of society? I have education but little wealth of my own. What gentled lady now would have me, rough at the edges as I have become? I confess, I have little taste for settled life in the town. With each passing year I grow less tame, but sister, pray I learn to use my temper more skillfully. I am *un homme du nord*.

I am young, but prospects are limited if sponsors are not forthcoming. My benefactors are deeply committed to the Trade. The life of a country gentleman would suit me better but there is little room in any of our family holdings. Grandfather Malcolm Fraser invests in land but there are no more seigneuries. Father is Catholic and Irish, not the best combination for success in an English colony other than managing the farms on the south side of the river. David has the greatest prospects because he does not have my temper, thus he deserves opportunity to study in Scotland. But who is to provide for his ambitions? You are a glory of the Ursuline convent, so enriched by your able mind and spirit with gifts for teaching in two languages. As for myself, I am thinking of coming down at least as far as Upper Canada or Detroit where I could begin again. I am not too old. When I do come down, I will visit the Beaver Club in Montreal and expect to be invited to banquet for I am now *un homme du nord*.

In this business, those with cash can reinvest and do well. Profits of the Trade are great this year. I am told that an initial deposit of £800 has increased by two-hundred percent. But who has £800 in cash? Not our family. We are land rich but money poor.

Sister, you write of the Holy Spirit that infuses your life. It would be too impolite, now that you are a nun, to fill your mind with stories about how Indians become infused with spirits that are less than holy but which rather have an inverse effect. A trader can become more like a priest of the devil than a Christian man of any faith. Corrupt men bred corruption among those they should advise. Kinship customs among the Indians are being destroyed with the continuous presence of the white man. He has many goods to trade and thus he receives preferential treatment, even encouragement from some Indian fathers.

I have been observing the natives of this area and think some of their belief in a Supreme Being may be a remnant from the French missionaries who traversed as far as *Lac Supérieure* during the French regime. Northern Indians continue an ancient burial practice. A stranger is asked to pull a length of hair from the corpse. It is then bundled and carried for the space of a year by the nearest relative, usually a wife or mother, until the Spirit is at rest. Men may have more than one wife if they can support their families. Fathers do not give up a daughter until she has borne a child so her young man cohabits in the same lodge as she was raised. His hunt belongs to the mother-in-law but he does not formally address this woman until a child is born. Children of sisters may intermarry but not of brothers. But our increased numbers among their societies affect these customs.

Many traders and Wintering partners have taken wives, as it is part of the trade. Some form family bonds that do not seem to require the sanction of the Christian religion to dignify the relationship. If our men go out from the high country, most provide in some way for the future of their country wives and children, usually by leaving some money or arranging another liaison. Surely it is the greater kindness. Our civilized society would not willingly admit these untutored females, as you well know. I wish these young girls and women could attend your school as they did in the time of your founder Marie de l'Incarnation. Many Indian girls and women in this country would benefit from your guidance. Your Ursuline teachers have proved their students are capable of learning. As they influence the men in their lives, they contribute to a more civilized society for all. Our more wayward men would also benefit from a preacher or priest to attend their sins. When drink influences them, many suffering unfortunates are abandoned. I hope the NWC enforces its new policy and withholds pay if men plan to go out without making sufficient arrangements for their families. But profits usually take precedence over morality when it comes to action.

Continue your good work, dear sister, and do not neglect me in your prayers. I have much need of guidance this Winter as I wait for the next Summer rendezvous with William McGillivray, an opportunity to negotiate with him a new contract, and news of the greater world.

With much affection,

Yr brother Jean Baptiste, *homme du nord*

1807/08, From the Ursuline Convent to Fort William for the next Summer rendezvous

My dearest brother,

Our brother David departed for Edinburgh University this past Winter. He will be interning in the hospital there at about the time you are reading this letter. I wish you could have seen our mother's face as he prepared to leave. Tears, of course, because should he succeed, as all hope he will, it is unlikely we ever will see him again. Her pride that both sons have become physicians is very great, as is Father's, although his is tinged with sadness. To be Catholic in our society is to move among exiles who live in their own land. To be Irish is to be forever a wandering, exiled spirit. To be Catholic and Irish in Quebec is to have rare opportunity to win redemption in Heaven because material rewards are not plentiful in this colony. Our Scots grandfather is pleased that one grandchild returns to the *auld* land and has pledged financial support, as have our uncles. Grandmère made David promise: *Je me souviens*.

Nevertheless, it is you, our dearest older brother, who is David's guardian angel. If you had not renewed your contract with the fur traders, you might have been with us now but our brother would not be going to Scotland for further study. You offered David a great opportunity and he will not forget your gift. I know your motivation. As I walk the Stations of the Cross in our quiet cloistered garden, I look into the face of Christ and see you. I think that some of His suffering acceptance will be engraved in your face when next we meet. It may be years before I see you but, when I do, I will gather you into my arms and make you feel the love that all of us, including Christ, have for you. David will work all the harder because of your example. His brother, only a few years older, was willing to make sacrifices so he might enjoy successes much greater than would be available here. He will owe you a debt for the rest of his life and will not forget. Father charged him to live up to the ancient McLoughlin code of Murtogh, our ancestor who was the first Christian King of Ireland: *Cuimbing go geallamhnaca* (remember your promise). There is no need to remind you. The quality is part of your natural disposition.

I am busy within my Community and apply some of the many advantages of being a member of our unique family. I am not afraid of handling money, having listened to so many arguments about it. My sisters have elected me *dépositaire* and therefore I am in charge of all business transactions. This trust and opportunity for service results less from my personal talents, I am certain, than from observing Grandfather and Father in their tasks of running the seigneuries. Among my religious sisters, I alone speak English and French, one as easily as the other. These are needed gifts for our Convent at this time. We need to communicate with the colonial governors as well as tradespeople. These communications are really negotiations about our status and future as much as any monthly transaction of payments.

In our school, I am fortunate to have as a companion, Sister St. Augustine, an Irish whose father came to this colony from New York after the Revolution in America. We share such delight and joy in teaching the girls and strive to cultivate both their minds and souls. As curriculum strategies, we use new insights that derive from learning in both languages, especially differences that make us laugh together. Our discussions include the natural sciences as well as classical literature.

The French revolutionary events flung our Ursuline sisters out from the mother convent at Paris, and destroyed our houses in Tours and elsewhere. They were scattered and the suffering was great. Five years ago, thanks to an English merchant, we received several sad letters, including one from Mother Ste. Saturnine who was *dépositaire* for us in France. She was then seventy-nine years and doubtless has now joined our Lord and His Mother in Heaven. Although few Sisters survived the tornado of the Revolution, those who remain are permitted since last year by Imperial decree of Napoleon to live in Community once again. They live in great poverty because their property will never be restored. They are too old to travel here so we could take care of them. One never can predict how children will support the parent!

The Revolution also affected our Community. Two hundred years ago Madame de la Peltrie, patroness of our Quebec Convent, deeded her properties at Alencon to sustain our mission. This revenue is gone forever, absorbed by the Republicans. Our Convent needs to manage its finances properly while at the same time we must nurture a spiritual flock that struggles to survive within an English colony. Undaunted, we arrange to transport a few remaining treasured paintings to safety within our walls so that some of our heritage is preserved. It is difficult this sailing season because French ships blockade the English coast and the British navy is certain to exert its power.

The financial pressures come from all directions. Within the walls of the Quebec House, we gathered to our bosoms sixteen Ursulines from Trois Rivières after their hospital, convent and church were destroyed by fire. Only the bake-house and day school remained standing a year ago but faithful parents began constructing new buildings as soon as the thaw began this Spring. During the recent crisis, we were grateful for the support of Bishop Plessis who acknowledges publicly "the invaluable services the Ursulines have rendered all classes of society."

I am certain our good Mother Marie de l'Incarnation must have been the model for my Sisters' calm deportment during the *incendie*. When this House was under similar threat two hundred years ago she organized everyone, abandoning her journal and letters to save some of the more pragmatic articles. The shivering little girls stood in the snow praying while they watched their dormitory and school burn. However, I pray that this Community will not have need to practice such restrained behavior in similar circumstances whilst I am in charge of the business of our Order.

Marriage, whether to God or man, is not always a path through a green valley filled with fragrant flowers. Long hours are now spent on examining titles and property management to develop a more practical system of economy. With prudent management I think we will eventually turn a profit from our seigneuries at Portneuf and

Sainte-Croix but at this season they offer not much more than a *foule de peines* that exceed revenue. It has been necessary to initiate a legal complaint against the Allsopp brothers because they charge a toll for passage across the river between Portneuf and Sainte Croix. It is scandalous to collect such money from the efforts of religious women and adds to tensions between our French who have little other than their Church. Except for one, Christ's disciples would never have stooped so low.

To offset these new expenses and at the same time to honor God, our Community has developed a new specialty out of old traditions. We gild wood tabernacles, statues and chandeliers so they reflect better the light of the Spirit and encourage the people to come more frequently to our churches. Our customers include the Jesuits at *le Séminaire de Québec* and most of our parish churches who also have little money to spend but who want to honor God and the Saints. Thanks to our novitiates we collect money from their handwork *en écorcé*. Lace ruffles are the current fashion and the English buy these items to decorate their gowns and waistcoats. I think that when it comes to managing money, I exercise my Scots blood. Grandfather would be very pleased!

Do you remember the old legend de la Rivière du Loup? The one about how the flowers "*sont nées*"?

> *Dans les commencements, il y avait un ange qui regardait la création par-dessus l'épaule de Dieu.*
>
> *Le matin du troisième jour, quand il vit la terre si nue sur le milieu des océans, il pleura tristement dans la barbe de Dieu.*
>
> *Dieu sécoua sa barbe au-dessus de la terre … et la terre arrosée par les larmes de l'ange s'est couvert de fleurs, de verdure et de fruits.*

(In the beginning, there was an angel regarding the Creation, near the shoulder of God.

The morning of the third day, when he saw the earth so naked in the middle of the oceans, he cried sadly into the beard of God.

God shook his beard above the earth … and the earth, sprinkled by the tears of the angel, was covered by flowers, greenery, and fruit.)

In Spring, I long to roam the fields among the flowers as freely as

I once did with you and young David. Now we are three adults sprinkled across two continents, and I cannot go out and search among the grasses for the transformed tears of an angel. It is sometimes difficult, *mon frère*, to remember that my prayers, properly offered, are flowers that help make the soul less naked. To avoid sadness, I teach this little story to my students asking that they translate it into English. See what a sinner am I! When you move amongst green hills in the high country, stop to smell the wildflowers. Send fragrant thoughts to me so that I might gather them as a mystical bouquet, an offering to Christ. Thus, shall we touch each other's hearts, even when we are miles apart.

Praise be to God,

Soeur St. Henri, o.s.u.

1808, From Sturgeon Lake, Winter; sent East in August

Dearest sister,

I am returned again to my Winter assignment, this time in a cabin at Sturgeon Lake. I am posted with Daniel Harmon, whose home is Vermont. It is still deep snow but soon we will go to check the traps with the Canadians and Indians who share this white solitude with us. I write to you as if you were a holy confessor, there being none for thousands of miles. As these words are for your ears alone, I do not keep a writer's copy of my letter because it grows dark early and our writing supplies are limited. My hope is that your sanctified prayers will help clear my mind for I am truly a sinner now. How difficult to express my confusion but how fortunate I am to have you as elder sister who cannot be shocked by my ways. When you inform our parents of my most recent actions, I know your soft words will help make their hearts less sore.

Mr. Harmon and I departed Fort William after the Summer festivities for our Northern location. His health is not the best so I am assigned to accompany him as physician as well as junior trader but we have found fortunate companionship in each other. We have some books but more leisure. After the traps were laid and the houses repaired, we caught excellent trout. Hung out of doors during the Winter season to freeze, we thaw a few fish every day. Sometimes we catch rabbit or shoot a deer, but neither is plentiful in this swampy place. A boring diet makes one more interested in the taste of good conversation. Mr. Harmon, a Congregationalist, is a moral person who is much attached to his young wife, Elizabeth, and their children. She is of mixed blood and about the same age as our sister Margaret, but this young woman already has lost several babies. Mr. Harmon commits to his family as much as any God-fearing Christian, which is to say much more than many of the traders and paddlers and about what we would observe on our own seigneuries.

Mr. Harmon and I have talked for many hours about what to do when we go down to civilization after leaving this country. A father has responsibilities to his wife and children. It is cruel to take only the children East for they need a mother. Mixed-blood women whose fathers have been traders sometimes have benefited from living within our establishments but they have little opportunity to become literate unless their fathers teach them. Lacking your gentle guidance and training, a native woman would have difficulty demonstrating the correct feminine deportment of civilized society. It is cruel also to leave these children and wives here. Native families honor kinship responsibilities but the life in their camps is harsh and the women work like beasts of burden.

In the unfashionable society I inhabit, a competent woman and an honorable man may forge a worthy partnership. What a good white man has to offer is a comfortable life and protection, better than she might otherwise expect. A country wife provides the daily support that makes life more bearable. In addition to household duties, she knows how to make moccasins and mend clothing and to interpret with trading families. Often she can read the stars and paddle a canoe. In council, she provides information about customs and kinship connections that are invaluable to us. However, there are so many of these families now and many men are ready to quit the Trade.

More and more NWC traders choose to "turn off" their wives and families, arranging with the Company for some provision from their share of the profits; thus the woman is not destitute and has, in fact, a sort of dowry. Some arrange good second marriages, a custom not uncommon among the natives because they have a tradition that a woman may leave her husband if he does not treat her well. When the woman has many desirable attributes such as beauty, cooking or sewing skills, and kindness, she quickly acquires another mate.

As we know, the influence of alcohol makes all men more animal than human. When no longer constrained by reason or virtue their actions cannot be considered civilized. Among Indian tribes many men fall victim to the same temptation. It is the Devil's work. You are a Bride of Christ, therefore I will not dwell upon the severe consequences for women and young children. Suffice it to say that some young bodies are not ready for womanly duties if they have gained less than twelve years. Not only are such young wives unready to bear children, they have not yet learned the skills that make them valuable partners because they were separated too young from grandmothers, mothers, aunts and older sisters. Their lives are usually brief or very abused.

Last Summer when I negotiated my new contract with William McGillivray, I became more trader than physician – do not tell mother. My chief motivation was not service to humanity, but a desire for money. After some "stratagems" on both sides, McGillivray promised £200 per annum with another review in three years. Thus, I have arranged for David to receive £100 as advance drawn on my credit. Our uncles will be relieved of that responsibility but I trust they will ensure the transfer. David carries the hopes for our family but my isolation is a great burden for me to bear.

I expect David will receive this assistance without difficulty but I have some concerns. The oral terms of my original contract were never confirmed in writing and, now that McTavish is dead, I am unlikely ever to receive the amount he promised. I am determined to use this injustice as a lever to gain ground whenever I am in new negotiations. In this wild country I have proven my skills in doctoring, trading, and administrating but now I have wildness in my soul. I fear I am like Faust and have bartered my future for a few pennies. I am twenty-three years of age and cannot again be my own master for several long years. With each successive season, comfortable options outside the Trade decrease.

Now I come to the core of my confession. During the festivities of the Summer season, I took a wife *au façon du pays*. It is an honorable commitment our family might have expected! Her father, who is a respected chief, brought her to the Summer rendezvous. She was pretty and liked to dance and made my single life more agreeable. You took a vow of chastity, not I! By the time her family returned to Red Lake, she was pregnant with my child. This past Winter after Christmas I trekked on snowshoes two hundred miles one way to visit them and to fulfill my obligations to her parents.

The baby is now born but he has no mother. I, the father and a physician, was unable to save her during childbirth. Possibly the pelvis was too small for delivery. Perhaps she was not sufficiently strong, so that her body could not withstand the long convulsions. As a man, I was lonely and homesick, and now a young woman is dead because of my carnal desires. The boy is named Joseph, after another Joseph who wandered in the wilderness until his years of service earned him a rightful place in society. He also demonstrated sufficient charity to forgive those who had wronged him. I also think of Uncle Joseph who faithfully farms at Rivière du Loup with father. Unlike his ambitious and prosperous brothers who wandered much farther, he labors in the vineyard serving his family. The Biblical story has much meaning to me at this time.

The child has been placed with a friend, Angus Bethune, who will act as foster father in the Scottish manner, just as we were sent away when we were young children. This familial arrangement is the best situation I can arrange for my son until he is older. Bethune's father was the first Presbyterian minister in Montreal so my child will be exposed to the same religious precepts that Grandfather Fraser and Mr. Nairne support. It does no harm for a child to learn the various arguments of religion – far better an exposure to the points of debate than no moral instruction at all.

I do not know what future my child will have. Perhaps he might go out to the Canadas for schooling if he proves worthy of such an investment. In this vast country he has many contemporaries but little opportunity for advancement. Our sons have small chance of being accepted as a gentleman even when educated. At least eligible daughters have opportunity for a good marriage with someone in the Trade. As your religious community has observed, girls with full Indian blood seem to do better when they take their lessons back into their own societies. If they abandon the freedoms they have here to live according to our customs, they remain strangers forever.

The first white child, a girl, was born at Fort Pembina this Winter to French parents. The Lamodgières add a new dimension and may settle here after his contract is completed. Both child and mother have survived the Winter but the Company does not want settlement near the trading routes. The mother traveled from Quebec disguised as a man, wearing trousers, with the father who is a Nor'Wester *voyageur* from Lower Canada. She seems to enjoy the life but I do not believe that an educated woman would abandon her musical instruments to participate in a buffalo hunt. God created women to be different from men and cannot be pleased if they attempt to be identical. Our species needs both male and female contributions if it is to progress from the current sad state.

Probably some day more white women will travel this far West but I think I shall be a man far older than our uncles before I meet one who would be an eligible woman I could court. As a physician and as a farmer, I have observed that life is easier when good men and good women mate with each other. Good quality more often results from good breeding and, one day, science will have proof of such selection. Survival depends upon natural culling. If that conclusion were true, then religion is a sometimes false category for classifying good breeding. I have met *sauvage* Indians with more good breeding than some Christian men but they are not considered civilized. I have met men from civilized societies populating this Earth like rabbits but who lack good breeding. Good character always can be cultivated but the seed grows best when the kernel also has quality. Even lesser quality seed can be made more productive and may flourish in new terrain. Regard how the *dente de lion* flowers have spread since the first French ships arrived in the waterways of this continent.

As a Catholic, I know you will worry about the soul of my child. There is no priest here, therefore if only a priest can anoint him on behalf of God then he is beyond God's reach. Whether or not my child has a protective Father in Heaven, I am his father here on Earth, who will provide for him. The children we are generating in this wild land would do better if they had education about religious principles, any religion. This situation is wherein the Protestant religions offer more solace than your faith.

Protestants believe these little ones cannot be condemned forever through an accident of birth and no fault of their own. Even without formal sacraments, they can earn their salvation. Catholic or Protestant or Indian religion, whichever has the faster gateway to Heavenly grace, my little son needs of benefit of prayers. I have sprinkled some water over his head in front of witnesses and attached my name to his.

Sister confessor, my guilt is great. Surrounded by temptations, and lonely, I have been unable to resist the temptations of a second sojourn. Through my weakness, I contributed to a death of a young woman. I helped produce a child for whom I now must care. I am indebted and more a disciple of Mammon than before. I am alone again and remain a lost soul. Pray that my sins be forgiven.

John McLoughlin, Nor'Wester

1809, From the Ursuline Convent, sent Summer 1810 to Fort William

My brother,

Your letter is a meditation on life that caused me much reflection. My prayers are for you and this child and also the poor mother whose heavenly soul certainly must be watching over him. We have many examples of similar arrangements in our own family to guide you. We also have the example of kindly, practical Joseph, the earthly father of Jesus, whose name your child also bears. It is not possible for the Church to always be present, but God is. He will surely care for your child. Even here in Lower Canada, priests are not always available so a lay person may absolve sins as much as is possible in the circumstances. God is always pleased when those who have dedicated their Earthly lives to Him make the Holy interventions but He does not refuse the earnest supplications of anyone.

You wrote of the happy consequences of good selection when a man and woman commit to guide their family well. Priests and nuns have the same responsibility for the souls of His faithful here on Earth. The Catholic faith teaches us that all human beings have souls which may be illumined through religious practice, either their own or by the intercession of others. What person is most holy? Not for me to judge, God will determine. Such contests of wills over which religion has the greater access to God! God wants people to be more holy, and He is larger than any religion that man could devise. Some of us think God might be viewed as female! Hildegarde of Bingen did!

I think that God also accepts the prayers of Protestants, although I believe he gives preference to the prayers of those who are the most holy supplicants. A true state of holiness is hard work, well beyond the ability of most sinners here on Earth. I suspect that God hears many more supplications from sinners than from saints! As a sinner and a daily supplicant to God who grants eternal life, I will pray for the soul of your child and for you. You will provide in material ways for him as best as is possible and I have faith that you will nurture his soul to the best of your abilities.

Think of our own family! Both our grandfathers were thrown up on the shores of Canada as part of the debris of war. Steady in his Catholic faith, Grandfather McLoughlin donated a small parcel of land to establish St. Patrice parish. As an officer in the Scottish Highlanders who helped General Wolfe win victory on the Battle of the Plains of Abraham Martin, Grandfather Fraser's tracts of land were more substantial. Sturdy Scots Presbyterian and friend of Governor Murray, he was allotted a seigneury at Malbaie. His good friend Mr. John Nairne has built a Protestant church for the people at both seigneuries and undoubtedly collects tithes from Grandfather Fraser. There are the Fraser seigneuries on the south shore where mother and father live, farm properties on Isle d'Orleans and a house in our *Ville de Quebec* not far from the Convent. Colonel Fraser disinherited mother, then me, from any direct titles to his lands because we profess the Catholic faith. He was not going to risk losing his investments to colonials who favor Protestant ownership more than Catholic. He has bred children by several women and had a wife who died in childbirth.

By the way, Maddy Nairne, Mother's great friend, followed her example and also married a Catholic Irishman, much to the ongoing chagrin of seigneurs Nairne and Fraser. The young Miss Christina Nairne seems disinterested in marriage but she sends you her best wishes. She is another example of a good life that honors God. Pity she is Protestant with no Catholic tradition in the family, and cannot consider my option. I wish more women could reap the fruits of Religious Community because the harvest among the Ursuline sisters is sweet and plentiful, although the ground sometimes is difficult to cultivate.

Having lusty grandfathers, uncles, and brothers, and a father, I understand well some of your needs. You were young, not much older than your own child must now be, when mother took us to Malbaie. You were to stay and be fostered with Grandfather

Fraser. She had too many children and he had an empty house. She knew her father would be lonely because Grandmère would not leave the south shore nor her French and Catholic relatives, although he soon acquired a housekeeper to meet his requirements. He wanted me to stay also but he was generous when he saw I had talent. He sent me to the Ursuline Convent School to be educated. Little did he realize how my soul as well as my mind would be captivated by my studies when he supported my application. He hoped ultimately for a marriage with a good family among his colonel friends. As Bride of Christ, I have made a greater one. You know the end of this chapter of my story well. Grandfather is so restless, flitting from one residence to another. When he was far away from Quebec, with the consent of Mother and Father, I professed my faith. I exchanged temporal love for a much greater passion, an eternal one.

Think also of King Henri IV, whose name I now bear. He also converted to Catholicism, hoping to effect a greater peace with Protestants. What a great price was paid! Like me, he knew that *a bon mot* could ease many tense discussions. Unlike me he was raised a soldier and became the first Bourbon King of France. The people called his marriage to his Catholic cousin the "scarlet nuptials" because so many Protestants were massacred on St. Bartholomew's Day within one week of that political wedding. "Paris is well worth a mass," united the kingdom. During the ensuing peace, he established a great culture. Through tax collections he rebuilt the economy but, most important for us, he had money to authorize Samuel de Champlain's exploration. Within a few years the new colony along the St. Lawrence was thriving from the efforts of talented Jesuits Brébeuf and Lalemant, martyrs both, and brave Mère Marie de l'Incarnation herself. *Le vrai gallant* Henri of Navarre was assassinated by a fanatic because he dared to say aloud, "Those who follow their consciences are of my religion, and I am the religion of those who are brave and good." I think it a courageous insight.

Grandfather is another sort of *galent*, exercising powerful seigneurial rights in public politics. In private, he follows the old clan custom that mutual consent is legal marriage if expressed in front of a witness. He acknowledges paternity of all his children regardless of whether their mothers live on one side of the river or the other. Powerful men live well, drinking deeply from the cup of plenty. But I suspect that amongst the daily chores of life, men such as King Henri and Grandfather Fraser must be more alone than our less advantaged father, who insisted upon a legitimate Catholic marriage with Mother. Perhaps God did not intend men to enjoy equal amounts of success in every dimension of life. Perhaps men cannot sustain complete happiness, but rather are meant to sample some joy and some pain. I, who am not a man, partake in a spiritual union but have rejected the temporal riches of our society. You, my brother, are sometimes lonely, sometimes successful but you seem certain of your obligations as a father.

One more example to think about. You know Angélique Meadows, Uncle Alexander Fraser's country wife. He established her at his seigneury when he retired from the NWC four years ago. He says he owed his life to her after she threw him her blanket so he would not be killed by Indian trappers. Now he builds a cabin near the river for her while he remains in the grand house where Pauline Michaud has become mistress. It seems a satisfactory and honorable settlement for all concerned. Will your story be written much like his? If so, continue to think about the resultant children. If a boy, his life will not be easy, even when provided with education. If a girl and pretty, prospects are good for marriage. If not, may God bless her because society may not.

We are informed that David has made good use of his studies in Edinburgh and now has a certification in surgery and a degree in medicine from the University there. However, your monies were delayed so he incurred debts and cannot leave the city. Mr. James Kerr, related to the Nairnes, has advanced £120 to keep him out of prison, and Grandfather has guaranteed the money. I know that you also guaranteed Grandfather the further payment. Uncle Alexander is angry that Father has not sold more of his land but prices are very low at this time and it would leave our parents at a very poor level. Uncle Simon huffs and puffs at Terrebonne but does not assist. The truth is, cash, in any currency used here, is not much available. We live well from the fruits of the land, with soil well cultivated, but we do not have much cash to send to Scotland. Thus, your promised advances have been most important to our brother but I do not know where the money is at this time. I know only that David is in penury, with one foot at the prison door, in spite of his good education. If enough money becomes available, he will purchase a military commission in the British army.

This morning, when I rose, the full moon was hanging down from the dark sky like a pendant around the neck of God himself. That same moon illuminated your life even if you were sound asleep. Let its light guide your dreams to Heaven and to conversations with God who surely will understand your confusions more than I.

Affectionately,

Your loving sister

*1810/11, Winter: From the West; sent East with the Summer
1811 canoe brigade*

Dear Sister Confessor,

The years pass and I have purchased a ticket into the high country
once more. This time my contract is more appropriate to my
duties and in writing. I will not share a percentage of annual
profits until made Wintering partner in the NWC Company but
will be due for that promotion next time. I also am appointed to
my preferred trading post at Lac La Pluie. I would have returned
to enjoy a more civilized existence among you all, I am certain,
had it not been necessary to advance monies for our brother's
final year of studies and his military commission. Living so far
removed as I do from society, I can only hope that David, who is
so fortunate as to live in the very center of civilization, will be
prudent. I long to read the latest books, to hear music played by
gentle hands, to have languorous discourses with gentlemen who
concern themselves with political and philosophical questions and
to share meals with friends in a good inn. I long to see our
mother's face, to listen to Father's songs and Grandfather's
stories. I yearn to affiliate with some religion although I am
somewhat fearful of making an accounting to God in his house. I
wish to partake in the greater political debates about governance
of the Canadas. I wish to be present when decisions about the
future of the Trade are made but, in this instance, I suspect I am
at the vortex of change.

My indenture price is a formidable commitment because the
undeclared war with the Royal Chartered English merchants
intensifies. In the far West, the Hudson's Bay Company builds
forts everywhere that we have established trading posts or we
build forts wherever they are located. Nor'Westers rapport with
the Indians is better, perhaps because of marriages *a la façon du
pays,* our boisterous Summer *régales* and our many seasons of

gifting trading goods. My efforts to reduce some pains that afflict these people have been useful. There is little I can do when they have a harsh chronic cough that signals chronic lung disease, or their bodies are dissipated by drink.

Nor'Westers and their *voyageurs* know this land and its peoples, having traversed it through so many seasons of toil. The English come in from the North at Hudson's Bay, thus have an advantage on the water, as the English always seem to. They navigate their ships well, the late break up of ice in the Spring makes a short Summer season. Their Atlantic Ocean traveling time is one season whereas our rotation, going by canoes through the Great Lakes to Montreal, then by ship to London, takes two years. Where freeze-up is six months of the year, HBC woolen blankets are much prized. The real trade is in liquor and women. Some Indians believe the false promise of liquor takes a much faster route to God than the slow challenge of a traditional vision quest. All disciplines of the soul, as you would know, promise an arduous journey. Country wives, too often young girls, establish kinship connections with a local village. This trust sometimes is abused by men who may form another set of relations when sent to another Wintering post. Honorable gentlemen and *engagées* make a greater commitment, especially if they are established at the same trading fort each season. Either way, every year there are increased numbers of women and children who are not living in any traditional fashion.

One good example of a good man is Mr. David Thompson, whom Uncle Alexander Fraser recruited from the Hudson's Bay Company at Reindeer Lake many years before I came into this country. Mr. Thompson and his wife Charlotte, a mixed-blood from Lac La Biche, have been surveying a southern route to the Pacific. Mr. MacKenzie's earlier exploits assured us of some northern possibilities to the Pacific coast but the geography is mountainous and arduous. It would be easier to travel by ocean. Simon Fraser attempted a more recent dangerous paddle along the cataracts of a great mountain river now named after him. His report has convinced us that another exploration further south would have the more advantageous possibilities. Mr. Alexander Henry leaves this month to explore the Saskatchewan River to its origins. We hope that it will not lead us into the hands the HBC claims.

If anyone can track the Columbia waterway link to the Pacific coast it is Mr. Thompson who has been sent to chart the route. He studies the stars as well as insects and birds and always he writes down his observations. He also studies the ways of the various tribes he meets and knows how to blend into the landscape when surveying. He takes his family with him during his vast tours of unknown territories. After the day's paddle, he reads the Bible to everyone on the brigade – in three languages, English, French, and whatever Indian dialect is best understood, Cree being most universal. He is an interpreter for God because at the evening campfire he finishes his Bible sessions with stories that explain the events of the day, and sometimes explains the constellations of stars. Always he ends by stating that although men will never understand all the ways of God, we may observe His many signs and become more thoughtful. It is a reflection that calms the camp as it prepares to sleep.

The Columbia River is a dangerous region at the edges of the Pacific. All along the edge of the continent, there is competition. Russians trade down from the northern archipelago and Spanish galleons have been sighted coming up from the southern hemisphere. American mountain traders begin to venture overland into that territory. Even the Indians are raiders. Alexander McKay, who was apprentice clerk on MacKenzie's trip to the northern Pacific, told me many times that local Indian river guides refused to go past the large rocks guarding their remote coast because the open waters are controlled by coastal Indians who paddle large dugout canoes and go as fast as our *voyageurs*. They wage war upon smaller boats for slaves and goods, taking them back to island villages.

Disaffected with the tense competition past Lake Superior, McKay did not renew his contract and has now retired from the North West Company. Although a Wintering partner, he was chagrined about his portion of the profits. Too much risk and too remote for too small share of the return! It has become a familiar refrain. You probably have heard that he and three other disaffected Wintering partners left Trois Rivières for New York! With their voyageur paddlers, they transported a large canoe by wagon down the long portage from the southern bank of the St. Lawrence River near Montreal to Lake Champlain. After traversing the lake, they loaded the bark canoe on another wagon to the Hudson River and paddled down it. This renegade brigade entered New York in fine style, chanting and in full regalia just as they would have announced their arrival at Fort William. I would have liked to have witnessed that arrival! Apparently it impressed Mr. Astor. He has invited them, with promises of good reward upon successful conclusion I am certain, to join his new Pacific Fur Trade Company. They have abandoned the canoe to travel around Cape Horn. This foray might result in them planting an American flag on the Pacific Coast, near the mouth of the Columbia. If so, it signals another competitor for the inland fur trade. I await the results of their adventure with interest because both Thompson and McKay are competent men and certain fame awaits the winner of this expanding contest in the Trade.

When the terms of my new contract were being negotiated, one possibility we discussed included going to the mouth of the Columbia River pending the results of Thompson's overland journey. It is the new frontier for the Trade, offering promise of great profits from an interior not yet exploited. I have declined for the moment. For this length of this contract, I prefer this trading region though the cycle grows more certain each year. Other men like traveling with the brigades, the exhilaration of reading the waters, the *voyageur chansons* that cadence the strokes of their paddles and make the long day seem more short. I am not yet ready to abandon all trappings of civilization. My country cabin sits where all who go in and out of the region will pass. I have established a garden where I observe the results of medical and agricultural experimentations. You and I both seem to be master-ing the art of managing people and establishments. Do you think it more an inherited talent, or the consequence of exposure to good advisors when we were young?

The North West Company has built a new fort near Red River just south of the long lake called Winnipeg, directly below the HBC Fort York at Hudson's Bay. We have named it "Gibraltar" to signify the strategic position it holds in this new territory. Our watery roads, the rivers and feeder lakes, change their directional flow, some going north to the Arctic and others south to the Mississippi. Together with smaller lakes fed by beaver-made creeks, these waters form a sort of twisting rope that is either a border or a pathway depending upon the faction. Lifelines that sustain the Trade are knotted here, goods from the Eastern colonies forwarded into Western Indian Territories and furs portaged out to the Great Lakes. This place provides our major food supplies when traveling further west. In addition to the North-South axis, Fort Gibraltar is at the edge of vast prairies that eventually are arrested by grand mountains.

Great buffalo herds move like an ocean, and the brown waves they form roll endlessly through the prairies. Indians use these great cattle for meat, hides, sinew threads and even make gunpowder containers from the horns. Our new Fort attracts the nomadic mixed-blood Metis families who gather to make dried pemmican from the meat and berries. The Cree call them *oteepaymsoowuyk*, meaning "In charge of themselves," for they belong to no culture. Their language is a melange of all they represent, Scots, Gaelic, Irish, French and Indian words. It is a fluid community, grouping together during the Summer season and fanning out in Winter. But the families always cycle back to the Red River region.

Other folk gather at the Red River crossroads as well. We are informed by the senior partners and by traders gossiping occasionally between the forts of the rival NWC and HBC companies, that many poor Scottish crofters are dispossessed when wealthy businessmen establish great estates that absorb their land. A gentleman benefactor of the poor, Lord Selkirk, buys up shares in the Hudson's Bay Company to sponsor some of these poor people as settlers who would farm near our new Fort. This would be a dangerous mix indeed. Fur trade and settlement mix like rum and fire. There is bound to be an explosion that does none any good.

For this season at least my daily tasks remain the same. After the Summer at Fort William is ended I go out like other gentlemen in charge of forts to supervise traplines and trade with Indians who bring in furs. I maintain peace among those who congregate nearby my fort. However, the job of the partner in charge of the posts that string north grows more difficult each season. Profits collect into the greedy hands of men who risk no more than a long evening of drinking in the Beaver Hall at Montreal. The new motto might well be "grab what is possible" because we exploit the resources of this region as quickly as we are able to do so. This past Summer, we were informed of Lord Nelson's final words, "I have done my duty," as he expired during the conclusion of the Battle of Trafalgar, near Spain, having destroyed the French and Spanish fleets. We now have paintings of both the battle and the man gracing the Great Hall at Fort William to remind us to also be dutiful. But this responsibility seems to rest with no higher an authority than the senior partners of the fur trade for there is no government here, except that which lies within our own hearts and character.

The Hudson's Bay Company, long protected by the King's Charter, is a great establishment that governs the fur trade, but it takes less responsibility for British subjects who live far from London. Adam Smith writes that a natural law in business and industry will regulate local marketplaces if powerful great monopolies are constrained. In this country, great monopolies are constrained only by weather and the scale of the land itself. Power when in the hands of an absolute few never works for the good of those whose lives are bound by their decisions. As an "officer" serving in this trading war I note little regulation in a territory where, on the one hand, no civil government is proximal to constrain abusive use of power by authorities, and on the other hand the lower classes live in an endemic lawlessness that always reigns when people live outside social boundaries. Such evidence of civilization as exists here is found within the Company wherever a good man is in charge. Our Trade provides a flimsy veneer of order which becomes more tarnished each year as profits dwindle. Those of us who face these challenges in remote locales should be properly rewarded for the risks we face and the lost opportunity to live a more comfortable life elsewhere. We are not slaves, although the Company controls our destinies while we are under contract.

My son Joseph did well with the Angus Bethunes. Visiting him at their home, I met a mixed-blood matron with whom I made a handfast marriage this Summer. It is one consequence of deciding to stay in this country for another five years by signing a new contract with the NWC. Marguerite McKay was wife of Alexander McKay but she chose not to leave when he went down to Trois Rivières so he turned her off as is the custom here, leaving her a free woman with status. Her father was Etienne Wadin, a Swiss-born free trader who was killed by Peter Pond in Indian Territory years ago, and an Objiwe wife. My good friend Angus Bethune is married to Marguerite's half sister who has a French mother that remained in Montreal. Another half sister, Josephete, is married to Alan Morison and we will foster their son, William, who wants to come into the Pembina trade. Thus, I enjoy familial relationships again, therefore am less alone in this place. Marguerite was very helpful in my medical ministrations at Fort William during the Summer. Her calm disposition makes my patients more comfortable even when that is about all that can be done for them. She is particularly good with women, having great knowledge of their complaints and local herbal remedies. She speaks French and several Indian dialects but purports not to know English as well as she does. My country wife is well positioned in community kinships with the Metis and is respected by the North West partners because of McKay in addition to what is earned by her own demeanor.

When married with McKay, they had four children. Thomas McKay, the son, was in school near Montreal until his father took him on the journey to Fort Astoria as an apprentice to the Trade. They now travel to the Columbia. Marguerite has three daughters but not all are with us at Lac la Pluie this Winter. The eldest recently married with Captain Guernoch McCargo, skipper on the Great Lakes shipping out from Sault Ste. Marie, and anticipates her first child this year.

You may realize that Marguerite Wadin McKay McLoughlin is older than I, about nine years. She is approximately the same age as our friend at Malbaie, Miss Christina Nairne, but what different lives they lead. Like Miss Nairne and you, Marguerite has the talent to assess many diverse types of individuals and runs a household competently. Her disposition reminds me of you and her advice will be as valuable. Therefore, I now have two guardians to guard my temper when I do not. With this contract of marriage, she and any future children are protected by the Company should something happen to me. Although we have not been united by a minister of God, I know that you will understand, my dear sister, and I hope approve. In this country, a woman of good character, and she is such, is a necessary comfort. She will be a good partner to me during these difficult years. For my part, I protect both her and the young daughters so they continue at the same level of society while she becomes mother to young Joseph, all being already well acquainted through the Bethunes.

Most important of all, dear sister, my wife has bore four children so I need not have fears of a life ending too early in childbirth. God gives life and he also takes it away, however much I strive to assist him in reducing the uncertainties of living. I cannot guess all the challenges my new household will face but I do not want to suffer remorse again for the suffering of a poor girl in a first childbirth. Some griefs, once experienced, provide sufficient lessons even for a poor soul such as me. If ever I do go out from this country, perhaps my family will come with me as I have the good examples of Alexander Fraser and Daniel Harmon to consider. My new wife will have a choice but I do not think she much desires to go East so she may prefer to remain here. If there is other opportunity in a few years, we will decide then what to do. For now, she has accepted me and I, her, and we are happy. We enjoy having little ones at a strategic post. All who travel East or West must stop for a visit. I hope to extend my scientific experiments by growing new plants and grains in my garden here.

I think my transition to the trading life is nearly effected but I long to come out for a visit and to polish rusting social skills. Given that I cannot, please remind all our family and friends of me. Let them know I am happy in my personal affairs as much as the professional challenges permit.

Affectionately,

J. McL.

*1811/12, Written from the Ursuline Convent in Winter;
received Summer 1812*

Dear bro.,

Congratulations on joining with a good and compatible woman
who will grace your life. I am not surprised to learn of your new
alliance. It is the decision of a man desiring the usual responsibilities of adulthood. You are a vigorous active man of twenty-seven
years. We know of many good handfast marriages made by
Grandfather Malcolm, Uncle Alexander and others. Even if the
commitment is not for a lifetime, for the most part, they are
honorable unions that protect resultant children as much as is
possible to do so in such an uncertain world. With this letter I
enclose a small regard of the affections of my Community. It is a
sample of the embroidery we teach the girls, knowing that this
handiwork helps to steady minds and concentrate hearts. Perhaps
it is concrete evidence of some development of the soul as well.
With some students, I am more certain this work provides proof
of their spiritual development than I am in other instances!

As an Ursuline religious, I receive the daughters of fur trade
marriages into our school, our blessed founder having established
a tradition of welcoming Indian girls. Possibly in some future year
I might guide the hearts and minds of your daughters so they
demonstrate both Christian charity and civilized manners.
Speaking as your sister, I think you will carry out the responsibilities you have undertaken with the same resolution you have
shown when supporting David. Be assured that I pray daily for
the well-being of your souls as well as your personal safety.

So many forces beyond any one person's control shape our
lives. This unknown continent is vast. The mighty commercial
monopolies of your fur trade seem to be battalions in a war for
supremacy of business and industry. Powerful empires in Europe
have battled for control, with England the winner on the high seas

at least. In Lower Canada we preserve remnants of a French heritage that has been lost even in Europe. American republicans think of little else than their own advancement.

In the Canadas we now have newspapers so one is more informed about the ebb and flow of these competing currents. One can read about corruption in either French or English languages although I am not certain it is an opportunity to edify our minds. Readers have little impact on the governance of Quebec. There is no true representative government for the colony, thus we attempt to influence the appointed officials of England as best as possible. Catholic women turn to our priests for guidance but Protestant merchants have much more temporal power than any Catholic in this town. Therefore, I learn the power of indirect diplomacy. Possibly this strategy is easier for me than for you because women long have had opportunity to develop such skills. We know how to influence the decisions of men in our families who then strive to influence the governors who then hope to influence the British parliament and nobles. In my Community, while sewing garments and making gifts from our hours of sewing together, we Sisters practice persuasive strategies of discourse. I may not be an imposing six feet four as are you, but I do have deft fingers and tongue.

As the first Canadian-born nun of the Ursulines to speak both English and French languages since the British Empire established its presence here, I am often asked to be present when the Ursuline Community must address local authorities. At these times, it seems wise to converse only in French and listen in English to their aside comments. This stratagem is especially useful if some members of the official group we are greeting are new to the colony. I doubt I could fool any of the old timers who know our Scottish Highlander grandfather! Of course, a mobile face is a disadvantage in these instances because one must not react to insults. As you will imagine, this form of control has been a difficult exercise for me because I like to laugh. I constantly beg that the restraining hand of Mère Marie reaches down from Heaven to assist me. We seem to have less difficulty when dealing with the Trade people and farmers because the intercourse of daily life creates common bonds.

My great friend, Sister St. Augustine, and I have initiated classes in the English language for our students. It is just pure joy to teach the young innocent ones. We have sixty to eighty *pensionnaires* and almost double that number as *externes* who day board in separate classes at this time. Our curriculum provides opportunity for these girls to learn languages, literature, music, embroidering, conversation and deportment. All signify virtues that will be useful when they establish their own homes. It is another way, I confess, dear brother, that we Ursuline Sisters employ indirect diplomacy to our benefit.

Under my title of *dépositaire*, I am happy to report that the finances of our religious community have become more stable. Thus we ask the priests to negotiate transport for the remaining paintings from the Mother Houses in France, those that were not completely destroyed by the Revolution. In this undertaking we are fortunate to have the support of Pére Phillippe Desjardins who has returned to France because this climate was destroying his health. You will remember he was most influential as I made my decision to take my vows. He encourages me to follow my vocation through the daily observances of the Ursuline Order of Sisters. In addition to advising how best to nurture my soul, he cultivated my interest in the new study of natural sciences. A great blessing, Abbé Desjardins is now *Vicar General* for France, although the position is much reduced from its previous influence. His younger brother, Joseph, however, requires some advance payments prior to incurring all the expenses. As you can imagine, the acquisition of a hundred French *louis* in cash is indeed a further opportunity to develop my eternal soul. Thank you for your generous contribution toward realization of this grand project.

I move quietly through calm wide corridors participating in daily routine and rituals, whatever the season. I doubt you follow such discipline! At least, not all days of the year. We rise at four for matins and maintain silence until we begin the daily chores that sustain the Community itself. We briefly take a *repos* for prayer, followed by some recreation. We prepare for our particular duty: teaching. Jesuits claim that if they are given a boy until the age of seven, they will have him for life. Ursuline Sisters have the same effect on girls. We have an established reputation in this colony thanks to the foresight of chére Mère Marie de l'Incarnation. More than 150 years ago, *petites sauvages* also benefited from the charity of the Community and our colony inherited successive generations from their womanly efforts. During the early days of our mission, Mère Marie noted how they enjoyed singing our masses and loved any physical activity while their faces during catechism were more rapt and attentive than many of the French girls who were more easily distracted. I believe that our current work with young mixed-blood girls has more consequences than any men in public life acknowledge. These girls and the friends they make will influence their husbands and fathers and sons, whether French, Scots, English or other background. This type of education is another form of indirect diplomacy, my fur trader brother. Remember it when you have daughters to raise and marry off.

As well as the particular responsibilities of our Religious Order and our Convent House, we have the daily Catholic offices of prayer to maintain. At times it is necessary to fast or make other abstinences. These duties have accumulated to include so many that we must rotate them among ourselves, some taking a shorter road one day while others the longer vigil. Never, ever does the light go out in the chapel and never is it left empty. Nor do I neglect my prayers for family, including you my brother. So know that in the vast silence that is your Wintering time, you must attend to your soul. These seeds of your nascent holy life are being guarded. God would not neglect such an important request, I am certain.

Your sister in love and in God

1812/13, Written at Lac La Pluie during Winter; sent East, Summer 1813

Dearest sister,

What a dark year this has become! I hope God illuminates the hallways of your Convent because his light seems not to shine anywhere else. The incoming brigade from Montreal brought only sad news about McLoughlin men we love. To have Grandfather McLoughlin pass away at the beginning of Winter and suffer Father's tragic early death at the end of that hard season is more than our mother should bear. I would that I could be present to represent the Irishmen in the family at this time but I cannot leave here. I have not heard from David at all so I do not even know if my lost years in this wilderness have been to his ultimate benefit or if he has perished in some battlefield of Europe.

Who protects the women of our family? All around our mother and sisters, American invaders initiate battles inside the British colonies so I worry ceaselessly about your safety. There is strife everywhere. We are told Napoleon crisscrosses Europe, but his retreat from Moscow has cost him so many men he surely must be defeated eventually. On the Pacific Ocean near the mouth of the Columbia River, Alexander McKay, along with others on the *Tonquin*, has been murdered. Marguerite's young son Thomas is left at Fort Astoria, too young to be alone. Here in the Indian Territories, tensions escalate between Lord Selkirk's farmers and our men because settlement and fur trade cannot coexist. Nowhere does Our Lady Peace find hospitality.

Grandfather McLoughlin had a good life. He was a free man whose two farms prospered. The Diocese he helped establish now provides him with a permanent resting place in St. Patrice cemetery. May God have mercy on his soul! But to lose Father is a great jolt, a bottomless grief. Our sisters are still young and our mother will have many years as widow ahead of her. May she not remember his drowned body for such a sight is not a pleasant memory. The St. Lawrence River now has claimed the lives of both our father and his sister, Honorée. It is a mighty force indeed. Never did I think that I would not see him again. I will ever regret that I had not more opportunity to express my affection for him. I would have let him know that his persever-ance in his faith provided an example of quiet strength and loyalty. Our Fraser family offered you and me and David with opportunities for advantage and success, but our parents provided the example of a good love match in their devotion to each other and to us, their children. I have asked Uncle Alexander Fraser to draw upon my agents for £50 to give mother until the future management of the farm properties is settled.

Our Fraser uncles, Alexander and Simon, exchange angry epistles about irregular transfers of the advanced credit I signed so that David was supported. I fear that my intemperate disposition has not been of value in these exchanges because I wrote a sharp rebuke to each of them. Now I must write Uncle Simon to apologize for this fault of mine. If they are too offended, they will not continue to look after my affairs at home. When you corre-spond with either of the uncles, I would be most grateful if you could contribute toward a more peaceful outcome than exists at the moment. I think their dispute extends beyond David's education to include their own mother's estate. Our father's death might further entangle Mother in that argument among her Fraser brothers. Grandfather may have a young new family on the north side of the St. Lawrence River but I think he will see to the care of our mother at Rivière du Loup. A family at war is no less dangerous than a continent.

Has anyone heard from David in Europe? He will have com-pleted his studies and should have his debts covered. How does Napoleon's war affect his career? My future in the fur trade is a consequence of the willingness of the Fraser uncles to support their sister's children, but David steps onto a grander stage because of my support. May he do well in a world more civilized than mine but I think he owes me letters that arrive on a more regular basis.

I make a request of you. When you see our mother, please talk about my new son, also named John McLoughlin. Perhaps this news will provide some small comfort. The McLoughlin family line thus is continued, both of us carrying the name of John. The baby is, of course, not baptized and he does have some Indian blood inherited from a grandmother. If Irish and Scots can mingle conjointly as they do in us, perhaps some native tincture added to the mixture will make it even stronger. He bears all my hopes. I will tell him of the grandfather and great-grandfather whom he shall never meet in person but whose strong characters he shall know through my remembrances. Please also give our mother an embrace from this errant son and remind her that one day I hope to be there in person to do the same. Pray for my soul and the future of my innocent infant.

I am grateful that Marguerite has this new son because we fret about her other son Thomas who is only thirteen years. He has been orphaned on the Pacific coast since his father was massacred and we do not know the situation. The American fur traders will care for him because his father's reputation and his own apprentice contract will be protection. I make inquiries through both the Astorians and the North West Traders and ask to have the lad returned to us here. Alexander McKay quit the NWC shortly after his brother William retired to Montreal. The McKays had a seniority that I have not yet acquired, so the lad has that protection as well.

McKay thought he had a better offer from Mr. Astor in New York but this expedition has ended in disaster. Captain Thorn, whom McKay thought a lunatic according to reports we received, used a pistol instead of the lash to keep order. It creates resentments when an officer bullies his men but, when he insults a trading chief over whom he has no authority, the situation becomes very aggravated indeed. Confident with his gun Thorn traded knives for furs thus providing the Indians with means to assault his crew. Even women paddlers in the canoes beat men who jumped from the ship into the water. That night four of the five survivors on board escaped in a long boat but they were tracked and murdered also. The lone white survivor was too gravely wounded to flee. The next morning when the looting

Indians returned, he blew them and himself up with the ship. McKay is mourned by all because he was a respected gentleman, even by the Indians who apparently murdered him first even before the captain.

This enormous loss of men and equipment was not a promising beginning for Astor's trading empire, and nor indeed for any of us. When David Thompson arrived at the mouth of the Columbia after crossing the continent to find the American flag had been raised just a month previously, we thought it a probable deterrent to our share of the Trade. I suspect that the Americans now will sell out to another competitor for it will not be easy to regain the respect of the Indians and both HBC and the Nor'Wester men push further inland each season. Each autumn, we establish cabin forts that we return to the next year before pushing even further west again. This event persuades me that trading with the Indians is better done on land than by sea. In spite of the trouble caused by men who do not honor obligations to their mixed blood families, human bonds are forged. We now call our trading regions the Indian Territories rather than the High Country because the higher mountains further west mark a new trading boundary.

Last year our Summer brigade to Montreal left in a great hurry because of the American threat from the south on the Great Lakes. We took a large harvest of furs by canoe through new locks at Sault Ste. Marie into Lake Huron, successfully avoiding armed vessels patrolling Lake Superior. It was a relief to hear this valuable cargo had arrived safely because we would have lost not only the profit from our work but demonstrated a weaker position to London buyers. The HBC already is much advantaged in England because their Directors are so well-positioned in society. This Summer, the threat to our Trade here came down from the North in another sort of bartered goods. Lord Selkirk attempts to establish hardy Scots farmers in the Red River area. In anticipation, Peter Fidler has laid out lots along the Red River in the old French way so that all will have access to the water but the system seems too narrow for this wide country. British subjects prefer the quarter system of dividing land. About a hundred people, including white women, build houses and plow land near the confluence of Lake Winnipeg and the Assinboine River. More are expected after Hudson's Bay thaws this Spring. These people arrived too late to plant any crop that could be harvested. They starve, so our men at Fort Gibraltar have supplied them with potatoes, barley, oats and other supplies. Mothers were selling their shawls so their children might eat and I have seen the results of frostbite on many fingers and toes.

I fear that the next test of these negligent policies will be here in the Indian Territories. Lord Selkirk has the ear of the HBC Council in London but his idealism is misplaced. There will be trouble soon with the half-breeds who consider this area as a base for their Summer hunting of buffalo. If our traders have pemmican food supplies, they can travel more quickly into the northern interior near Fort Chipweyan. In spite of our great harvest of furs from there, Montreal NWC men did not plan for the future but rather spent profits lavishly. Their attempts to influence the British government for a royal charter or to purchase shares in the Hudson's Bay Company are late strategies because each year our profits have been reduced. If through competition, we reduce the profits of the English HBC Directors and if the settlers abandon their attempts to adapt to this harsh climate, our NWC Trade will survive. However, levels of consumed liquor increase while the quantities of good furs do not. Liquor is not a good fertilizer for the trade of furs and we exploit to our disadvantage.

Many of us who have lived for years in this country now have wives and children so that it becomes necessary to think where they could be safely housed. One wishes for schools, for churches, but these represent settlement and must be sufficiently distant from abundant traplines. There are too many mixed bloods to absorb at our small trading forts. Having lived a lifetime in the fur trade, the women do not belong in Indian villages and the promise that these children might do well in civilized society is not assured. During the old French regime, the government at Quebec encouraged marriage between Indian and colonist to increase the population of settlers. In this territory, there is no government excepting that of mercantile princes and population increases are a threat to their kingdoms. It is a wilderness of soul as much as that of land.

News arriving from the Canadas reports battles that threaten our town of Quebec once again. We mourn the fall of brave Colonel Brock at Queenston Heights and wonder what new violences have taken place. It is difficult to comprehend that an American fleet has burned the Parliament Buildings of Upper Canada and taken the church silver plate and books from York. I do pray you are safe in your Convent. Remember the Battle of the Plains of Abraham and how your buildings were damaged by General Murray's cannon. Perhaps you should plan to retreat to Murray Bay where Grandfather and the Nairnes and the distance itself will offer some protection. Is young Tom Nairne in the thick of the fighting? He seems the only male of our generation who is in residence and able to protect the seigneuries. The burdens of daily management will fall on the shoulders of the Misses Nairne and Mother. Well, you all are proof that women can handle large numbers of people and supplies with small amounts of monies. I try to imagine a settlement of women without the protective hand of strong men, but derive little comfort from the exercise. May God continue to be a Good Shepherd watching over you all.

The times seem to call more for the skills of a politician than physician. Machiavelli has suggested some applicable strategies. His book provides me with as much comfort as my prayer book and Holy Bible. However, I pray God hold you and all of our remaining family in his wise hands until we meet again.

Yr concerned and distraught brother

1813/14, From the Ursuline Convent, Quebec; received Summer 1814

Mon cher frère,

The sad cycle of these years continues unabated although Mother was gratified to learn that your child was named John, a comfort to her during this past long Winter. She joins with me in hoping that all is well with your family. Mother continues to live at the Big Farm with our sister and her family while Grandfather Fraser has passed more time than usual at Mount Murray because of the sad situation in the Nairne family. Tom is dead, killed in battle. Since his father's death, our grandfather had advised the young man as if he were a foster son. Unlike our surgeon brother, David, who seems to be serving with an army somewhere in Portugal, Tom returned to the Murray Bay seigneury with the intention of managing his country estate. It is an ambition you claim to prefer but not many young men educated in Edinburgh would accustom easily to such a role when only in their twenties.

With war against the Americans becoming both a land and sea battlefield in the Canadas, our friend could not at first decide whether the colonies or Europe was his proper stage. Tom was commissioned as Captain after he decided to stay. Events here have been so serious that even our ancient grandfather once again mustered militia for the defense of our Quebec. At Mount Murray he is commissioned to take oaths of allegiance from the *habitants* whose loyalties are sometimes suspect because they pay tithes to British seigneurs. Some of the local gentry have made plans to travel to the seigneuries at Murray Bay should hostilities accelerate as they did in 1774 and 1759, but I do not think our mother will leave the south side of the river and my duties remain with my Convent Sisters and our pupils.

In the war against the Americans, the initial victory was ours. Our young Captain Tom Nairne marched his prisoners through the streets of Montreal to a derisive rendition of "Yankee Doodle" but a few weeks later General Brock was slain at Queenston Heights. Tom asked for transfer to the 49th Regiment on the front line and saw much fighting. Finally, the strange last chapter of his life was written. On November 11, his mother, at work in the kitchen at Murray Bay, fell into a faint, crying out "Tom is dead." And, indeed, at the battle near Chrysler's farm where our British forces were greatly outnumbered, Tom was shot in the head. He was buried on the battlefield but his body has since been returned to the Nairne seigneury to lie beside that of his father.

It was one of those very sad occasions when Catholic and Protestant unite in grief. At Murray Bay the priest, himself an escapee from the incendiary of the French Revolution, comforts this Presbyterian family while all who possibly could attended the dignified military funeral in the Nairne kirk. I said additional Masses in our Chapel. Tom Nairne's mother and sisters are now alone on the seigneury and Grandfather has written to inform the Kerrs in Edinburgh.

We pray that our David is spared a similar fate in Europe. He bought a commission to have officer status but he serves as a surgeon. How you men do love your whistles and marches. I think it an evil way of tricking you into unwisely challenging death. It is also a failure to develop good minds that know how to negotiate skillfully other means of settling disputes. Too much is made of the heroic clarity of a young man's military death. Perhaps it is because those who live longer muddy themselves in the more murky waters of diplomatic resolutions and greedy business bargains.

Sad events seem sometimes to unite families more than happy ones. Since our father's drowning, Mother has become even more close to Maddy Nairne McNicol, their stories are so similar. Both married men who owned land but not status, they could be *cultivateurs* but not seigneurs. Both women married Irish Catholics, both braved their Protestant father's wrath, and both were so beloved that they were forgiven their "sins" by those fathers. Both have watched cherished sons go off to risk deaths in war or wilderness. As for me, I meditate often upon the courage of our beloved father. Alone of all the family, he came to the convent when I received my white veil as Bride of Christ. Truly, our father "gave" me away to the Holy Son although it was me who made the decision to accept His invitation. As well, I know what it means to stand firm in the Faith because I had the example of Mother who weathered Grandfather's storms when she married Father. Although one hears of legendary Irish tempers, in our family it is the Scots blood in such as Grandfather and you who are best known for fierce tempers, especially when roused by unjust actions. Father was more calm and sought to maintain relationships when justice must be done. David is more like him – a sunny, smiling singer.

In acknowledgment of all mothers and fathers who bear the burden of their children's vicissitudes, I am making a pilgrimage to Ste. Anne de Beaupre this Summer in time for the *Fête de Ste. Anne*, July 26. We go first to the village of St. Joachim, named after the father of the *vierge Marie*, to deliver some gilded altar vessels and embroidered vestments. These beautiful pieces that our Community produces add to the glory of God in tiny churches where villagers worship, but they also provide necessary income to sustain the work of our Convent. Prior to the feast of Ste. Anne, we will make a nine-day Novena near the miraculous fountain. During that retreat I will pray for your Metis family as well as for all those who are part of the Nairne and Fraser-McLoughlin seigneuries. Ste. Anne, mother of blessed Mary, has long been patron of these shores. Since the earliest days of settlement, the Huron-Wendat peoples have joined us in pilgrimages and they think of Ste. Anne as grandmother or wise woman. She does seem to have special regard for this site. Many stories of rescues from the river and reduced suffering are shared each year. My prayers cannot return Father or young Tom to us but perhaps Miss Christina Nairne who recently has been in such poor health and others among us whose sorrows are not so evident will find relief through our intercessions.

Here is the request I will make of Saint Anne to God most often during the pilgrimage. God willing, you will receive my letter during this special time. Therefore, pray, share these words from Saint Luke with those around you: "To give light to them that sit in darkness, to guide our feet into the way of peace…"

War is an expensive endeavor that affects even those who live in a cloister such as ours. Because of the English and French tensions, my dear mentor, Abbé Desjardins, is no longer permitted to write letters to me or even to the Duke of Kent, his Royal friend in this colony. Our ability to obtain even the final ornamental vestiges from the Mother House has trickled to a stop. Nonetheless, at times when one passage is blocked another opens. The Irish regiment, stationed here because of the military hostilities, provides music at Mass. Their chaplain, Monsieur French, an appropriate name *n'est-ce pas*, has arranged that we inherit musical instruments that the band no longer uses. We, in our turn, offer improved and more frequent music lessons to our boarders and day students. This augmentation of income is most welcome and makes our voices rise ever more lightly and highly toward Heaven. I think that this war has drawn French and English colonists in the Canadas together in a more general bond, like a family. The military activities of the new Republic seem excessive to those clustered under the Union Jack, however reluctantly. When the constraints of civilization are abruptly severed as they have been in France and in the former American colonies, a cultural wound appears. It takes time for any injury to heal and often scarring results. Certainly, France is no longer an enlightened nation of *philosophes.* The Napoleonic Empire seems but a fragile constellation, while the British Empire lights up even the Eastern skies with steady expansions to new and unknown lands.

Dearest brother, you often must regard the skies at night, searching for clarity of direction to guide your steps. When you do so, know that I also search these same dark horizons, attempting to read hidden messages from God among brilliantine groupings of light that beckon all of us on to new endeavors. When you observe twinkling beyond the softer glow of moonlight, think of me, here at my Convent window beseeching God that you remain safe and also praying for David, our brother somewhere in Europe.

May God respond to my humble pleas and guard you both.

With great affection,

Your elder sister, Mary

1814/15, From Fort William, Winter; sent East that Summer

My sister,

I write you this year amidst political events that swirl about all who live as British subjects. These currents are more difficult to read than troubled waters at the confluence of rivers and oceans. With respect to the affairs of men and countries, these are treacherous whirlpools, difficult to navigate. Now that the English are less distracted by events in France, their Lords and merchants turn a fierce attention to the resources of this New World.

Never would I have thought the restoration of the Bourbon monarchy after Napoleon's final defeat would have such effect upon my life. It seemed that David, somewhere in Europe, would be more involved. Worse, the enmity developing along these lakes and rivers places Scots in conflict with each other. It is not hardy clan lords against other warrior clan lords but poor wee crofter families sent out by Lord Selkirk of the Hudson's Bay Company who disrupt the North West partners, traders and *voyageurs*. The North West Company cannot paddle all the way from Montreal to Fort William and then be stopped at our Fort Gibralter on the Red River before accessing the beavers along fertile northern rivers! Selkirk has some experiences with establishing colonists in Upper Canada. Does he not realize the danger in sending women and children directly into the path of our commerce?

To make the mixture more dangerous, Metis regard this territory as their homeland and will not be idle observers as prairie land is plowed under. This land grant Lord Selkirk procured from the British government extends directly across the waterways where the Metis prepare buffalo pemmican for us. It is a system that has worked for all. With this necessary staple NWC men travel long distances more quickly without stopping to hunt and prepare their own supplies. The best furs are now in the North and West so we follow circuitous inland rivers and lakes as we always have. Summer is a brief season there and paddling routes to good trapping lines get more distant each year. Thus the nexus at Red River becomes ever more important to the success of our venture. Furthermore, the Metis are a people we traders have generated through our interaction with the Indians. They are not NWC Wintering partners, but they are kinship families to many of us. They edge half-wild horses into massive buffalo herds with a nervy skill we dare not emulate – they seem part Minotaur. Their oxen and carts lumber around our trading forts. Their fiddles make our feet dance and their *joie* enlivens many a long day for trader men. However among Selkirk colonists when dour Scottish wives take time to look up from their vegetable fields, their stern faces do not smile and their apprehensive husbands reach for sticks and guns.

Now that France is well and truly withdrawn from this continent, the British and American governments will settle the boundary question. No one knows how far the Pembina territory extends below the 49th parallel but the small interlinking lakes have provided an easy access to good trapping. The HBC Governor and Committee in London have little understanding of the vast territories they hope to control, even with massive support from their parliamentarians. They have better knowledge of Arctic island bays and iceberg oceans. These Indian Territories are not the populated continents of the Far East and Africa. These are lands that discourage, that demand new understandings of space and time to traverse, lands where sparse gatherings of people represent settlement because the soil will not support a dense population and remain fertile. This is a land where Nature only dominates.

Red River becomes a lawless conflict, Godless as well. This Spring, Governor MacDonell of Selkirk's Colony placed a proclamation on the gates of various North West Company forts stating that the arriving colonists would need all the buffalo pemmican and no fur trader could access provisions from the Metis. To make his point even more clear, he seized fur cargo from two of our canoes, threatening us with the possibility that our annual exchanges will not pass through until some stability is procured.

To win some victory in this undeclared war, at our Summer meeting, the NWC established policies that require us to be less humane. Our men in the interior are no longer permitted to visit the HBC forts, even on holidays. We are not to sell supplies or assist Red River settlers even if they are in crisis. Most of them barely survived the Winter. The senior partners sent one of our traders, Duncan Cameron, former Captain of the *Voyageur* Corps, a militia unit in the recent War of 1812, to visit settler farms. He offered them free transportation out of this troubled area to Upper Canada. In the colony, these destitute families would receive free land and free provisions for a year, plus a cash payment. NWC Partner Alexander MacDonell, cousin to the Governor of the Selkirk Colony, has been less diplomatic. Our MacDonell contacted the Metis, encouraging them to make a more hostile visit but warned them to stop short of butchery. Thus, the numbers of fires to farm buildings have mysteriously increased, Spring crops are overrun with stampeding horses and buffalo. To curb further confrontations between the obstreperous governor cousins and their various supporters, Duncan Cameron exercised his magistrate's authority under the Indian Territories Act. He obtained warrants and arrested Selkirk's Governor Miles MacDonell because of illegal threats to destroy our NWC forts. The colony's sheriff, John Spencer, is also arrested. These two men Selkirk hired had authority, but not wisdom. They leave with this Summer's brigade to face trial in the colonies. Most of Selkirk's settlers have accepted the NWC offer and depart on the same brigade. It also carries this letter to you. Lord Selkirk has a great dream but he would be wise to reflect upon these harsh events because further escalation will result in greater frictions between all parties.

When gentlemen compete and dispute, there are many ways to use power and reduce tensions before violence destroys our efforts. The best policy is to establish an expectation of correct behavior and thus arrest undesirable actions before they occur. Penalties for minor infractions must be public so that all know about them and, if challenged, reinforced at the most minor level possible. Some good humor helps and, as always, music hath charms to calm savage and beastly men. A good time is talked about during many a dull evening which great anticipation of the next one. It helps me to have a large and strong physique – that is threat enough for most. If there comes a point past which violence may be the only way to test strength and principles, there are courts of law and professional military men and militia volunteers. Fur traders, Metis and settlers have enough challenges fighting to survive. Unfortunately too many powerful men chose the weapon of violence as a first resort, but they seem less likely to lose their lives and property in the ensuing fray.

Thus, in spite of the tensions, we held our annual dance at Fort William this year. The settlers who travel east with the brigade joined in the festivities while Miles MacDonell, their erstwhile governor, fumed in a nearby jail dancing an angry jig to a rather different tune. NWC, settlers and arrested gentlemen, all must travel out on our canoe brigade together and perhaps at portages, the travelers will learn to support each other. If the level of hostilities increases at Red River, the next chapter of this saga will be written by the hand of death. Therefore, I entreat you to continue your supplications with the Jesuit priests that they may send one to us before that sort of bloody conclusion is drafted. We will have a difficult time to reduce aroused emotions at Red River and do not know what Lord Selkirk's next moves might be.

As you undoubtedly know, Uncle Alexander sent his son out here last year into the Trade. I had opportunity to visit with our young cousin who went to Fort Gibraltar, situated right in the midst of the hostilities. I think this is an unwise posting for a young man of mixed blood. It will be difficult enough for the lad to prove himself as a trader without the influence of other such youth who live in the Metis camps. Thomas McKay so recently returned from the Columbia, joins with other young bloods who thirst for action to prove their mettle. Their leader is Cuthbert Grant, another of these mixed blood offspring of the Trade who returned last year. His late father provided monies for the lad to have a good education in the Canadas, but the grown son now influences the Red River Metis. He brought his wife to talk with me and Marguerite because he is good friends with young Tom.

Therefore, I have many opportunities to hear about their idealistic plans for a new nation. Sometimes they appear to be the visible manifestations of unseen forces that push us all toward more confrontations.

I do not think this second generation will live a nomadic life as free as their Indian ancestors, nor enjoy the more civilized comforts of their European heritage. To realize their dreams, they will need a place of their own and they congregate at Fort Gibraltar. Too wild and restless to settle on farms, too *bois brulée* to succeed as civilized gentlemen, they must carve out a new society. The Red River crossroads may offer a modicum of hope for these youth. However, given the current lack of restraint, I think young Alexander could have been kept in the East for a longer period of time because he was taken out east at a younger age than the others. My concerns about his welfare have been forwarded in a letter to Uncle Alexander who has not replied. Knowing that you meet often with mother who lives but a few miles from his seigneury, I hope that you might explain my views, perhaps better than I have done. If these youth do not find adequate opportunity when given the chance through proper education and guidance, they will return to cause further trouble here and we have enough as it is.

I speak from experience after twelve years in this trade as both businessman and doctor. I am now past thirty. Although I dream of seeing you again, this year has been gratifying in my family life. Marguerite safely delivered another child, whom we name Marie Elizabeth. Mother will be pleased, I hope. Our little sister who died so very young now lives again in name at least, may her spirit also bless my child. Although I will never see our father and sister again, I evoke their presence when I call my children to me. After several seasons at the Lac La Pluie posting, my wheat crops have resulted in good quality flour from a little mill that I had built. These results are proofs that we can develop productive settlements for those families who are attached to this country. Not all our men want to retire to the eastern colonies, and the Metis might learn to mill these crops. Like wild rice, their management is not so intensive as potatoes and beans. To develop this idea further, good judgment must be exercised by men with more power than I. Events of this past Summer revealed me as idealistic as Lord Selkirk but I am not as poor a judge of character and timing. Of course, I also am not so wealthy, nor so noble as he either. Do you suspect there is some monetary connection between the ability to dream and the ability to realize these visions?

My fortunes are now tied to the profits of the North West Company. Although I think about the life of a country gentleman and admire Mr. Nairne and Grandfather Fraser's accomplishments on their seigneuries, I have not yet earned such freedom. At the end of the 1814 accounting year, profits were reduced. To pay us our share, it was necessary for the NWC Company to draw from the McTavish, McGillivray & Company subsidiary. Five of us Winterers were overdue for promotion to a junior partnership. This obligatory transaction was honored, but other contract negotiations were necessary during the conclave this Summer. Things being what they are, no partner wants to go to the Athabasca so the unanimous vote was to appoint me! I had expected to continue managing the fort at Lac la Pluie and my experimental farm but did not persuade Mr. McGillivray of the value. Kenneth McKenzie almost convinced me that I should do a term in the Athabasca to gain experience of governing such a vast district and the possibility of increased profit if the job was done well. I threatened to go down – there are father's farms to manage and David is graduated, so everyone knew I could do so. I refused to continue to practice medicine without payment for my additional time and responsibilities. After I immediately discontinued my medical services to the men of this department a few weeks ago, the senior partners were persuaded it would be advisable to keep me at Fort William. It is a central and safe situation for me and my young family. I have a good cabin in the doctor's quarters with pine furniture and green armchairs and can keep an eye upon young relatives who aspire to success in this wild country they consider home. Although NWC profits diminish I will receive a partner's share of the annual trade and ensure the shares of others are guarded. I'm not a Laird of the land but often reread the copy of a poem Mr. Nairne gave me before I departed the Canada colonies:

> May plenty still around thee smile
> And God's great help thy foes beguile,
> In Wisdom's path be sure to tread
> And her fair daughter Virtue wed.
> My compliments and love sincere
> To all our friends both here and there.

May Lady Peace rest at your Convent house and send her doves to the troubled Indian Territories to watch over our hearts and actions.

My compliments and love sincere, fair virtuous sister,

J. McL., NWC Chief Trader, Wintering partner

1816, From Sault Sainte Marie, after Seven Oaks

My beloved sister,

So much has happened since my last letter to you that it is doubtful your annual letter will reach me before I greet you in person at Quebec sometime later this year. I hope to collect my thoughts and perhaps acquire some understanding of the events of recent months by chronicling them for you. Also, you will be prepared when you see me for some great changes in my appearance. I write to you from a bed at Mr. Cadot's house in Sault Ste. Marie where I am grateful to be alive.

As I share the story of the past year, prepare yourself. In my last letter I outlined the stormy negotiations with the NWC that resulted in my posting at Fort William as Doctor and a Chief Trader for the Winter season. Our frictions with the HBC increased so it was not an easy time for governance. Harassment between our representatives at tiny posts scattered throughout the Athabasca territory attained new forms of refinement that become the stuff of camp legends. One example is that of Mr. Black from Aberdeen. His tactics helped set the stage for much darker deeds. His activities included the setting afire of wood piled in reserve for Winter, using a cutlass gun to startle ducks so hunters misfired their guns and endangered their own parties. He even threatened to cut off the ears of an Indian wife who wanted to follow her husband when he left an HBC fort to come over to our side of the conflict. Observing such behaviors by so-called gentlemen, mixed breeds and Red River Metis needed little direction when encouraged to discourage Selkirk's latest crop of settlers.

Even at Fort William, it has been necessary to enforce discipline. This Fall, a newcomer from Upper Canada, hired as blacksmith on a three year contract, attempted to sell skins he had trapped privately to an American free trader. I gave him a drubbing, a blacksmith is a worthy physical opponent. Then, he was locked into a cell near the latrine until he was sufficiently chastised. It is a common practice in the Trade, a punishment that probably is no worse than a late night stroll in most streets when the chamber pots are being emptied. Bearing a great name but of no great character, this Alexander Fraser, for like our uncle and cousin that is his name as well, soon capitulated. After ten days confinement, he agreed to continue his work with our Company, including an extension to his contract. Exhibiting another fine element of his character, he was the first deserter to Lord Selkirk's camp when the Laird himself arrived at Fort William in a great rage after a great tragedy.

Miles MacDonell was replaced as Governor of Selkirk's colony, this past Spring. Governor Semple proved to be an inexperienced British Loyalist moved north from the United States. He never did understand the men and situation into which he was thrust and he has paid the ultimate price for that ignorance, dragging all of us more deeply into the muck of this now truly bloody Trade. Semple's appointment included direction of the HBC Northern and Southern Departments and it was in this capacity that his actions have been judged. Soon after arrival at Spring break-up on the Red River, Semple ordered the destruction of Fort Gibraltar, our NWC trading post. Logs from the buildings were burned or carted away while the horrified Metis watched. For them it was symbolic destruction of their culture and land. Led by self-appointed "Captain-General" Cuthbert Grant under their new flag, which is St. Andrew blue with the figure of eight infinity symbol, the Metis met at HBC Brandon House, thus ensuring everyone knew about their actions. They marched toward the blockade Semple had established to guard Selkirk's colony. Thomas McKay was with them. They met Semple's men at dusk on June 19. Leaders of the two groups argued, shots were fired. Fifteen minutes later, Governor Semple and twenty men of his party were dead. One Metis was killed. Though various pomp and charades, hostilities in the Trade finally had escalated to the point of mass murder of gentlemen by those who were ready, with some incentive, to fight for their land grant. Once life is gone from a body, no man can close the wounds and restore that which cannot be undone. Sometimes, however, it is possible to avert further hostilities. This, the North West Company tried to accomplish.

Lord Selkirk's brigade was traversing the southern part of Lake Superior when he learned of this tragic event. He diverted his canoes and came to take Fort William itself. He had with him a large contingent of military men, a hundred Swiss mercenaries and officers. In the Canadas, the colonial governments had refused to provide guards for his settlement so he paid these soldiers' wages himself. They arrived August 12 ready to fight fifteen senior NWC partners and our men. It would have been another massacre, so we surrendered.

Selkirk is ill to the point of dying from tuberculosis, or he would demonstrate more calm. McGillivray and the rest of us have been charged with treason, conspiracy and accessory to murder. Lord Selkirk ordered the NWC partners back to Upper Canada in shackles, but finally agreed that Kenneth MacKenzie and I could be bondsmen for the Company until the dispute was resolved. Selkirk has taken up residence in Fort William, there being no settlers at his colony. All who remained after the exodus of last Summer evacuated this Spring to more reasonable safety north of Lake Winnipeg near York Factory. McGillivray now goes out to procure legal and financial support for our side in what will certainly be a long, sensational trial somewhere in the Canadas. He carries this letter part of the way. The likelihood of being intercepted is very high because that type of theft seems another consequence of this vicious dispute.

Not much honor in this tale remains on either side. Records are destroyed, reputations tattered, and lives terminated. Trading practices beget no honor and follow no honorable rules for the exchange of goods or of behavior, including the gentlemen responsible for maintaining order. Corruption erodes profits and the souls of the men who strive to gain any final advantage. Even Lord Selkirk is caught up in the greed now that he sits in the Great Hall at Fort William.

And so I finally come to the part that most closely relates to my own survival. Having accepted to act as bail, Kenneth MacKenzie and I were to be transported by canoe to the colonies for trial. Near *Isle aux Erables* in Lake Superior our convoy was struck by a storm on August 26. The overloaded canoe that carried us capsized. MacKenzie, a good man and friend, was drowned along with eight others. I, being of greater height and strength, survived. But – just so. It took some time to revive me and the shock was great. At thirty-three years of age, I am now crowned with a head of white hair and have an injured hip, but I still live. When next aboard a canoe, I will not be given iron manacles for humiliation. Given the white crown I now wear, my hands need not be bound. All who see me will remember the story.

It is difficult to write about this temporary escape from death. Would it be too strange to confess that I am certain that I heard our father's voice refusing to let a watery grave claim me. He would not let me pass to the other side so soon after he had slipped into the chilly arms of a cold river. Also, many living kin called to me with vibrant demands: Mother, David, you, my other sisters, my children and wife. Marguerite has survived the loss of two murdered protectors, a father and a husband, so she is firm about not wanting another such loss. This immoral business I am involved with can be made more orderly but I will not be martyr to that cause. Family and faith are worthy infusions. What I have suffered is less than the horrors endured by Jesuit martyrs Brébeuf and Lalemant who were tortured and burned not far from where our canoe overturned. They were steadfast to an ideal of God and Christianity that would make this savage wilderness a more civilized place in which to live. Unlike Kenneth MacKenzie and thirty other men, I am alive. Why?

I am mindful that the crucified Christ himself was the same age as I am now. He made the ultimate sacrifice for love of humanity. I have not demonstrated any particular bravery but God has spared me, thanks I believe to the intercession of our own father himself and perhaps thanks to spirits of the brave Jesuit martyrs as well. It is not sufficient to have superior physical strength, not enough to have the benefit of education, nor an ability to convince men to listen and obey. One makes the world a little more pleasant for having lived in it. I do not have a calling to the priesthood as you have had to the Church but seem to be a successful businessman and a reasonable physician. I strive to be a man worthy of communing with God but I needed this good warning from Him as to who has ultimate power over life and death. I, a much weaker vessel, do not live just so that the heads of civilized Europe are warmed by beaver hats. There must be more purpose for my restored life. *Que Dieu me vienne en aide*!

For several weeks I have been recovering at Mr. Cadot's home near the cemetery at Sault Ste. Marie. He is yet another with old grievances about his NWC Wintering partner contract. Because he was friends with Uncle Alexander, Alexander McKay, Colin Robertson and others, we have had many interesting talks. Before I resume my journey, I will have time to reflect upon how the past decade has benefited a mighty few and injured many. Justice must be brought to bear upon the situation. British authorities will not tolerate murder of British subjects, even within the Indian Territories beyond colonial rule. Although not shot dead at Seven Oaks, I am another victim of that event. We who are Wintering partners might be the human caulking that mends the breach between the HBC and NWC. They have quicker access to European markets, we the overland trading expertise. Perhaps I can assist in negotiating some sort of contract between this ancient, but timid, Charter Company and our brave adventurers and traders from the Canadas. The fur trade as we knew it is ended but trading of beaver pelts will continue as long as there is a profit to be made.

It may be some time before I hold you all in my arms after so great a voyage to the depths of my soul. Please, pray for a safe passage from this place and for my state of mind. Assure Mother and our family that I survive and will recover. I left precipitously, a chastised youth. I return more slowly as a mature man. Along with other NWC partners, I am still under arrest but will be released on bail when I return to the colony. I will visit you before this year is over.

Ton frére

Interior view of Fort William, sketched by Lord Selkirk, 1817. John McLoughlin's medical office and cabin is on the right, near the gate. Source: Archives of Ontario.

Interior view of the Ursuline Convent – corridor.
Courtesy of le Monastère des Ursulines de Québec.

II: Evolving Challenges, 1819–1837

Now in their thirties, the brother and sister assume mantles of leadership, developing associated skills and expertise. Both arrive at important crossroads. Ensconced within cloistered convent walls, Sister St. Henri, o.s.u. must maintain links with colonial leaders amidst increasing tensions between the French and English cultures. It is a rebellious period of dissatisfaction and unrest prior to political reorganization of the Canadian colonies. Chief Trader John McLoughlin becomes leader of the dissatisfied NWC Wintering partners and travels to London as their representative, taking time to visit their brother in Paris. As a consequence of amalgamation between the NWC and HBC, he accepts the position of Chief Factor, Columbia Department, far from the increasing power of George Simpson. By the end of this middle phase of their lives, Dr. J. McLoughlin and Mother St. Henri are acknowledged successes as outstanding administrators of their respective domains and deeply involved in the education of his children and their cousins.

England and the United States have signed a treaty that provides for joint occupation of the Pacific coastal region until an international boundary has been established across the continent of North America. In both the United States and England, a new generation of leaders comes to power, resulting in expanding continental ambitions for the Americans and increasing international predominance by the British. The sun never sets on the British Empire because on every continent in some colony the Union Jack is raised at sunrise. But clouds are forming.

Rindesbacher's sketch of The Governor of Red River, Hudson's Bay Voyaging in a Light Canoe.
Source: Library and Archives Canada.

Interior view of the Ursuline Convent – the science classroom. Courtesy of le Monastère des Ursulines de Québec.

*1819, Letter was probably written shortly after his return to
the Indian Territories past the western tip of Lake Superior
and sent with the express canoes to Quebec in Lower Canada*

My beloved sister,

I am once more active as a trader and doctor in the high country,
this time with a false charge of treason and murder against me. In
spite of the public storm, the charge against my name should be
cleared. No one has enough finances to transport all the necessary
witnesses back to courts in Upper Canada. The case against the
great Alexander MacKenzie, the explorer Simon Fraser, me, and
nine other NWC partners was transferred from Lower Canada to
be heard eventually at one of the colonial courts in York,
Kingston, or near Sandwich on the Niagara Falls Peninsula.
These delaying tactics cause the McGillivray Bros.' expenses to
become excessive. Fighting the inherited wealth of an English
nobleman is an expensive game, perhaps too costly for fur trade
bourgeois. Lord Selkirk speaks persuasively into the ears of the
London establishment. However, William and Simon
McGillivray have an audience in the Canadas. Upper Canada
colony is not yet so well established, as Quebec is in Lower
Canada, but its leaders understand the value of the Trade. The
NWC is the largest business in both the Canadas and the senior
partners have several sub-companies that add further revenue to
colonial coffers.

The moral responsibilities of Empire are not long ignored
when British subjects live next to American citizens. In this chess
game of political power, the British government will not want the
names of Lords and Members of Parliament tainted by more
unrest and bloody confrontations, inferring scandalous business
dealings across the ocean. Those of us who serve as gentlemen
traders in the Indian Territories are but knights and rooks that do
not fare much better than the sacrificial pawns, the Metis and

Indians. Like all men with some rank we knights represent honor, nor can we forfeit demands for justice. I talk with other members of the rough knighthood of Wintering partners around various tables. We are not anxious to continue in the destructive enterprises of the past decade. One massacre at Seven Oaks more than suffices as a warning about the value of constraint.

I, at least, am permanently scarred. Given the gift of life for a second time when I survived the waters of Lake Superior, I now present my newborn daughter with a patronage that grows ever less respectable. Even if free to participate legally as a respectable citizen again, what type of clientele would such a physician attract in society? My name and hands are forever dirtied because of the murder of Governor Semple and his men. I am better off among the fluid and freer company of the High Country, exercising any talents I have in managing establishments and markets.

However, I return here with my personal affairs in order. Given the disputes between Grandmother, Mother and our uncles, I have spent more than 500 Halifax currency to arrange their support. You are to obtain money from John Fraser of Ford who acts as agent to ensure that our mother will not have problems with her sons so far away. Uncle Simon will be executor of my estate should I have a fatal accident. If I had more capital, I would have accepted a secret offer to enter into a business partnership in the southern Great Lakes area. Had Mr. Simon McTavish kept his word when first I shipped west, there would have been no difficulty on my part to accept this offer now. I should have shared in the greater profits of an earlier period when more furs were easily accessed and competitors were more distant if I wished to fund such a partnership.

Even with these feuds, I am better positioned than young Cuthbert Grant who has become the scapegoat of the current dispute. An intelligent lad o'parts who received a sound education in Inverness, Scotland, as well as Montreal, he bears the public penalty for being leader of the Metis' rebellion. Wisely, Mr. Grant chose to jump bail in Montreal to join our return brigade at Ste. Anne's for the journey to Fort William. That hasty departure meant I did not have a final visit with Uncle Simon and his family at Terrebonne. Should young Grant ever return to the Canadas, he will be sentenced for murder and probably hang. He has a love of freedom and a wild streak that will not be tamed with time. His father died too young and his McGillivray mentors are proof that the raising of a child is best done by immediate family who are bound by loyal blood more than money obligations. Grant reflects a good education but not good fostering. My stepson, Thomas McKay, another mixed blood who lost a father too early and too tragically, is much taken with him and was also caught up in the fight. His name was not so muddied by participation in the Seven Oaks affair but we have sent Tom west of the Rocky Mountains for his own safety. As a consequence of their violent involvement, I fear their futures as gentlemen in the Trade will be much constricted. This concern causes me to think further about the sons I have fathered.

I have come back also to protect my shares in the NWC. A Wintering partner has but one place to ensure some profit and that is in the Indian Territories. There is some opportunity, with much to restore at Fort William since Lord Selkirk's illegal occupation, the worst of several mistakes he made during the past few years. Now that Lord Bathurst has got the British government involved, this dispute between traders and philanthropists will be settled in London, not at Norway House or Fort William. The monopoly of the ancient Royal Chartered HBC is in question. The Honor of the British is at stake. And, since no one is making much money, the unholy competition will be terminated. Expenses incurred from legal warfare are as costly as those of economic warfare. Even the greatest estates might falter before this expensive intercontinental game is completed. I go back to talk with the other knights in the field and learn their opinions about how to move around in this chess game. My colleagues and I have much to discuss during the long months ahead before next Summer's rendezvous and the signing of new contracts.

More than this I cannot say and will not say in later dispatches because we know not whether the seals on our letters will be respected. Each side blocks passage of the other Company's documents ever since the great burning and occupation of Fort William. Perhaps the priest who recently arrived in Red River,

Père Provencher, will become a Bishop in our game and help bring to close this hitherto unholy game. At least he will protect some of the pawns who have become so consumed with alcohol they abandon any respectability or tradition. Father Provencher and I will have many reminisces when he comes to say Mass at my post. He says you are acquaintances because his parents live at Kamouraska village, so near to home. His benefactor is Lord Selkirk's Montreal lawyer, Mr. Samuel Gale. Maybe he will advise this knight about how to make some advantageous moves. When religion and business become mixed, the stakes become very high indeed – our immortal souls are risked.

Thank you for your prayers as I re-enter this dangerous world. Even God cannot have ignored the affairs of the fur trade during the past three years. You undoubtedly will argue my case persuasively in the great and final court before which we all must appear one day.

With affection,

Yr bro. John

1820, Letter from McL. written on board ship for mailing from London upon arrival in December to be delivered in Spring 1821

My dear sister,

I write this on the *Albion*, a Western Ocean ship that takes us to London, for mailing after we arrive. We didn't sail from New York until November 10 so you are unlikely to receive this message until the new year. The *Albion* is a comfortable packet boat with an interesting passenger list. Those who travel as gentlemen have ample time to present our arguments when we dine together because there are not many of us. Our enforced leisure stimulates discussions about the vagaries of loyalty and the vicissitudes and victories of life. I presume that the holds of the ship now filled with the produce of our endeavors will be crowded upon return with passengers with less opportunity to eat as properly or as well. Nevertheless, our tables have their own tensions and I think wistfully of the meditative calm that must pervade silent meals shared between your holy Sisters.

Monseigneur Carriere, a fellow traveler, presents as a politician as much as a religious leader. I told him that I was baptized "Jean-Baptiste" and assured safe passage if he would send a priest to the Indian Territories to perform the same sacrament for my children. He informs me of his great respect for your school at the Ursuline Convent, having sanctified marriage vows for many brides who had benefited from being your pupils. It is too many years hence to imagine a future for the daughter whom I left in your care but I suspect Eliza will not follow in the footsteps of her older cousins, who profess a Catholic vocation with as much girlish commitment as you once did. Therefore, I must ensure she has a dowry that will attract a proper husband.

Have you even doubted your decision to profess as a religious? Not that I expect you to answer such a question, it is impertinent even to voice it. Such a query is evidence that this brother is less a gentleman than he was seventeen years ago when he was a hot-headed naïve youth who was hustled away from Quebec. Although my options were few, I also was tempted by the lure of oral promises made by a gentleman whose word had brief temporal value and less moral weight. May McTavish long repent his sin of exploiting young men who trusted him for advancement in their career. I am now more businessman than medicine man.

I travel to London as a leader negotiating on behalf of the NWC Wintering partners. We want to receive fair recompense for risks incurred in our isolated posts, risks we incur equally to our lives and souls, risks that have long brought unjust profits into the pockets of those who dwell more comfortably in high society. While they sip tea we chew pemmican. Our Chief Traders carry the flag of civilized ideals to unknown territories and lands. Life in *les pays d'en haut* tests the metal of men, sifting pure value from base overlays. Our wild Garden of Eden provides many temptations, so many that it becomes difficult to determine who is civilized and who is savage. We rarely listen to Christian narratives but if these ideals are not part of a man's character, his behavior is unlikely to be ideal.

What makes a man civilized? "It is to be a citizen who cultivates his character, his property and who protects people who reside on it," responds the Englishman. The late Lord Selkirk, so recently deceased in Pau, home to your King Henri IV, might be an example. Both of these idealists, each in their own century, attempted to improve the lot of those poor who had little opportunity for a good life. The powerful winds of religious fervor and economic instability proved too much for their talents but these noblemen were much admired for their attempts. "A civilized man loves life, liberty and the pursuit of happiness," claim French Republicans and their admirers, the Americans. However, the French Revolution is remembered more for its excessive terrorism than for its enlightened governance while Americans exploit others through enslavement so their cotton plantations and mills may thrive. "True civilization rests upon reasoned inquiry, a knowledgeable observation of facts and a rational probing of religious mysteries," states the Scholar Priest (including beloved sisters who teach). But even they must eat. In our age the businessman is an explorer, probing wondrous frontiers, but is he civilized? Perhaps my sojourn in Europe will assist me to find answers to this question.

I travel as businessman to propose a reorganization of the fur trade in North America. Unlike our dear David whom I will see in person in a few short weeks, my journey is to bargain, not to study. Mr. Bethune, my traveling companion and colleague, visited Canton during the early days of his NWC contract. He enthuses about expanding our trade in furs, especially ermine, and profiting from return voyages with the produce of ancient cultures in the Orient, especially tea and spices. The HBC Directors are well acquainted with the successes of the East India Company but it does not have a royal charter and soon must renegotiate the terms of its monopoly. They are situated to expedite appropriate political arrangements in England. For centuries, men like Martin Frobisher dreamed of finding a northwest passage to the Far East but their expeditions always ended with ships trapped by ice flows. Henry Hudson found the great bay that now serves as the HBC depot but the inland passage is overland, not by water. The way to Eastern riches is through trading furs and NWC men have centuries of experience trapping in the high country.

As for me, the Governor and Lords will study the face of a man who understands the Indian Territories, who treats the injuries of lonely traders, whose loyal family assisted the British crown to acquire and hold its North American colonies and whose very life was held hostage because of their policies. They will be respectful of the eighteen signatures I carry giving me power of attorney. These are proxies from men whose service is essential to future profits. If the Royal Charter is to be anything but a piece of paper without any real value beyond the frigid Hudson's Bay, we will be listened to. It is unlikely Mr. Bethune and I will have a front-row seat when the directors of the HBC and NWC negotiate at the same table but I think we *deputés* have influence. Business is the study of people and finances as much as it is the exchange of goods. In these arenas the banner of civilization is often contested. These contestants are *gentil* only in social station, they are more like wolves ripping at a carcass that still breathes.

As you know, I have paid the price of such contests. Travel by canoe to drafty and remote cabins has no further charm for me, if it ever did. My labors, whether the treatment of disease and consequences of disorderly behaviors or the management of trade goods, have resulted in unseemly profits for other men whose greatest advantage has been their access to the ears of those with power. I am fortunate to be alive. Other men of my temperament and age have died and not because all were intemperate or ill-tempered. The loss of all the men on the *Tonquin* ship along the Pacific Ocean coast in 1811, and in 1818 the premature deaths of brave young Frobisher who starved near the south Saskatchewan River, and young MacKenzie's drowning in a Lake Superior storm, mark years of increasing violence across the breadth of the vast Indian territories. These are stories of talent snuffed too early because of unwise and intolerant competition. I have no desire to complete the narrative of my life so young. My body is already an aching testament to the travails of the past few years.

One dining companion aboard ship is Mr. Colin Robertson, once a Nor'Wester, now in the employ of the Hudson's Bay. Like me, he survived a recent near-drowning and was held as a captive to be ransomed in the trade wars between the fur companies. In fact he is on this ship because he avoided arrest in Montreal by flinging hot biscuits in the faces of his NWC captors and escaped to the USA. We agree not to discuss our respective petitions to the HBC Governor and Committee members but we share similar views about how Wintering partners should be reimbursed for their successful exploitations. He encourages the HBC to become a profit-sharing company, with shares distributed among men in the field as well as among the men who sit in the London offices effecting intercontinental sales. If he succeeds, the protection of a royal charter will make the Hudson's Bay Company a monopoly with resources against which no one else in the known world could compete. Mr. Robertson's position is not much different from that of Mr. Bethune and me. But he does not know that we will present a proposal from a majority of

Nor'West Wintering partners. It is the fault of the Montrealers themselves that they lose our loyalty. Had promises been honored to young recruits about a fair reward based upon a sustained financial plan, the McGillivray Bros. would not have the NWC in the position it is now. Where once a few men could make fortunes in a few years, many men must now work for years in harsh conditions, scattered across the continent. More complex conditions make both ends of the trading transaction risky. These risks do not diminish so profits must be distributed more equitably. Our perspective requires a longer view than a capricious annual cycle and undercutting rivals so that no one profits.

This year truly has been one of passages. Sir Alexander Mackenzie is dead and can no longer influence the Trade from his Scottish estate. Lord Selkirk has died but his Scottish settlers remain at Red River to pursue his dream. Mr. Robertson informs me Andrew Colville of the HBC Committee sponsors a new man in the Indian Territories. After disembarking, it took Mr. George Simpson only seven days to journey upstream from New York to Montreal but I doubt he could describe much detail of the terrain. Before going to Norway House, he made a long detour to Fort William. Now that he has seen the place for himself and met the men in charge, he will undoubtedly make a report to his mentor, Lord Colville, in London. Mr. Simpson carries letters signed by Lord Bathurst of the British Parliament addressed to both the HBC and the NWC indicating that the British government will not favorably regard further hostilities by either company. I met George Simpson at Fort William on his way to pass his first Winter in the North West as I was preparing to depart for my first Winter in London. A tiny accountant, he seems destined to be a Napoleon, much given to plotting long days for men and supplies so they move in accordance with more profitable goals. I think Simpson respects ledgers more than men but if he survives a Winter in the field he will bring much-needed skills to any amalgamated company.

Another generation takes over affairs. I am certain Cuthbert Grant is destined to influence the new Metis nation forming at the Red River. My son Joseph and my stepson Thomas are among the young bucks aligned with him. These mixed bloods ride as freely through the prairies as others might stride familiar city streets. We must develop good relationships among the diverse fur trade offspring and settlers in the lands beyond the Great Lakes. Whatever society they build, education and religion are certain to provide the best moderating influences. As you know, that expectation is why I brought my namesake son out to school at Terrebonne and my young daughter to the Ursuline Convent where you are *Mère Supérieure*. Living in Upper and Lower Canada during the formative years of their lives better positions them for an advantageous future. I hope they will have roles upon a larger stage than in our lawless arena.

You, David, and I much benefited from the support of our uncles and grandfather. In their time, seigneuries along the St. Lawrence shores were the new estates to develop. Some of the knowledge I absorbed from business affairs in the Trade helps me to manage responsibly the farms that we now inherit. When I see David in Paris, I will ask our brother to sign power of attorney so these family establishments might be more profitably managed. Cousin John Fraser will oversee the annual operations.

A part of my heart will always beat more quickly when I arrive at the St. Lawrence River and I would like a quick ride to enjoy merry evenings among friends. I know my wife prefers western waterways. She births our fourth child while I am in Europe. Always in good health, she has lived more than forty years so this infant is her final one. Mine is a small family compared to those of our sisters' families in Quebec but I strive so that we all enjoy good lives.

Such ambitious plans are expensive, as is this trip to Europe. I await my reunion with Dr. David, decorated surgeon of the Continental Wars, with anticipation. He will show me all the wonders of Paris and where the Revolution was fought. Perhaps we will observe the debates of elected *Deputés*. Mr. Robertson has accepted an invitation to visit us in Boulogne some time next year. He can debate the merits of Shakespeare and Wordsworth while David presents truths from the *philosophes* and new breed of scientists. This open disputation is a type of conflict more preferable to the shadowy corridors of English politics that I must haunt. I do not know how long my negotiations will take, nor how my health will fare, but I am overdue for furlough and eager to learn more about civilization as it is manifested in the great cities of London and Paris.

Upon my return to Lower Canada, be certain I will transport some items for your school. However long I am away, please keep me in your daily prayers so that I might succeed.

Your adoring brother

1821, Letter sent by boat probably with Angus Bethune while John remains in Europe

My beloved sister,

A new era has begun! On March 26, the amalgamation agreement between the HBC and the NWC was signed. There is but one ruler of commerce in all lands included in the Royal Charter of 1670. We are now "Adventurers of England" trading into Hudson's Bay, the St. Lawrence and the Columbia Rivers, including trading contact with the port of Canton. All this for five shillings! I witnessed the British Parliament confirm on July 2 that the Company has an exclusive charter for trade in all of British North America excepting the various Atlantic colonies and colonies of Lower and Upper Canadas.

We will have a period of twenty-one years to exploit the un-known resources of these vast territories, perhaps to bring some civilization to remote cabins, and to stabilize the small societies within our purview. Although the monopoly is also renewable, it does not result in peace for the Promised Land, however. Americans are canny traders as Astor has demonstrated and the Indians have learned to bargain to their advantage. This competi-tion does not always mean consistency in annual returns. Mother Nature has not agreed to be kind, so we must plan to survive lean Winters. Most of all, settlements of farmers and harvesting of furs are not complementary occupations although they could be more so than the experiment of the Red River colony has indicated thus far.

I return to Canada as a Chief Factor, and, like others with this office, hold two of one hundred shares in the HBC Company. Most senior NWC Wintering partners received similar awards, so together we have fifty-five per cent of the total number of shares. Our feisty NWC men own the field while the HBC controls the executive decisions but I think it a good mating of the strengths of both companies. The new order makes promotion more difficult because there will be fewer positions. Not everyone will emerge as winners. Those gentlemen in either company who exhibit appropriate promise and temperance will have a better future as consequence of their labors and deportment. *Voyageur engagées* will be treated better because there will be less harassment along the brigade routes. Notably, not one of the mixed-blood Metis is listed by name in the gentlemen's agreement. The most likely candidate, Cuthbert Grant, was specifically excluded because of his past politics. These young men will have difficulty even to be appointed clerks in the new regime.

The HBC sends one of its committee members, Mr. Nicholas Garry, to the annual rendezvous at Fort William with William McGillivray so that the new face of the old company is seen in the assembly. Mr. Garry is a young bachelor, very sensitive to diverse types of people, and interested in visiting the Indian Territories. He will be a good representative. His report will be awaited with interest here at "home", meaning London for all British subjects, even though our hearts might be elsewhere.

By remaining in London, I miss the last great rendezvous at Fort William but next year must attend the first annual meeting of the joint companies at Norway House. Governor and Committee understand that since nearly drowning because of Lord Selkirk's intemperate actions, my aching joints, especially my hip, constrain desire for additional long voyages.

My attention to scientific observations has been stimulated by many lectures here in London and Paris. Conversations with David remind me of how much I have missed. In France, our respected brother is the first British subject to receive *la Légion d' Honneur* because he established a hospital for French soldiers after being captured by them. Emperor Napoleon is exiled from Paris but the upper classes of France consult the distinguished *docteur*. And now that it is safe for English nobles to visit France, his medical practice is further extended. I am gratified to observe how well Dr. David applies the skills I helped him acquire while I learned about survival in another type of bloody war. He will be my ambassador at court when I return to some distant trading post.

Another skill I polished while at the center of the world is diplomacy. Mr. Bethune and I supped well during many evenings, first with the McGillivray brothers who this past Winter grew more willing to listen to the concerns of the NWC Wintering partners than they had been in the Canadas. Then we dined in opulent gentlemen's clubs with Grandfather's old friend and business partner, Mr. Caldwell, now the Receiver General of Lower Canada. He proved to be very close to Mr. Ellice of the HBC Governing Committee, a Montreal crony from the peak period of NWC profiteering. Nicknamed "The Bear", Mr. Ellice has put his great fortune to good use and married well into Whig circles. He is a new MP who has the ear of Lord Bathurst, which undoubtedly aided the parliamentary rite of passage for our grand new scheme. Mr. Bethune and I will not step into the pages of history for our background contributions but we did help bring a bloody chapter to a close and anticipate a positive conclusion to the story!

This past year permitted me to make first-hand observations of differences between the English and the French as well. Mr. Garry might return to England with tales of our wild dominions, but I have stories about Europe. The attentions of the British people are fixated on the long-delayed crowning of King George IV in England. The new King attempted to install the husband of his mistress as Lord Chamberlain but Prime Minister Liverpool blocked the appointment. Queen Caroline returned from Italy to fight her divorce petition in Parliament, exciting much sympathy among the common people and even within the Royal Guard. Her actions delayed the coronation ceremony for a year. Ultimately the Queen was barred from Westminster Abbey both for the taking of the oath and the celebratory banquet. Within the following month this lady was deceased, a rapid exit from center stage.

In an attempt to produce heirs to the throne, the King's two middle-aged brothers had been married off in a double ceremony at Kew little more than two years ago. The Duke of Clarence, likely successor to the throne, still has only illegitimate offspring. Our old acquaintance, the Duke of Kent, recalled back from Quebec City to produce progeny, sustains the dynasty by leaving a tiny daughter, Victoria. If this infant survives, she might become Queen of England one day. I imagine that you are not too removed from society to appreciate how Grandfather Fraser might comment upon the cold sanctity of legal marriages and the comforts of illegal liaisons.

Meanwhile, in an attempt to reverse their misfortunes and end the ceaseless civil terrors in France, the Republicans restored the brother of Louis XVI. This so-called bourgeois revolution has ensured a return of the clergy. Our David mingles amongst the better classes in France but protests his untimely discharge from the British Army and remains on half-pay until the dispute is resolved. Much to the dismay of his superior medical officer, we have used our Royal connections to arbitrate the conclusion. I have been of some assistance because the Duke of Kent remembered our grandfather well from their merry youthful days in Quebec and us as little boys who pestered them.

The first observation of anyone arriving in London would be the great docks. Massive East India Company warehouses all but eclipse the new HBC buildings. London is a wealthy merchant city, all stuffed with global influence. Wives and daughters move elegantly through fashionable townhouses and country estates. Merchants become members of private clubs, invitation only. In their smoky libraries they discuss the weighty burdens of Empire and the discoveries of natural science. By contrast, Paris is a collection of charming villages in which *glitterae* gather to listen to music or readings at elegant *soirées*. Some ladies ride thoroughbred horses like *amazones* through the Bois de Boulogne, not always sitting sidesaddle. David has a bachelor's *garçonnière* but I hope soon to encourage him in the establishment of a more prestigious *apartement* so that he might host visitors more appropriately. His years in Scotland and France, plus a youth in Lower Canada, offer a hint of the exotic that is quite fashionable in this city but such a background would be less well received in England. *Parisiens*, women and men, dine publicly together at little *café bistros* along the boulevards, enjoying the sunlight ambiance among the trees and dappling in their own flirtations. Although French women are more free to appear in public, they do not seem to benefit materially from political revolutions. The Napoleonic Code restricts legal rights of inheritance, thus making women more dependent on their families than they were in the earlier days of direct inheritances. You are undoubtedly aware that increasing numbers of women have been attracted to the newly restored religious orders in France. The situation offers, as you know, a sort of personal independence not available elsewhere. My wife has more liberty! Mgr. Carriere and his colleagues scout for priests to replenish their numbers in Quebec and the results of their hunt are poor. Would you care to speculate why the numbers of women religious grow at the same time as the commitment of men decreases, my accomplished sister?

I have been absent from the company of white women for so long, I am shy in the presence of these glorious creatures, whether English or French. With some pleasure, I shop for the women I know best. The collections of fashionable patterns and woven cloth for my wife and our sisters are admirable at least in my eyes. David introduced me to a good tailor so I shall appear quite foppish upon my return from a whiff of the prestigious. Dressed always in the white wimple and black robes that Monseigneur Laval proscribed, you and your Sisters are perhaps not so inter-ested in these vanities. Therefore I will not go on in detail but do remember to admire the new outfits that our mother and sisters will undoubtedly wear on a future visit to the grill of your Convent. I would not be adverse to similar flattery should you approve of the refurbished appearance of your gentleman brother, HBC Chief Factor. To tempt you I bring other types of presents that David helped me select.

Here in the great capitals, there is experimentation with painting, with sculpture, even with furniture and architecture. The bourgeois class reflects a confidence and wealth. When a man has enough wealth to purchase land from his risky ventures and to build magnificent houses while managing the establishment and people on it with grace, he then wants more of a voice in the politics of governance. It is a franchise that increases participation in the public policies. Among the decanters and crystal glasses, the harps and cellos, the imaginative novels, I note unrest in London and Paris. Too many people work from dawn to dusk in factories while an ennobled few at the apex of power benefit. Infections and sores among the poor who walk sewery streets are obvious to anyone who has eyes and who will look on their rags.

It is the exciting domain of ideas that I will miss most after my return to the colonies. The engine of Empire is not the product of industry, the outputs of factories, the final exchange of woolen blankets in exchange for beaver pelts. Progress results from the ideals that motivate men to persist in the face of difficulties and the values that women instill in children to make a civilized society. In his novels, Walter Scott revives the mists of Scottish culture as much as he describes the glens. The enormous painting of Gericault in Piccadilly Square has an allegorical message. *Raft of the Medusa* is a more disturbing warning about the dangers of revolution than any glorious monument to a dead hero. Faraday explains how magnets attract and repel, inferring a thousand applications of this force. Adam Smith demonstrates how the wealth of nations rests upon the harnessing of individual effort in mutual gain for individual and society. Dickens reminds anyone who can read that poverty is enslavement but neither a predestined or moral situation. These ideas compete for our souls as well as our minds.

City life demands too much daily nodding and bowing for me. The country life of a gentlemen is more balanced and attractive. Whereas Grandfather won his land as a consequence of war, and Father gained his as a consequence of marriage, I must win mine through industrious management. I return to a place where the stars act as lamplights and rivers are roads for our traders, where people dance more for joy than for propriety and pomp. Mr. Darwin's words about survival of the fittest in a species has new meaning. The English organize their society for the stout purposes of worldly success and good governance. The French are more of the moment, a *je ne sais quoi* attitude. The New World that you and I inhabit could be constructed from the best intellectual offerings of the old and our own raw resources. We must be as competent when sifting ideological wheat from chaff as we are at evaluating furs that the Indians bring to our stores! Continue to navigate skillfully the cultural cross-currents of Quebec and bring your students safely to new understandings!

Confirmation of my next post awaits reports from Mr. Simpson who is much regarded by the HBC directors. His assessment of the situation at the rendezvous might affect my posting because I have influence with the NWC Wintering partners. I return with surprises for all of you but, as I do not know my exact departure nor the place of arrival, I may not transport these gifts in person. Please assure my daughter that I am concerned for her progress and will forward a letter upon my arrival. Many thanks to you for the influence your prayers have had upon our business affairs.

With great affection,

Yr bro.

1824, Letter sent from Rainy Lake to Quebec

Dearest Mother Supérieure,

As a consequence of the new order in our remote world, I am in charge of the rural factorum at Rainy Lake. (Whether to continue using French names, such as *Lac la Pluie*, is the new contest.) As seigneur, pardon me, esquire and Chief Factor of this establishment, I continue to devise activities that might result in a more harmonious amalgam of settlement and trade. It has been an interesting experiment but I anticipate moving onto a larger stage. This letter will be forwarded by express canoe to Lower Canada because we leave soon for the annual meeting at York Factory, Fort William no longer being our major *entrepôt*. Mr. George Simpson has succeeded in reorganizing us again, always of course to his benefit but, in this instance, also mine. He will be in charge of the Northern and Southern Departments of the HBC while I take command of the new Columbia Department. We go directly to the Pacific Ocean at the conclusion of this gathering, therefore I leave Marguerite and our younger children at Norway House near Playgreen Lake, from which point we turn west to go over the Rocky Mountains. I look forward to being in charge of my own department because the Trade here will be run according to the same principles as industrial establishments in England. Some of these ideas are efficacious but I think that people govern regulations; rules don't make people.

My report about the natural science experiments conducted at Rainy Lake is completed and is to be forwarded to London. I look forward to receiving comments of the Royal Academy of Science as well as the HBC Committee and Governors. Natural history is the new focus so acquaintances I met during my furlough will be interested in our results. I attempted to cultivate a sort of plantation that might provide income and food for the increasing numbers of people who regard this country as home. Once an area is trapped out of furs, the next generation must plant and harvest seed to supplement the hunt. Selkirk's settlers might be subsistence farmers hoping to till better fields than they had in the old country, but the Metis are nomads who require less in the way of material goods and more space. However, they observe the settlers' efforts more thoughtfully since Seven Oaks made it obvious that the British government will not abandon these territories even though future policies remain uncertain.

Americans are more direct in their aspirations. President Munro articulates a doctrine as imperialist as any colonial nation and claims most of the continent. Their free traders move into our trapping territories but there is no need yet to initiate another trade war. I suspect that our commercial trade may not be as weighty a consideration as stability in relations between governments. Mr. Simpson will advise the London Committee how to influence the British government when the survey of this area is completed. It would help to establish a boundary line with the American government. The Boundary Commission established a precedent at the 49th parallel after the War of 1812 in Upper Canada. If so, the southern Pembina territory granted to Lord Selkirk and any trading posts south of the 49th Parallel will be lost to American settlers. Thus our Red River and Rainy Lake depots become even more important to subjects of the British Empire. My report includes a description of the Indian tribes who live in this area because the British government must take some responsibility for their welfare when international boundaries are declared. As I leave Rupert's Land, I wonder how the French culture in this region will fare. This contest of culture will be fought in the churches and schools. My son John is immersed in the English style of life and my daughter Eliza in the French. Time will reveal the harvests of such experimentations.

Now that the fur trade has moved into the North and West, Rainy Lake trading post is not as strategically important as York Factory on Hudson's Bay. The people who remain here must become more self-sufficient because pemmican supplies are reduced, and even the buffalo have moved West. We have grown culinary herbs that help diversify the diet and provide medicines. Near this post, I had a little mill built. The harvested grain demonstrates it is possible to provide bread for paddlers of the express brigades and settlers. Many of our men have taken early retirement since integration, sometimes unwillingly. Red River seems to be a good settlement for those men who do not wish to leave their country families. Priests and ministers have arrived to remind us of Godly expectations for our souls and they open schools for children. The Metis nation, following the leadership of Cuthbert Grant, establishes its own hunting community and governance. And the abandoned Scottish settlers struggle on, fierce about establishing deeper roots. Indians camp at the edge of these three disparate societies. A little store, a small church and a tiny school brings all together but only for wary short periods. Perhaps it is better that way because these societies have no common government except that which the British government delegated to the HBC Governor and Factor to act as magistrate but not judge.

As for me, I turn a profit and look to further expansion. Having refused the Columbia depot when there was grave personal threat and little possibility of safe delivery of our furs, I now go with Mr. Simpson to determine how best to develop the Pacific coastal trade. It has been necessary to use all my European influences to confirm this appointment. My friend Angus Bethune will go to Moose Factory and may not stay much longer in the Trade. He will try on the HBC colors to see how well they wear on him but wishes to retire to Upper Canada in a few years. Many men and wives who travel with us are old Nor'Westers so we will form a sort of colony of old timers and will have some cohesion.

Marguerite goes with me although there are grandchildren to enjoy before she departs, perhaps forever from them. Her McKay daughters have married. Nancy resides at Sault Ste. Marie where her husband, Captain McCargo has a good reputation because he hid his ship to avoid capture during the recent American raids in the war. The middle daughter, Catherine, will leave the territories when her English soldier completes his tour of duty. The youngest, Mary, recently became wife of trader James Sinclair and will reside at Red River. We look forward to a reunion with my stepson, Thomas McKay. He will greet us on the other side of the Rocky Mountains where he was hired to prepare horses and boats for transporting our brigade from the Athabasca mountain pass to the Pacific Ocean. My son Joseph stays at the Sault Ste. Marie portage with his stepsister for another year to benefit from schooling, although he does not show much inclination toward book learning. I expect more from our two children who are boarded at good schools in the Canadas, including yours. The two little ones travel with us but I may send them out to you and my Fraser uncles when they are older and could be separated from their parents.

This freedom on the other side of the mountains will feel like a warm westerly wind. I follow David Thompson's steps along his grand river but have not much desire to return on an annual brigade. The challenge is to build my own department in a territory wherein Indians are more numerous and hostile and trading competitors are diverse. The challenge excites me. If one is going to be in the Trade, then it is best to be senior officer in a new area, with a staff of old friends. I will have the weighty support of the HBC Governing Committee, the British government and, most of all, occasional visits by the British navy. Mr. Simpson, a man of industry, keeps a tight eye on inventory and likes the politics of making money talk, especially with the governors. I prefer the example of the Lairds and seigneurs who managed great estates and kindly people. If one is to live within the British Empire, one does well to be associated with a company positioned to turn great profits. Perhaps when my pockets are as full as my stomach, I will think differently and retire to Quebec. But this year I go the HBC annual meeting to take the pulse of Rupert's Land and say farewells. An initial diagnosis of our Trade: patient is recovering after a serious illness but will be more robust in a few seasons.

It will be many years before we meet again. In the interim, I take pleasure in making your monastery an offering that I know will be offered to God. Watch over my children. Seek my image in their faces for they are our future. Do not forget us in your prayers for God watches his sparrows wherever they fly. In the Columbia, although we will have not the guidance of men dedicated to God's work, surely He himself will be present to bless our activities and assess our actions.

With great affection,

Yr brother

1824, Letter sent from Ursuline Convent to Fort William for forwarding to the Norway House meeting

Mon Frére Royale,

This letter is forwarded with the hope that it will reach you before the departure to the mouth of the Columbia River. It carries tangible evidence of my affection and prayers. Mother Marie de l'Incarnation expected her letters to be private communications with her son and so she opened her heart in them. I write to you in English, so that I might maintain fluency with this part of my soul. My packet is infused by prayers offered in the French language. Know my dear brother, that, as always, I carried this letter to and from many Masses with the hope this blessing might guard you. When we sang to commemorate the souls of martyrs Brébeuf and Lalemant on March 16 my thoughts traveled to the site of their sacrifice and your survival from death in those nearby waters. Our epoch has dangers of its own. In spite of all the time that has passed since the martyrs were tortured and our own elevation to lesser responsibilities, you also travel to territories where the church does not yet have ministry. Whether French or English, Catholic or Protestant, a Christian commitment will be most important because you will be the father of your flock. It will not be an easy crown to wear. Strive to be an example of how a man should behave as leader.

I am assured that the HBC requires senior officers to read the Bible every Sunday to all in their establishment. This religious observance is better than none at all. However, perhaps you could speak about God in French as well as in English for the sake of your men and the families they bring with them. You wrote that David Thompson and other gentlemen in your trade honor Christ, His Father and Mother, and the Holy Spirit by sometimes telling stories from the Bible that are translated into Indian languages. Ursuline Sisters have used this teaching strategy since the time of Marie de l'Incarnation. Once a soul is brought to God, even if that person falls from grace, it is never permanently lost.

Together with a rosary, I enclose a reminder, one that your wife will be pleased to know your daughter has memorized. Almost two centuries ago, Mère Marie bade us offer this little evening prayer to close each day. As we kneel in our Convent near the banks of one great river of North America while you traverse the continent to the shores of another mighty waterway, perhaps you might sometimes offer this prayer at sunset. It links us to each other and to great Mysteries that only God understands.

> *Répandez Seigneur, vos bénédictions, sur mes parents, mes*
> *   bienfaiteurs mes amis et mes ennemis.*
> *Protégez tous ceux que vous m'avez donnés pour maîtres, tant*
> *   spirituels qui temporels.*
> *Sécourez les pauvres, les prisonniers, les affligés, les voyageurs,*
> *   les malades en les agonisants.*
> *Convertissez les hérétiques, et éclairez les infidèles.*

> (Pour forth Thy blessings, O Lord, on my parents,
>   benefactors, friends, and enemies.
> Protect all those to whom Thou hast confined my
>   spiritual or temporal welfare.
> Have compassion on the poor, the prisoner, the af-
>   flicted, the traveler, the sick, the dying.
> Convert all heretics, and enlighten all infidels.)

This April at our annual meeting, I became *dépositaire* again after completing two terms as *Mère Supérieure*. Like you, I will spend many weary hours reviewing ledgers and letters. These duties draw us from the people we love, those for whom we have responsibility to nurture and oversee. During my term as leader of our Community, I was honored that all the young novitiates that I supervised remained steadfast in their vows. Thus our numbers grow, although we recently said Mass for two deceased, the most elderly of our Order. With the passage of one, Mère Josephete Lafontaine de Therese-de-Jesus who came directly from France, our grand artistry of decorative embroidery becomes a lost tradition. The French Revolution destroyed all Ursuline Convent workshops so this craft has been sustained by those of us in the colonies, a much more poor offering. My Sisters are competent needle workers but not fine artists. You will remember the vivacious centerpiece medallions of our precious priestly vestments and altar cloths. Each recreates familiar Bible stories in beautiful images, evoking a fresh dedication among the faithful. My favorite is a lively scene of the Holy Family, who seem to be one of our parish families. My companions and I must now preserve these treasures for we will not see their like again. They will be carefully stored and used only for great occasions at special Masses.

Nevertheless we are not without some culture in our visual arts and music. Mr. Bowman, from Boston, instructs our pupils in crayon and oil-paintings. The altars and shrines are decorated weekly by their efforts. The piano you gifted us is much used. Our music classes have expanded and the requests for instruction bring us additional money. Mr. Glockemayer from the Anglican Cathedral supervises these classes. We attracted his services because he enjoys playing the instrument so much. When your daughter sits at the piano, I remind her that you provided the instrument. The greatest talent Eliza exhibits is with her music. No doubt she is inspired by this thoughtful gesture of yours. I think her playing so sufficiently developed that I have requested she assist our novice teachers in the classes. Another new arrival is musician Theodore Molt, who was in the Napoleonic Wars. His talents supplement Mr. Glockemayer at the Cathedral but he interests himself also in the old habitant songs. He is the first person to spend time writing them down.

You and I have often talked about the noble ideals and efforts of Lord Selkirk to settle destitute Scots in the Indian territories. Our *Ville de Quebec* becomes increasingly Irish! More than 20,000 people have arrived since 1820 and that doubles the total population of our town. We have moved the class of little Irish girls enrolled as *externs* into the same hours as the children who board with us. The Governor's Education Society and these new immigrants generate numerous demands to admit even more children. We need more English-speaking nuns to immigrate! Through the efforts of my great friend and companion, Mother Cecilia O'Conway, we have opened correspondence with the Ursuline Convent of St. Mary's in Waterford, Ireland. Therefore, in addition to our music lessons and our science classes, we hope to be provided with wonderful teachers of literature written in the English language. We are very proud of our efforts to intertwine these English and French traditions. It makes a stronger tree to harvest.

One fruit is a book by a former pupil, Judith Hart Beckwith. She has authored *St. Ursula's Convent or the Nun of Canada, Containing Scenes from Real Life*. Dedicated to Countess Dalhousie, the story is placed within the geography of France as well as the Canadas. It covers several generations and therefore is realistic enough. The novel is the first to be published in English in British North America.

Thus the colonies in the Canadas grow ever more literate and cultured. Your previous mentor, Dr. John Fisher, has been appointed to the new position of King's Printer. He composed the Latin inscription for the Wolfe-Montcalm monument in the Governor's Garden. I am told it reads:

> *Monumenti in memoriam vivorum illustrium Wolfe et Montcalm*
> *Fundamentum C.c. Georgius comtes de Dalhousie in septentrionalis americae partibus ad Britannos pertinentibus summam rerum administrans opus per multos annos praetermissem (quid duci egregio convenientius) auctoritate promovens exemplo stimulans munificientia fovens.*
> *Die novembris XVa A.D. MDCCCXXVII*

Like your establishment, there is no doubt that the dominant culture of our colonies will be based upon the English empire. Most new immigrants speak some dialect of that language and England has a world of oceans and lands to exploit. But our French people are hardy and their roots will not wither. I think the Metis nation provides interesting evidence. Your little sons and daughters are a melange of Scots, French, Irish, Swiss, and Indian. It is indeed a new world we cultivate, you in your commerce and I in my classes. Whatever customs we cherish, whatever ideas we pass on, whatever ideals we value and how we express them to each other, these all become foundations for our inheritors. I pray that the Holy Spirit guides us all in our endeavors.

May God protect you during your journey, your family and your men and your interests after you arrive in the Columbia Department.

With great affection,

Your loving sister

1825, From the Columbia Department

My dear sister,

This letter goes out with George Simpson's return brigade until the Red River settlement. Then he turns north to York Factory for the next HBC annual meeting while the letter awaits the express canoe that goes along the old route to Montreal. Mr. Simpson is very proud of his ability to travel rapidly and, indeed, has earned a reputation for pushing his men through long days and distances. Perhaps his size helps. It is easier to paddle a small man in a canoe – and all more comfortable – as the *voyageur engagées* know. On our journey west, my party was more heavily loaded with supplies and family. Although Governor Simpson's brigade departed later, he caught up with us one morning laboring through Methy Portage, which is about eleven miles long, mostly uphill. He chose to follow the river named after Lord Nelson, while I chose Lord Hayes' river. Nelson died fighting at Trafalgar after defending the interests of the far-flung British Empire whereas Lord Hayes earned much profit from his investment in the Chartered Company when it was newly formed and then retired to his great Kent estate. Perhaps the river routes that Mr. Simpson and I chose foretell our futures. Thus, I lost my first great wager with him, but not the final one I hope. One week after we began to travel together, he placed himself under my medical care because he admitted to feeling "extremely unwell." During his prescribed half-day rest, he busied himself drafting letters to the Governor and the Chief Factors in his departments. He demonstrates thereby a human mortality as well as an industrious temperament.

Even with children, our conjoint brigade cut three weeks off the previous record! To arrive early at our final destination where the Columbia River joins the Pacific Ocean, we paddled from 10 P.M. until daybreak. Then we worked all day against a head-wind and arrived at Fort George to find the Chief Factor and

119

Trader enjoying an afternoon of sailing. Our new Governor-in-Chief was not amused. Mr. Simpson now intends to return in time to chair the HBC Winter partners' annual meeting at York by setting the travel standard very high. He knows that if he delays the start of the arduous trip, he can work the men with less complaint at the *finalé* because they do not want the last choice of campsites or dancing partners during the rendezvous. Mr. Simpson's favorite phrase is "steady and active management." Therefore, his return trip will initiate further changes in our entire organization. He prefers York boats but the expeditions lack *la majesté* of the *canot du Nord* without the graceful cadence of canoe paddlers. God alone knows what will have been inaugurated by the time I next make a trip across the mountains. It is a three-month journey, even with Mr. Simpson's hurry ups.

Changes in route reflect other changes in our routines. HBC industry brings more efficiency and profits but, throughout the territories, all employees are less secure in the Trade. Those employees who read and write and are thus considered civilized gentlemen are responsible for men as well as profits. Undoubtedly loneliness and drink will continue to tarnish and deplete the sterling in many a man's character. My department is supported by North West Company survivors so we form a sort of alliance, although our gentlemen's club is much different from those I visited in London. Traders are sent out in large parties because Indians tribes here are plentiful in numbers and their previous contacts with various white men have not always resulted in advantages to any involved.

To the North are Russian competitors, to the South, Spanish, to the West, the Orient, to the East, Americans. Of these, I think Americans are most dangerous because they travel overland as independent freemen trading whiskey and establish an unscrupulous presence among the Indians. According to the Treaty of Ghent, British and American traders have eleven years of joint occupation, a brief time-period in which to exploit the resources of this area.

Mr. Ogden, whose family you know, is now restored to HBC favor although it took some time after his actions during the tensions at Red River. He is in charge at Spokane House, our inland supply depot and uses horse brigades to trap out the Snake River drainage areas. He undercuts American mountain men with the quality of our goods and advantageous bartering. We will create a fur desert for those who work against us. The financial resources of the HBC may seem as vast as their territories but we create a buffer zone to delay direct competition and discourage lawlessness such as was experienced among the competitors at Red River.

There is a dispute over ownership where the river joins the ocean. I carried Sir Alexander MacKenzie's gun with me to the Columbia and plan to brandish it on any occasion necessary to assert British rights to these coastal waters. Fifteen years ago Nor'Westers hired by the Astor Fur Co. raised an American flag just weeks prior to Mr. David Thompson's arrival. Our North West Co. men purchased the fort from the Americans during the 1812 War and a British naval officer arrived soon after to raise the Union Jack as reinforcement of its dominion, but the contest for title continues.

My men build a substantial trading fort on the north shore of the river that cannot fail to impress gentlemen visitors from various countries as well as the local Indians. We have named it Fort Vancouver. At the mouth of the river is a large sand bar that makes it difficult for ocean vessels to enter during tidal changes. An anchored ship with cargo and crew becomes vulnerable to raiding parties from Coastal Indians as well as the ravages of nature. As a consequence of these serious uncertainties, Fort Vancouver is located a hundred miles upriver where it is more protected. The alluvial soil is rich land so we will cultivate provides opportunities for generating a supply depot for those who arrive on ships and who travel to the interior. Also, our location is more strategic. Horse brigades can more easily deposit their furs and river traveling Indians can access our goods without fearing raids from tribes along the coast.

Unless our Columbia Department returns an immediate profit to the Lords in London, they will not be persuaded to lobby the British government to establish the international boundary along the Columbia River where it joins the Pacific, too much below the 49th parallel. It is the responsibility of Mr. Simpson to equally impress the Governor and Committee in England, a task I am certain he will carry out with his usual vigor. He is their most trusted eyes and ears in North America. He and I are agreed that New Caledonia be joined with the Columbia Department, so after this plan is proposed at the forthcoming annual meeting your brother will have charge of a territory larger than all of the British colonies in the Canadas and the Atlantic. Inform your geography students they will need to redraw their maps of the Pacific coast after we have been established here a few more years.

I am determined local Indians shall understand that fair justice is administered in my corner of the British Empire. Because of past violent contact with traders and because our numbers are few, local Indians are kept outside the walls of our post unless employed by us. Already a little village congregates not far from the doors. Two old useless cannons from the fort at the mouth of the river have been placed in the center yard of Fort Vancouver and they look impressive. Ritual is important to maintaining order, as you know. A wise Chief with many wives and comely daughters governs the largest tribe in the vicinity. I think he and I will have a common interest to assure they are properly pledged to good men and not abused by roving sailors and traders. Therefore, I will carefully select examples of misconduct to punish in public and thereby reduce the frequency of occurrence. Unless a British subject is murdered, I am the final arbitrator as Justice of Peace. I plan to apply as many strategies for celebrating peaceable trading exchanges as I will use to reduce unfair practices. All our important holidays will be celebrated with a lively and generous potluck. We will exploit the opportunity, not the people.

The morning of March 19, everyone assembled in the yard of the new fort. Mr. Simpson cracked a bottle on the flag post and ceremoniously declared: "On behalf of the honorable Hudson's Bay Company I hereby name this establishment Fort Vancouver. God Save King George the Fourth!" Mr. Simpson and I agree that local profits in the short term will be well worth this effort but the long-term outcome is more difficult to predict. Until we know the consequence of the moratorium between British and United States governments which ends in 1828 we represent the interests of the British government as much as the HBC. We built Fort Vancouver near a southern tributary of the Columbia but on the north side of the great river I will send men to establish posts further north near Walla Walla and to explore the mouth of Fraser's River. In several years, the result of our current stratagems will be evident and we can think about trading further along the coast and to the Orient, as Mr. Bethune recommended when we were in London. If successful, I will require more men and financing to consolidate the enterprise but Mr. Simpson is unlikely to promote this point of view. He has plans to expand his own domain, not my depots.

The establishment here is much like Red River in some aspects, except we have no impoverished Highland farmers to worry about. The numbers of Indians are much greater and past contacts with visitors have turned them into raiders more than workers. Salmon, not buffalo, is the staple food. These Indian tribes prefer dried fish to meat and are not much motivated to trap beyond their immediate needs. They honor salmon fish as spiritual manifestations of their ancestors and become very angry if our men do not respect their customs surrounding the annual spawning cycle. Among themselves, they use slaves captured from other tribes. These unfortunate men and women perform the same undesirable tasks as slaves everywhere always do, although it seems more a form of humiliation than hard labor.

In addition to slaves, most chiefs keep several wives so the skills of women differ from the prairie and the Eastern tribes. A woman's desire for iron utensils and abilities to comfort men who have no other companions are no different than anywhere else. One peculiar custom of the Chinook tribe is that both men and women have cone-shaped heads because a baby's skull is pressed while in cradleboard. It makes them appear more tall and stately, with much the same effect as a beaver hat does in London streets. Since there are many great trees, coastal natives build comfortable large cedar houses that have space for several families. Their usual costumes reflect the mild climate. Shells are used for ornamentation and ceremonial outfits are quite beautiful although they lack the embroidery designs that you so much admire. They do not use horses as much as in Red River but some are skilled boat makers and can travel great distances along the coast. Because of the frequent rain during Winter season, HBC point wool blankets are much desired.

HBC claims on behalf of the British Empire are established but now that Simpson departs those who remain will revert to French for our daily exchanges because it is the most comfortable and common currency for communicating among all classes here. It seems a long time since the spruce bark baptism ceremony during which new *hivernants* promised to respect the country wives of the *voyageurs* and to cherish each other. However, we will have a *jolie* time on Ste. Jean Baptiste Day in June and prepare a celebration.

Fort Vancouver environs will soon produce good agricultural harvests, and, given the mild climate and alluvial plains, excellent wood is plentiful. Should I describe the width of trees, you might question my ability to report accurately upon our situation. Suffice to say that all of the family I have here could join hands around the trunk of one gigantic tree and still not encircle it more than halfway. I plan to build a two-story home for my family with a small library room and commodious space for an officer's dining hall. My main room will be sized to impress the longhouse Indian leaders and visitors, whether British, American, Spanish or Russian. We will have a verandah so that we might sit outside and enjoy the evening air. The Bachelor Hall will be located outside the Big House so our ladies will not be overly disturbed by their activities. Although we have no church, some semblance of civilization will be sustained. The effects will, I hope, ripple out into the hinterlands of the continent until they touch those emanating from Red River, no longer the most distant outpost of the King's Empire.

Please inform Mother that we settle in, possibly for some years, and that we establish homes that remind us of those we knew along the St. Lawrence River. Perhaps ask my musical daughter to let us know what melodies she prefers. Although we have no choir, long rainy nights will be passed with greater joy when fiddles and flutes are put to use and we will select songs that bring us closer to those who are far away. Our hearts will beat to the same rhythms. I trust my son John is diligent in his studies and hope to send the boy to David in Paris should our uncle agree. The worst of this life is the uncertainty of knowing how beloved family members fare when long distances separate us. Our remembrances of how they look and move are frozen in time but remain living testimonials to our love for them.

With affection,

HBC Chief Factor, John McLoughlin

1826, From Quebec to the Columbia River Depot

Dear Chief Factor of the Hudson Bay Company, Columbia Department,

I do hope that I have addressed you correctly, *cher Royal Frére*.

This letter is forwarded with the expectation that priests at Red River will use their friendships among the gentlemen of the HBC to ensure safe delivery. I am informed that several children from your Columbia Valley were sent out for education either at Mr. West's Presbyterian school or at the one that Mgr. Provencher sponsors. After Mr. West left for London in 1823, he published *The Substance of a Journal during the Residence at the Red River Colony* which lays bare tensions between the Roman Catholic Church and the Protestant religions in that area. Within five years of his arrival, Mgr. Provencher recorded baptisms for 800 infants and adults, celebrated or recognized 120 marriages, and provided 120 first communions between Saint Boniface and Pembina. So you see, the Catholic Church thrives under the protection of the HBC much as it has done in Quebec under British colonial governance – thank you for your support of our efforts. Sometimes it seems that the old battles about religion are destined to be replayed by every successive generation in our family.

Those responsible for administering vast geographic areas inhabited by a few baptized souls or for cities stuffed with new immigrants know that religious observance assists in maintaining political stability as much as it develops personal Grace. Therefore, it is most important to have regular opportunity to participate in any religious observance, whatever the faith. The congregation learns how the lessons of love will curb base, cruel impulses. It is not just a matter of penance for sins but of daily practice to grow with Grace, as Mother Marie wrote many years ago. When I chose the Founder of the Convent of Nouvelle France for my spiritual model and made my political cause the same as that of my icon King Henri of Navarre, I did not imagine how interpreting two languages and faiths to each other would remain lifetime themes so relevant to our family and communities.

Our Priests are overextended because the Holy See has organized Bishopric dioceses for all of North America excepting in your remote corner of the continent. Are you certain that you did not escape to the Pacific coast just to remain in a personal wilderness, *mon frère*? Rest assured, I believe that you extend an appreciation for Christian virtues wherever you reside. Expansion of the Church in the United States differs from in the Canadas. In the American republic, the majority of Catholics live in Baltimore. These faithful are not French so it is a cultural challenge for many of our Bishops. The American government distinguishes between separation of church and state in ways that are not acceptable in either of the Canadian colonies, so money for education such as we have obtained from the governors is not as readily granted. I believe that our colonial society progresses in a more orderly fashion as a consequence. Our school prepares the wives and mothers of the next generation of civic leaders. And our girls learn both French and English, although demands for schooling in one or the other language have increased.

Nonetheless, the basis of political representation is too narrow here. Even in Lower Canada, new immigrants are Irish or English so the percentage of those British subjects of French heritage decreases even when mothers continue to raise large families. And when all these children grow to adult status, their new families will want land and a vote. In spite of political discontent, I think the Catholic church here has more freedom to observe the tenets of our Faith than in either England or France where it would be pleased to be as central to the community as we have been for nearly two centuries. Although electoral representation remains but an ideal, in Quebec City we move forward on other fronts. Dr. Morrin, mayor and president of the college, has organized the first medical society for doctors so they may share observations to stimulate discussions about new treatments for old diseases. You would enjoy joining them,

Dr. John. Perhaps it is possible for you to be a member in absentia and receive any reports. I will ask.

Tensions in society seem also to ripple through our family. Uncles Simon and Alexander once again conclude another battle over Fraser inheritances. After Grandmère Allaire's death, our mother inherited title to the manor at Rivière du Loup and, in accordance with tradition, her female children are to inherit it from her. Our sisters have married and provided me with four spiritual daughters who enjoy nurturing your own Eliza, although she is not inclined to a religious profession. Ursuline *Soeurs* benefit from the charity of our family, but we cannot inherit titles to property. The manor at Malbaie seigneury goes to Grandfather's second wife's children and the house in *Ville de Quebec* to his daughter from his McCord marriage. I think part of the problem between our uncles is that Alexander has a growing second family with two new infants since you last went west. His eldest son, Alexander, whom you had sent home from the Indian Territories, became great friends with your son John, until he was shipped out to Dr. David in Paris. Perhaps young John could be encouraged to join them. The schism between our Uncles permits your young son to move about too freely without consistent guidance from either. Uncle Simon has tired of fostering so many children from his sisters' families. He refuses even to accept our nephew from the Michaud family at his Terrebonne establishment – perhaps you might write some persuasive arguments.

This letter must end. The sentiments are too heavy for someone whom the priests say laughs more than most in our Convent. Your wife is now chatelaine of a riverside manor and you are the grand seigneur of an establishment that prospers. I doubt either of you expend much time in the kitchen except to check on the cooks. You are HBC gentry and, therefore, must eat from an English table, which as God knows will never be as tasty as a French one. You inhabit a countryside where berries must be plentiful. Allow me to offer this recipe, which comes originally from the *pays de Maria Chapdelaine*. If translated the flavor will be lost! I trust you remember the French tongue sufficiently well and if not, when you eat this cake, your own tongue will recall the bountiful hills of your childhood.

GÂTEAU AUX BLEUETS DU LAC ST. JEAN

1 tasse de sucre
1/4 tasse de graisse
2 oeufs
1/2 tasse de lait
2 tasses de farine
2 c. à thé de poudre à pâte
1 c. à thé de sel

Garniture:
1/2 tasse de sucre
1/3 tasse de farine
1 c. à thé de cannelle
1/4 tasse de beurre
2 tasses de bleuets

Procéder comme pour un gâteau ordinaire.
Étendre la moitée de la pâte, recouvrir de la moitee de la garniture aux bleuets, mettre le reste de la pâte et recouvrir du reste de la garniture.
Managez bien!

Sr. St. Henri (whose tongue is firmly stuck in her cheek)

1827, From the Columbia Outpost

My dear sister,

This letter goes out on the same brigade as my wife and children. She also cares for two young children of my stepson, Thomas McKay, who return west to be placed in a school. Should a letter from Simpson or the governors be forthcoming before Marguerite and the children cross the Rocky Mountains at the base of Athabasca Pass at Boat Encampment, they will return. I remain at Fort Vancouver awaiting confirmation from the Governor and Committee regarding our future. The terms of my contract must be clarified and confirmed, not violated. Without reassurance from the London gentlemen that my department will be properly sustained and that I have support in decisions I make regarding the Trade west of the mountains, the uncertainty is too great to warrant yet another year in this far-removed country.

Little George Simpson went off to London last year. How I would have liked to have been in attendance. I know from experience that whomever has the ear of the HBC Committee fares well. While I wander in solitude among firs and furs, my voice does not resonate as powerfully as Mr. Simpson's who stood in the board room at Fenchurch Street. The problem is about clarifying the contracts for those gentlemen in the field, what the NWC called Wintering partners. We all have been prevented from profit sharing until outstanding financial affairs incurred by the old NWC have been addressed. I am told that Mr. Ellice moves onto the Committee and the McGillivray bros. will be removed. In 1821 at amalgamation, the McGillivrays did not hesitate to cut a deal with the HBC while undercutting the NWC Wintering partners. Those votes I controlled so there is little love lost or regret lost in the McGillivrays' downfall. However, although the integration of the two companies has been formalized for six years, details of profits from our new trading partnerships under the old name are still being processed. Since the great merger, capital stock in the HBC has increased four times and dividends rose from four percent to ten percent in one recent annual cycle of profits. As a younger man, I learned to ask the Governors for assurances in writing because, without that evidence, a wealthy NWC gentlemen's word might not be so honorable. I now await written assurances of just how honorable the HBC will be with respect to my future involvement. If I do not have the original terms respected and my current productivity acknowledged, I would turn to other business like many other former NWC partners have done. Mr. Bethune has departed from the fray and I may follow him.

By contrast, little George Simpson has received a bonus and a salary increase, plus a new title. As Emperor Napoleon of Rupert's Land, he now marches all over the Indian Territories as Governor of both Northern and Southern Departments. The Governor and Committee in London are alert to even more increased northern profits because the Anglo-Russian Treaty was signed last year. The Russians will stay in their Arctic corridor. The United States government also concludes treaties, thus moves into the South and West. Therefore Spanish influence decreases, just as did the French sixty years ago.

England has only one inland competitor on this continent: the American republic. Financial and political resources behind our private HBC business concern give us a great advantage over the independent American wandering-free trader. We also serve as harbinger of the British Empire in this area. My responsibility is to demonstrate how early returns from the Columbia indicate even more opportunity for we who are HBC shareholders. However, as Mr. Ellice knows, my personal responsibilities at other levels are considerable. After paying all debts, supporting development on the Québec farms, and maintaining two children at boarding school, I still am not solvent. Until the returns from the profits of the past several years are properly paid out, I incur more debts on company ledgers and become again ever indentured to this Trade. Nevertheless, I will not sit here next to the Columbia River while Mr. Ellice in London and Mr. Simpson in Red River garner excessive wealth and powers. That situation is exactly what occurred after the XY Company merged with the

NWC at the beginning of my career. It is what Bethune and I tried to arrest when we met Ellice and others in London before the HBC-NWC merger. I am too old to be squeezed by such games but have enough experience and maturity to join another venture if necessary.

We have no schools, churches or missionaries here. It is dangerous for so few of us to live so closely amongst so many Indians. I forbid groups of Indians inside the gates of the Fort because past events with other traders have bred distrust. These injustices become memories that live on in storytelling chants that can provoke many youth to reckless actions. We might anticipate violence if too close contact at an early a stage is permitted. Let all comers be impressed from a distance at the size of our establishment. With time they will be reassured that my actions under the British Union Jack signify fair trade and quality goods. We offer better prices than the competition. I do not allow arms, ammunition, and spirituous liquor for trading articles although competitors do so. Some Indians demand them, having lost dignity through too much addiction. If the HBC Committee in London values its profits as consequence of having "equal freedom to occupy" lands where no English-born gentleman wants to come, it then must reward colonial-born gentlemen who make it possible for them to discuss weighty public issues in safety and comfort. The joint occupation agreement between the United States and Britain established after the war in 1818 will result in extending the international boundary to the Pacific Ocean. My establishment procures access to the Columbia River watershed, no small consideration.

If I retired from the Trade, I would see family more regularly. My son John seems to be antagonizing Uncle Simon with his behaviors. As a father, I would exert a more direct influence upon this young man in whom I have placed such hopes. I could become involved in colonial affairs. If I were even as far west as Red River, I would have more social discourse and enjoyable company and my children would be guided by their participation in church and schools. If I went to Detroit or St. Louis I could become an independent merchant. In any event, I shall not expose my family to many types of hostilities from various enemies while a little man positions only himself to advantage among the London Committeemen. Our brother David will plead my cause among his acquaintances who have influence in Paris and London. I await the arrival of the next ship after it comes around Cape Horn and the news it brings from London. I am past forty now and will not wait much longer to learn of my fate in this new organization nor expend energy again to make wealthy men more rich from excessive profits. Perhaps I shall be visiting in person not long after you read this letter. By the time you receive it, my fate for the next few years will have been decided. Please say some additional prayers for me and my family.

Very best wishes,

Yr affectionate bro.

1828, From Quebec to Fort Vancouver

My dearest bro.,

Three thousand miles continue to separate us in person but three thousand words flowing between us maintain our bonds of love, which are much more than mere familial obligations. We write as friends, adults who enjoy a lifelong affection built from the foundation of shared childhood experiences.

Do you remember going into the woods to tap maple trees? How you and David and I would carefully monitor Mr. Dupre's fire on the boundary of the seigneury. He encouraged us to find exactly the right size of branch to maintain a temperature that warmed the sap so we could make maple toffee in the snow. Clever man! He saved himself a great deal of work and taught us how to boil the sap into syrup at the same time. This Spring was an exceptionally good year and we received our share of the harvest at the Ursuline House. When I roll the taffy slowly around my mouth, I meditate whether you have found a worthy substitute. Since neither of us may go to sugaring-off parties, let us visit them in memory at least. I also will remind Dr. David of what he is missing whilst sitting in his fashionable Paris cafes.

You are not alone in thinking about the effects of governance by British leaders so far removed from the colonies and territories. There is a breeze that threatens to become a storm raging throughout Lower and Upper Canada. It is a warm wind that blows up from the south, helping to heat tempers. Radical ideas spread like seeds in this wind and we do not know what will be the harvest. As our population increases and prospers, people want more direct representation. It is not just literate and responsible men who chafe at the limitations of the old order, it is a national sentiment among the people. I am told it is the same in England and France, where new classes of wealthy merchants and educated professionals challenge inherited political prerogatives. During our lifetimes, England learned much from the loss of its

Atlantic colonies, and the French Empire now has retreated to the edge of the Atlantic in Europe. Consequently, our colonial forebears are more conservative but individualistic ideals incubated in the New Republic sprout among us because of newspapers and travel. The remaining colonies need some form of more representative government, perhaps not as republican as in the United States. The Catholic Church has a much greater influence in maintaining stability in this colony than in France or England or the United States. Irish priests join with French Canadians in a common chant about shared grievances. All join in a louder chorus, which is carried further by these currents of change. Do not permit your ears or tongue to respond to the call. Guard your temper. Be canny.

It is difficult to determine whether such disputes about proper governance result more from increased numbers of people in our cities or from desires to increase profits among the captains of industry. Both forces contribute to rebellious attitudes and actions. The new shipping canal along the Lachine Rapids near Montreal links Upper Canada more easily with Britain but it is the wealthy English merchants of Lower Canada who were the early advocates and winners. Many prosperous men, now recovered from the ravages of the 1812 war with Americans, sit in their fine houses debating the financial merits of the Republican style of government versus limitations set by colonial appointees whose interest in our daily business affairs is primarily collecting tax revenues. Thus the demand for more self-governance is not likely to abate. It is fueled by rich and poor alike although the latter are more likely to take to the streets in protest because their small houses are uncomfortable.

Mr. James McGill's bequest to establish a university in Montreal has received little attention and less action in Lower Canada. On our colony we have not such a desire for secular or English language universities. Nothing happens although young people need the opportunity! The more pressing concern is the transportation of poverty and mouths to feed on immigrant ships. Some of these people fought in the Napoleonic Wars and have been granted land in the colonies as reward for service to their country. If they are Catholic, they wish to stay here in

Lower Canada, but the majority are Protestant so they move on to Upper Canada after they recover from their voyage. In that colony, the official Church of England and members of the dissenting Protestant congregations fight among themselves. Here at the first port of entry, we are forced to lock our doors because we cannot support all these impoverished newcomer demands for assistance. Mother Marie might have thought of another solution but I cannot. My Sisters and I have great guilt because our Community has always had a pot of soup ready for the hungry and needy, whatever their background. These newcomers are so numerous, we cannot serve them, excepting to provide some schooling for their daughters. I pray for God's guidance because the governors are unlikely to respond to our humble pleas for assistance. Better that we become bankrupt, less trouble for them.

Do you remember the story of American prisoners of war who were quartered at Malbaie, guarded by Mr. Nairne and Grandfather Fraser? Some escaped and rowed across the breadth of the St. Lawrence – twenty-one miles – to Kamouraska, only to be returned by the *Canadiens* who lived along the south shore. It was the Catholic priests' influence that guaranteed loyalty but the imported British governors must ever be reminded by us about that debt. Some deep pockets may jingle, but the heart responds to a different song. It beats to the rhythms of hearth and home, a love for the curves of the land and sunlight caressing shimmering trees.

In our mission to maintain morals and cultivate souls by educating little girls, the Ursulines have learned that music is one of the best approaches to a better life. It transcends differences that languages foster and evokes joy and gaiety that honors God. Such activities ease us through more difficult days. Since the welcome gift of a second piano, we extend our recitals. One of our instructors, Mr. Molt, a veteran of Waterloo, corresponds with Ludwig van Beethoven, the German composer. Beethoven has composed a canon for Mr. Molt who has just published some of *les paroles des anciens chants du Québec*. Bedard's old ballad is an old favorite that you and your men must not forget.

Sol Canadien terre chérie
Sol Canadien, terre chérie
Par des braves tu fus peuple
Les cherchaient loin de leur patrie
Une terre de liberté.
Nos pères sortis de la France
Etaient l'élite des guerriers
Et leurs enfants, de leur vaillance
N'ont jamais flétris les lauriers.
Qu'elles sont belles nos compagnes?
En Canada qu-on vit content.
Salut aux sublimes montagnes,
Borde du superbe Sainte-Laurent.
Habitant de cette contrée
Que nature veut embellir,
Tu peux marcher tête levee
Ton pays doit t'enorgueuillir.
Renverse le pouvoir perfide
Qui ne cherche qu'à t'écrasé.
La liberté est ton guide,
Sous elle tu peux triompher.
Ne fléchis jamais dans l'orage.
Tu n'as pour máitre que tes lois
Tu n'es point fait pour l'esclavage
Le destin veille sur tes droits.

(Beloved Canadian soil
Beloved Canadian soil
By the brave you were peopled
They were searching for their country
A land of liberty.
Our fathers came from France
And were elite warriors
And their valiant children
Will never forget these glories.
Where is our beautiful country?
In Canada where one lives contentedly
Saluting the sublime mountains

Bordered by the superb St. Lawrence.
Inhabitant of this place
Whom nature has rewarded
March with your head high
Take pride in your land.
Resist the treacherous power
That seeks to erase your culture.
Liberty is your guide
Under it you will triumph
Don't wince in the storm
You have your laws
You do not have slavery
The old destiny is your right.)

My beloved brother, you, within your Honorable Company and I within my Religious Community have some power over our small domains. Perhaps by our actions we may retain a semblance of peace, establish order, and further solid governance. Let us provide a haven safe from the worst of the gathering storm to protect the most worthy of our cherished heritages. For certain, God observes your efforts at the shores of the Pacific Ocean and mine near the Atlantic. He will guard your soul and that of others within your care. If He becomes distracted, the Holy Mother will prompt him, just as our own mother guided her children.

With great affection,

Yr sister (re-elected *Dêpositaire* by her Community this past April, appropriate penance for her sins)

PS. A letter from your daughter is enclosed. Ignore my dispute with Uncle Simon regarding payment for her additional music lessons. It is an accomplishment in which Eliza has demonstrated sufficient talent to gain a proper *entrée* into society. She is thus better prepared for marriage to a proper husband, but you also need to think about providing a dowry within a few years.

1829, From the Columbia courtesy of Gov'r Simpson's brigade

My dear sister,

Mr. Simpson's express brigade will carry this letter from the Columbia to your part of the continent. He may go directly to London after the annual meeting at York Factory so perhaps others will carry it east of Fort Garry. If he does come to tea with you, please ensure that my daughter gives him a piano recital. He might be persuaded to support the education of more of these children.

Governor Simpson has been here five months and seems pleased with the results of his inspection. He has been so thoroughly picayune, I have wondered at times whether he was going to count out the steps our men make between the river dock and the warehouse. There is no doubt that we prosper more with each annual return. That success is a strong bond tying us all together as tightly as the furs we press for transportation to market. Dividends from the Trade are estimated to be twenty percent again this year. Mr. Simpson promises me that the Governor and Committee will be properly informed of my contribution to their purses. Thus, I also hope to turn a greater personal profit after the charges against my account are paid and the dividends are calculated. Fort Vancouver will also receive the necessary furnishings to appropriately represent the company and Empire at the dinner table when various guests arrive.

We expand Fort Vancouver and establish a larger house for the gentlemen and executive officers. I expect to have increased staff after the annual meeting as a consequence of our demonstrated success and planned expansions. I warmly anticipate that Chief Trader Mr. Douglas and his family will join us. He is a most promising young gentleman with a West Indies heritage who has a Metis wife and family. They will be welcome company for

Marguerite and me. After much sampling, even Mr. Simpson seems to have somewhat settled and has selected a country wife. Much to the pleasure of my wife, he brought Margaret Taylor, sister of his piper with him. They have several children who remain at Red River.

The future of these mixed-blood children is a concern we have much discussed. Mr. Simpson is not optimistic about their possibilities. I believe they will be excluded from society unless well-socialized as educated gentlemen and ladies. It is welcome news to know that our nephew Alexander Fraser has done so well under David's guidance in Paris. I regret that reports of my son's recent behavior are less encouraging. Perhaps it is a matter of being young and too far away from home but needing some freedom. Uncle Simon is now aged seventy and too elderly to understand this new generation of *jeunes gens*. His only son John has never been west and is a more rarefied European strain of humanity. Mr. Simpson has kindly offered to place my young John in the HBC counting house at Montreal as a consequence of his expulsion from school. Thus Simpson provides the boy with the same opportunity that gave him a great advantage. However, if John does not have that sort of temperament, and I do not think he has, the youth will be sent this October to join Dr. David on condition that John continues his studies in Paris. David will prove to be as good a mentor with his nephew as he has been with our young cousin and provide appropriate opportunities for the enjoyment of youthful pleasures. I keep my other son David closer to me until he is older. Like our brother, he does not have pressure such as that which falls upon a first-born son, but he must have some opportunities to achieve.

Mr. Simpson and I also spent long hours discussing the collapse of the McGillivray Bros. Empire now that Simon is dead and William declared bankrupt. Simpson carries my power of attorney so that I might be disentangled as soon as possible from any past obligations for the debts of the NWC. Some of the earliest days of the Trade are perpetuated in these ongoing conflicts. Perhaps the dynamics are much like a river; water sucked into ocean tides is the same as that which trickles from a high mountain lake but the forces that pull it out to sea are not.

In the days when the HBC was content to be at the edge of Hudson's Bay, the NWC had tensions with its dissatisfied partners because of inequitable profit sharing. These men formed the XY Co. and were led by Alexander MacKenzie. Alienated partners returned to the fold when the NWC extended the terms of its partnership agreements and the XY Co. was absorbed. As the territory in which we traded expanded, competition between the NWC and HBC overextended both companies and you know the role I played in that merger. Now, unwise and unholy competition has been reduced. From one coast of the continent to the other, HBC men and profits thrive on a larger scale, pushing back other competitors. It is backed by the power of the British Empire and, as long as that support is sustained, we benefit. In both instances, it took the early deaths of central characters to make the change, and in both mergers the word of a gentleman as bond became less important than the written contract. Had Simon McTavish kept his word to me and other young men when we first signed up as Wintering partners, the NWC would not have split from within. Had the McGillivray Bros. built a reserve fund for the NWC Company, their ascendancy might have been sustained and control of the trade remained in the Canadas. If the British government listens to Mr. Ellice now that Sir Alexander McKenzie and Lord Selkirk are gone, then it will likely retain its vast territories in North America.

The recent Anglo-Russian boundary agreement gives evidence that that HBC influences British government policies. In addition to protecting the northern boundary, establishment of the Spanish boundary so far south provides further hope. The Columbia River might become the lower British boundary, leaving a corridor for the Americans to access the Pacific Ocean below its southern shore. Inland, our Company can deflect the efforts of American mountain men and entrepreneurs such as Mr. Astor, but only time will tell whether the struggles in the corridors of power in London result in comparable successes.

With each ripple, the Trade becomes more rational, more grand, more intercontinental. That expansion puts more coins in our pockets but there is less freedom and less of a personal bond as a guarantee of an honorable gentleman. A gentleman's handshake is his bond when he is face-to-face with those with whom he negotiates but, when they are continents removed, it seems less a breach of trust to twist words into something less firm and agreeable. Accouterments of civilization do not travel as quickly as the detritus, therefore the tactics I employ here are similar to those used in London in their intent. I trust that my application reflects the best, not the worst, of our civilization.

None of the HBC officers permanently stationed here were born in England, but we are the commercial face of the British Empire. As Master of this establishment, as Justice of the Peace, as HBC Factor, I determine punishments that are understood to be British justice. Although employed in a business monopoly, I administer British governance. I am not a politically appointed Governor but I strive to be an honorable gentleman and to establish order among the men who are employed in this Department. A British subject does not like humiliation but bears privation like a badge of honor. With no civilizing tools such as educational establishments and Christian churches it is easy to become more savage than civilized. My punitive tools are public examples of negative consequences. Officers are directed to lash men if they cheat or are irresponsible. If our men do not conduct themselves according to Company policy with each other or their wives or the Indians, I have the offender stripped, bound to the cannon in front of my office, and flogged. It is a better use of that monster than firing it. On occasion, we thrash misbehaviors, a good beating is an impressive demonstration of strength. More hurtful, more effective, are verbal put-downs and diminishing actions. In anticipation of this type of constraint, I built the jail near the privy, just as we did at Fort William.

Therefore, I polish an array of leadership tactics, both negative and positive. This past year, after Clallam Indians murdered a clerk on Puget Sound, we burned their camps, necessitating some deaths among them. This year when the supply ship, *William and Ann*, was wrecked on the bar at the mouth of the river, and Clatsop Indians stole the trading goods, I sent an armed schooner and in the *mêlée* some of their men died. When American traders come to our fort, I make an assessment of their characters and if they are not good examples, they do find it difficult to procure supplies and are not invited to dine with our officers. Thus, I have earned a new title. In my emporium, I am known as the "White-Haired Eagle" after the large raptor that surveys his territory from the top of the largest cedars that line the waterways. As violent incidents decrease, I hope to build a school and have asked that Mr. Simpson provide at least an extended visit from an ordained minister. Every Sunday, I read from the Bible in French, so that those who cannot read will be reminded of some Holy phrases and virtue. Our farms prosper, game and fish are plentiful, so we avail ourselves of every feast day in the calendar. It revives the spirit and memories of when we were young and at home.

Mr. Simpson proves himself a master of Scottish ritual. He was informed that even the King has been seen in the Scottish Highlands wearing a kilt. Therefore, in full regalia Colin Taylor now announces the arrival of the Little Emperor with a swirl of the pipes that carries far out over the river whenever the Governor's party arrives at one of our trading forts. Simpson's select *voyageurs* grumble at the pace he insists upon in his specially built grand express canoe. The old competition to see who can best the others at carrying the packs disappears because York Boats require fewer men to transport more goods. The great advantage of the North West fur trade was our relationships formed with local Indians who procured the furs. Nevertheless, Simpson is also firm about using ships for the Pacific coastal trade and, although we traveled to review the Willamette Falls prairie, he does not support establishing a sawmill there at this time. This country is too mild to produce good pelts, but the interior and the North require men who will live according to the harsh style and conditions of the country. It demands resiliency and breeds independence. Weaker men become drunkards and more savage than the *sauvages*. However, strong men are granted glimpses of a life more free from false constraints and veneer of the excesses of civilization than anywhere else in the world. Their mettle is tested and with them it might be possible to build a more ideal society. I collect some of these men here with the hope that perhaps we can realize some of these ideals. And so I close, signing this letter as a man more content than one who has periodically written more of his misadventures.

Yr bro.

1830, To the White-Haired Eagle from Mère St. Henri

Dear White-Haired Eagle,

That title and image is rather grand! It evokes confidence about abilities to sail through high currents of air, sharp eyes fixated on minute scurryings of earth-bound creatures. You do resemble an eagle in carriage and character, white-haired, black suited and strongly visaged. For my part, I fix my white wimple over black robe and think how to embody such fearless majesty after being elected once again to the position of *Mère Supérieure*. I kneel at the altar praying to be still, so my thoughts might soar higher to Heaven where He looks down upon all His creatures. May His eagle eyes approve of my scurryings! Your astute observations about how men's affairs ebb and flow in increasingly wider circles around the globe remind me that God's power flows in exactly the opposite direction, spirally ever inward, calming the heartbeat of a single creature. It is a Mystery to reflect more deeply upon, dear brother.

You will have received news about the arrival of the new Governor of Lower Canada and his wife. Lord and Lady Aylmer are friends of our dear Dr. David, having known him in Paris. Therefore, they did not hesitate to call upon us and we anticipate further visits. Lady Aylmer takes a particular interest in our students and promises to examine the more advanced students at the end of this term. Your daughter Eliza will assist me with the reception for these graduates. I believe Lady Aylmer will advocate our plans to complete the renovation and expansion of our buildings so that our school sustains its reputation for educating according to the latest curriculum. The Seminary of Quebec holds public examinations this year for the first time and the Ursuline Sisterhood has a similar ambition for our students, but we require a setting to display their talents with appropriate elegance.

The continued support that both you and David provide is of immeasurable value. Until the students examine shells, tiny skeletons, and furry hides, so many of our young girls have never thought much about natural history. It is important to develop observational skills according to this new field of science and your gifts help bring the out of doors into our lives. They also bring you closer to me, knowing that I am touching objects that you have carefully selected for shipment. David sends copies of poetry and literature that excite much interest among the girls and develop their dramatic skills in deportment and oral presentations. But the most appreciated subject is music. Their young voices are like choirs of angels and affect all who listen, including God's heavenly hosts, I hope.

The political problems that consume Lord Aylmer are most wearying and we pray for some resolution. It is *une ère d'agitation*. Lord Aylmer attempts to include the Assembly in his deliberations but has inherited a buzzing hive. Electoral reforms last year provided representation in the Legislative Assembly for English-speaking residents of the Eastern townships and raised the total number of counties to forty. The appointed Executive Council, however, has but nine members, of which only two are French and only one is Roman Catholic. Lord Aylmer intends to add members from the opposing representatives but the legislative and executive authorities make demands upon each other that cannot be easily reconciled. In other reforms, Lord Aylmer proposes legislation that removes judges from the Assembly and, most importantly, prepares to divest the Crown from receiving provincial revenue. This will be good news for the municipalities because monies for road repairs and maintenance are sorely needed.

The lines of debate are not entirely about language or finances, as powerful as both forces are. Reformers in the *Parti Patriote* want more local power and less British "home" government. Mr. Neilson, quite the vociferous editor, generates much support among the Scots for such independence, as you would imagine. There is agitation also in Upper Canada. Newcomers from the United States who must be more republican than they realized speak against the Anglo-British "family compact," a few families that have much civic power. I pray that these campaigns for self-government in the Canadas will not result in the violence of the French and American revolutionary convulsions. Our French, all Catholics, have nowhere to go if they wish to practice their language and their religion with official sanction. The British crown, distant as it is, remains the best guarantee to perpetuate our culture. Lord Aylmer rotates most uncomfortably at the center of this squeaky colonial wheel. Your HBC officers at least are Lords of the Manor unless Mr. Simpson's "carriage" descends one of the mighty river highways.

You also undoubtedly have heard by now of the latest family tragedy – young Alexander Fraser's untimely death in Paris this past January. Your advice to send Uncle Alex's mixed-blood son to our sophisticated Dr. David was accepted. He would be removed from violent situations in the far country and exposed to civilized companions who would open the doors of society for him. To die brawling in a bistro on New Year's Eve about the Catholic Emancipation question in England is too early an exit from life. I hope that your John absorbs the deeper lessons from this sad incident and I have written to David to be explicit about the need to set a moral example.

Ultimately the issue of self-governance resides within the person. It is not possible to have a populist democracy or in-creased political representation unless a majority of citizens are in command of themselves, regardless of station in life. From what I hear the majority, neither within the grand nations of Europe, nor the republic to the South, nor the British colonies and its commercial emporiums, is truly ready for such freedoms. Nor are they likely to be within our lifetimes, dear Eagle. However, the demand grows. In the various services that the McLoughlin trio of brothers and sister provide, as businessman, doctor and educator, we must support each other and those who look to us for direction. Our guidance comes from the unseen forces caused by the extended hand of God who granted freedom to err but who abhors violent death.

Your family is, as always, in my prayers.

Mère St. Henri

1831, From Fort Vancouver to the Ursuline Convent, Quebec

My dear sister Mary,

After all these years, it seems somewhat odd to call you directly by the English version of your name, but sometimes you assume an Anglo countenance. As we all live under the veil of the British Empire, I thought I'd address you as a proper country gentleman would. Or, perhaps, I am just playing with words because the issue of what constitutes a proper marriage has once again become contentious in Rupert's Land. Our little Governor has returned from his latest visit to the old country importing a new English treasure, his young bride. With great fanfare they journeyed by canoes to Red River. Unaccustomed to a white lady moving among their midst, the *voyageurs* even let her step on their backs to go ashore without getting wet. Near our old anointing place on the trail, Lac la Pluie is renamed "Fort Frances" in her honor. They traveled with John George McTavish who returned with a similar trophy. Prior to their arrival, Margaret Taylor, the "commodity" as Mr. Simpson now called her, was hustled away to the Metis camp with their children. At Fort Garry, Governor Simpson plans a new stone mansion in which to hothouse his fair English rose. Mr. Simpson has scored another first!

My quiet wife has had much to say about this unkind treatment of her friend and the children who knew nothing of his marriage. Simpson will arrange that they are cared for but his manner of deposing his Metis family wins him no friends among the old crowd of Chief Traders. Mr. Simpson has had several children by different women but his longest liaison was with Margaret Taylor and the Metis nation will be watching closely to observe how he and McTavish conduct themselves. If Mr. Simpson does not establish his fur trade family appropriately, we all will have difficulty with our men as well as their wives because he is the Governor-in-Chief in all but name and sets the example. According to the 1823 HBC policy, all employees are obliged to make appropriate settlements for their dependents. We do enforce this policy, sometimes applying the whip to replace a tongue-lashing if scolding is not effective. The Company will see to the wife and children of men who drown or die in the service but, when the men go out, it is their own responsibility. The women have the right of refusal as well. You know quite well that not all our gentlemen take their country wives and children out with them because it is so difficult for everyone to become established in society.

Mr. Harmon, with whom I wintered years ago when a young man in the Trade, has published a book since he returned to Vermont with his family. He confesses his affection for them and writes of the lived entanglements that encase the heart just as ivy vines curl round an oak trunk. But he, David Thompson, and Uncle Alex are exceptions among the gentlemen. Most of our men who have lived with country wives for many years and who care about their children prefer to retire in the Indian Territories. They have lived a long time themselves without fine accoutrements and are more comfortable with women who have never known such graces. Until the arrival of Mrs. Simpson, the only white women at Red River thus far have been hardy Scots who can pull a plough in the fields and a few French wives who lead a nomadic life with their husbands. They learned from Indian and Metis women how to identify local grasses for cooking and healing. Perhaps the little Governor who has two acknowledged children in Great Britain and half a dozen others scattered throughout the territories at trading forts may exhibit a different behavior now that he has been bridled in marriage and sanctified in church.

Red River needs the hand and heart of a Marie de l'Incarnation to guide its development. It is at the forks of society as well as the forks of a continent. Simpson sets himself up to be Lord in place of Selkirk but I think his attempt to be Laird of the place will not work out. One good appointment has been that of Cuthbert Grant who becomes HBC Warden of the Plains. His position buffers the immigrants from the Indians while providing better sustenance for the growing numbers of young and old within this so called "new nation." Grant has the charisma and education to build pride in his people and will encourage settlement for them now that the buffalo hunt has declined. The fires of freedom seem to flame on the prairies with as much liveliness as along the levees of Lower Canada and the streets of Upper Canada.

At this far edge of the continent I am ever more concerned with ships. The *William and Ann* floundered in the delta of the Columbia and all men and cargo were lost. I think the Captain and crew were too eager for drink and women. On our ships, the young apprentices are more problem than value. They might even be better off enslaved in Yorkshire cotton factories but for certain most are too young to be among men whose character is often as shifty as the waves they chase. On land these lads would mix with some resemblance of family; as apprentices they are induced by ragtag sailors to the edges of society. We should not leave young lads very long in shipboard conditions. It would not be possible to make much of a whole costume out of those pieces of humanity. Do say Mass for their souls and for future successful traverses.

We must master these tidal waters of the delta. I need navigators like those who live along the banks of the St. Lawrence. *The Eagle, Dryad*, and *Isabella* survived their voyages around Cape Horn and form a veritable fleet. Many of my men are fully occupied providing them with provisions and fuel instead of extending our farms. Now that the Snake River country has been trapped out, eliminating profits and competition, Mr. Ogden goes to establish a fort along the coast north of Fort Langley and will next challenge the Russians. How he is to replicate a fur desert corridor by traveling along the rolling white waves of the ocean is a vision that only Mr. Simpson sees clearly. I maintain that a line of small forts is less costly than servicing large ships. It builds closer relationships with the natives and makes them loyal to us but this argument does not hold water, so to speak, with our Governor. After observing the arrival of an American brig when he was here at the Columbia, he appointed his cousin Amelius Simpson to head a new Pacific Ocean marine department. However, the sad and untimely death of this amiable man a few weeks ago slows implementation of this ambition. Young Mr. Simpson brought with him from England some apple seeds that we have planted near Fort Vancouver as a tribute to this young gallant and Mr. Ogden's new trading post will bear his name.

In addition to problems on board the ships and the long waits or losses we have when they arrive at the ever-hungry and lapping tongue of the delta, we have suffered many drownings upstream this past year. In July, we lost nine experienced canoe men in the Dalles whirlpools. In October, we lost six newcomers from Lower Canada, again in the Dalles of the Columbia, as well as another experienced man who was returning to Lower Canada. Sixteen lost souls, in addition to the sailors, makes an impression on those who remain on this earthly outpost. The bodies of drowned men make a difficult burial, as I know well. The memory shapes our decisions and destinies.

An unexpected visitor I have welcomed is Mr. Jebediah Smith, an American trader, whose party was raided by the Umpqua Indians. After we assisted him to recover his fur packs, he spent the Winter before returning to central Missouri for the Rocky Mountain Rendezvous, a *levée* much like the ones we enjoyed at Fort William a decade ago. Mr. Smith, a Methodist, and I are agreed about the dissipating effects of liquor when it is used to escape the demons that reside inside a person rather than to develop an ambient conversation. Another American, more *outre* in character and dress came North to escape some Spanish adventures. His stories flow as freely as the tails of his captured horses. I am less enthused about his august company so the doors of Fort Vancouver are closed to him until his background is verified.

We also have had troubles with some English transplants within Fort Vancouver. Mr. Dease's death of a stomach hemorrhage on his return trip is a loss that hangs heavily about my shoulders because we quarreled before he left. I need no repetition. Dr. Hamlyn, who journeyed here with Mr. Simpson two years ago, is not well suited to the type of medical practice our situation provides, so he goes out this Fall although his contract has not yet expired. Fort Colville remains ever a hotbed of complainants who inform Mr. Simpson of any difficulties within my Department.

We are never very far from death here but the arrival of Mr. Douglas and his family has provided a much welcome addition to our establishment, which is located on a Point named Belle Vue. To the south near the falls in a small, beautiful place we call French Prairie, a sawmill has been constructed. I have permitted some retirees to build cabins there, thus a little settlement forms. I encourage them to lay out their claims in the British style of quarters rather than the French form of long strips because of the conflicts we observed at Red River between the two styles of settlement. These homestead farms buffer the activities of Fort Vancouver and are in little danger from Indian attack, given their tribal connections. Men who have lived here since the Astorian days, men who have grown old in the Trade, have formed bonds with this land and their country wives. Their children know no other home. Although the land may eventually become American territory when the boundary is determined, the HBC has some responsibility to assume for their future. Some day, my own wife may persuade me to join them.

In a few years, Fort Vancouver will have many of the same demands for settlement that now exist at Red River. The longer our men live in this pleasant country, the less they wish to return East, even to the Forks at Fort Garry. It is possible for a landscape to decorate the interior of a mind as much as ideas might forest it. The soil is rich, waterfall cascades sparkle, Winter storms are brief, game and fish plentiful. All call to the hearts of those who live in the Columbia River region. I have petitioned Mr. Simpson and the London Committee to approve this decision to let our Canadian retirees settle in the Willamette Valley. Therefore, it is time for you to ask the priests to come and cultivate our souls. Their harvest would be as richly rewarding as our diversifying trade. Possibly you could even spare some Ursuline teachers.

Your brother,

Jean Baptiste

1832, From Quebec, Lower Canada

Dear fur-trader brother,

This year is one of the few that I have been glad you are so far away. If you were in Quebec I know that your temper would be an ingredient fomenting current disputes. The days when Grandfather and his war buddies or club members could glare and insult each other and then cool off by returning to their big houses for a few months have gone. Now angry rhetoric is sustained by newspapers and public meetings that attract crowds. On the streets these gatherings then develop energies of their own. Mobs breed violent behavior. When the minds of men become too fevered, their bodies become instruments of aroused anger. It seems that tempers are inflamed everywhere. As seasoned leadership steps off stage, newcomers stride forward shouting their demands. Their noise draws the eyes and ears of restless youth while the sad silences of the lesser powerful are ignored. Our Lord would not be so distracted from them therefore this servant of His will not ignore their predicament. However, as you have noted in other letters, when unrest becomes violence, it is better not to impress thoughts into letters that must travel. Therefore, I beg of you to read between these lines to find what must remain unsaid unless we sip tea together.

Here in Quebec, the numbers of starving Irish families increase with each arriving boatload but there is little work for the men now that the Lachine Canal near Montreal is completed. Amid the squalor and dirt of immigrant homes, a fever spreads and the contagion is deadly. In *Ville de Quebec* alone, we buried more than 3,000 victims this year and may have nearly as many by next Summer because most of the sick will not survive the Winter. These are shocking numbers! Their Catholic faith is all that sustains them as they crowd into our cities and towns. Their distress makes our inhabitants afraid for themselves, therefore the priests must hold many separate Masses. Families separate in fear from other ones, and these become cultural distances, encouraged by political leaders.

Rebel demands for more power have grown so extreme that Mr. Neilson has broken with the reformers. His influential newspaper had done much to bridge the English and French communities. One cannot help but have empathy for some points made by the Reform party, especially when they argue for a more appropriate alignment of property, taxes, votes, and civic decisions. Within the legislature, our lawyers and doctors play the politics of republicanism. Under the leadership of Mr. Papineau, they have prepared ninety-two resolutions and drafted a Declaration of Rights, inspired by the American model. Needless to say, this situation creates many difficulties for Lord Alymer and his Council.

However, in the United States, our Boston Sisters tremble in fear and the Ursuline House has been the target of many anti-Catholic threats. I hope that the destruction that came to pass in France during the height of the revolutionary terror is not repeated to the south of us. The new leaders of these United States have wealth based upon imported black slaves and are convinced they have a manifest destiny to dominate the continent. What would that mean for us in Quebec, our religion, and our language? What does that mean for you in the distant Columbia delta?

In France, your son John writes his cousins that he witnessed political insurrections there in June and that, when shots were fired, people standing nearby were felled. Undoubtedly John thought it exciting but our brother restricts further involvement and insists that the young man focus upon his studies. That responsibility would not be easily enforced as you might realize. In England, Lord Bathurst has retired and the King becomes ever more withdrawn to his country estates while his advisors remain in London. They are uncertain about how to assume the mantle of Empire and do not know what to do about the unrest in the colonies. So they dither, and their delay becomes a festering sore for us.

Women cloistered within a Quebec Convent cannot afford inaction. We oversee the expansion of our building with great anticipation of the Holy Benediction ceremony. Our boarders shall not complain that their bodies will be more comfortable in the newer classrooms. Lord Aylmer has been most consistent and supportive of all our efforts. He greatly assisted in the legal settlement of the Ste. Croix seigneuries. Therefore, I have now signed letters of patent that ensure our ownership should the system of land allotment be revised. This is a great relief to us and our prayers have been answered as much as is possible in these unsettled times. On the other hand, Mdme. Papineau is a former student who remains much interested in music. Therefore, we continue to have tea from time to time, after which she returns to remind her honorable reformer husband of our needs and concerns. She holds many salons during which politics is threaded among musical notes that awaken listening minds. It is difficult to juggle these differing perspectives because each has some right in their viewpoints and each stands firm on some wrong opinions.

For the sake of our colony, I pray that the quiet cadence of our daily routine provides sufficient counterpoint to the public meetings of men who shout aloud in at least three languages. I expect God prefers the soaring voices of choir nuns against the raucous discontents of discontented citizens. May He favor the requests of our melodic offerings to maintain peace in our cities, even also throughout the unsettled lands where beloved brothers dwell. Your financial benedictions are as necessary for the nurturance of our minds as the priest's are for our souls. You are forever remembered in our daily prayers.

With God's blessings to you,

Mère St. Henri

*1833, From the garden of the Columbia River Valley to the
garden of the Ursuline Convent, Quebec*

Chère Soeur,

My wife and I have just returned from a walk through the gardens
around our establishment. Perhaps it is not so different for her
than a walk you would take around your cloistered Convent
gardens. Marguerite's daily life is enclosed within the walls of
Fort Vancouver. In some ways my wife is as cloistered as you.
Marguerite rarely leaves the palisades of Fort Vancouver but she
enjoys the company of Mrs. Douglas and our daughters. They
arrange meetings and make gifts with women who live as wives
with our Canadians and Metis. Their families have been a part of
our lives since the early days. Our respectable wives dress soberly,
as soberly as you, in black dresses with white lace about their
faces, although they have no veil and are more interested in ladies'
fashions. I prefer to wear their moccasin footwear, much more
comfortable. Company rules forbid that women join the officer's
tables so we enjoy tea together but not dinner. If you took tea
with her, both would enjoy a discussion about spiritual practices,
educating children, music, and women's needlework. You would
make astute observations about the behaviors of mighty and
powerful men. I fear that you might also enjoy discussing my
foibles so perhaps this continental divide has benefits I have not
heretofore sufficiently considered. I am a fortunate man to have
such wise women as trusted advisors.

Your community of women has more seniority than the
HBC's old charter from the King. A royal charter establishes a
trading monopoly but the Ursuline Sisterhood graced by the
Holy Spirit has served a greater God for a longer time. As you and
I realize, this longevity rests upon the good management of
human and financial resources as well as noble intentions.
Although the purposes of our grand compounds are quite

different, both result from primitive and eternal dynamics among human beings. Spiritual teachings about mysterious forces and honest exchanges of material goods are components of cultures much less civilized than ours. When these great impulses are in some balance, wondrous societies evolve. Our times provide such possibilities, may the leaders also provide the guidance. I need your prayers: You benefit from my profits. As you kneel in prayer before the altar of God please do not forget me, and I will forward specimens of the wondrous array of species that inhabit this continent for your students.

Our little garden tour was an inspection of the herbs that might be used for medicinal purposes because the fever you noted in Quebec has extended its long fingers of death to our coast. David comments upon the growing epidemic in London and Paris as well. Our Indian tribes have little resistance and entire villages are depleted or abandoned. Mr. Tolmie is the new physician at Fort Vancouver and we have decided the fort must soon be closed to all but the few who must pass between the gates. Within the fort we made quarantine quarters but it is little more than a hospice. Once the fever takes hold, there is little we can do except offer kindness and some water. Therefore, we attempt to maintain cleanliness and distance.

Elsewhere, I have less control and I have heard of some who think that taking the body of a young girl might cleanse such fever. You will not be pleased to learn about this behavior. I do not condone such abuse within my jurisdiction and favor only those traders who respect my policy. Drink is another false comfort for too many and I do not tolerate anyone imbibing during the day within my establishment. Such injustices might never be eliminated. Therefore, beloved sister, I think demand for our respective commitments to nurturing the spiritual and economic domains will persist long after you and I have written our final letters.

Contact with American citizens continues although it makes our Londoners nervous. Disgusted with the excesses of drunken captains abusing British lads and Indian women, I hired one of the best captains along this coast. Mr. McNeill came from Boston. He runs an orderly ship and has sailed these waterways for many years. Our trading access is more assured when his anchor is dropped because he is married to the daughter of a chief from a northern coastal tribe. My men string four small HBC forts along the northern shores of the continent to bring Indians into our trading stores more easily. Mr. Simpson is not pleased with this land-based approach. I hope that our brave percentages of profit provide some counterbalance to Mr. Simpson's eloquence when the Governor and Committee meet to decide our policies. Thus far they have supported me but I must go out on furlough to meet with them again within a few years.

Another Boston man has passed the Winter with us at Fort Vancouver. An erstwhile competitor, Mr. Nathaniel Wyeth had many grand plans but they all have gone awry. His ships filled with trading goods did not survive the storms at Cape Horn. His overland traders asked for release from their contracts since attending the mountain men's rendezvous or suffering a long march to our posts. Mr. Wyeth leaves with our outgoing brigade, having written Mr. Simpson of his intentions to try again. He promised to trade only south of the river and not within a hundred miles of any of our forts. The little emperor thinks this is too close to our stores. I have encouraged this plan because Mr. Wyeth is a reputable businessman and I prefer compatible gentlemen in our buffer zones. When the last of Wyeth's men went to Honolulu, one of them, Mr. Ball, decided to remain at the fort. Thus, he becomes the first schoolmaster in Oregon, which is the local name for this region. A graduate of Dartmouth College, Mr. Ball indicates that my David and Willie McKay, Tom's son, have potential for more schooling. He also has been kind to my young daughter, Eloisa. We will keep her at home to have one child near us. My wife needs her and I enjoy the lively imp.

Mr. Wyeth has interesting ideas about transportation and politics. In Massachusetts, he had been much teased about his plan to construct amphibian wagons. He was somewhat deflated to learn that, a generation ago, the Metis of Red River evolved carts for which the wheels could be removed at river crossings so that the body of the cart became a raft. Mr. Wyeth assures me that sentiments for change in the new republic go much beyond

Catholic and Protestant schisms. Slavery abolition debates have resulted in the establishment of a new political party to resist "King" Andrew Jackson who centralizes power in the republic. Some think he attempts to usurp individual freedoms that the former colonists fought to win. It may be the Manifest Destiny of the American people to imagine a new form of democracy, but here along the Columbia River we have greater possibility than most to create a utopia. The Willamette settlement now has four farms with crops that prosper. What counts most is the quality of settler who wants to stay. I do not think many British subjects will come so far now that the Highlands have been cleared at such dear expense to nobleman and laborer alike. Besides, the English have a globe full of colonies, some are less isolated than this place. The French have retreated permanently from any colonial dream in North America and would likely not do any better at cultivating soil than English laborers, they expand their cities. Thus, the Metis roam a vast Northern prairie while Spanish Mexicans ride through the South. The Western continental push will come from land-hungry Americans. I hope that when Mr. Wyeth tells his Methodists about this fair place he includes mention of our hospitality and desire for peaceful conclusion to the boundary dispute along the Columbia River.

This year my Department expands our profitable cattle operations from breeding to beef and tallow exports. There is disagreement about whether the HBC charter should handle these operations as a component of its monopoly or whether they should be contracted out. Simpson's efforts at Red River were not successful but our early returns from the expanding herd here suggest that, if we do not capitalize on this prosperity, the next groups of arriving Americans will. Mr. Simpson will undoubtedly try to convince the Governor and Committee that I be not allowed to venture where he has failed. I await news of whether scientific reasoning or personal influence has been most persuasive.

We are informed that Mr. Simpson's young son has died and both parents are much distressed. There is talk that he will withdraw his English wife to Montreal and build her another mansion near Lachine where she might have more companionship. This death will be very hard on Mr. Simpson as it was his only legitimate heir, so I am certain he will continue to protect her. The Indian Territories become more settled but only the most hardy of transplants thrive in it. Young David will be sent out with this express to Quebec and will call upon you this Summer. John's studies go well in Paris, so perhaps David will join his brother and uncle in a year or so. I wished to have gone with him but cannot leave Fort Vancouver for such a long time when there is expectation of new arrivals and the cholera fever continues.

Pray greet my youngest child with warmth. He carries kisses and embraces from me to you.

Your bro.

1834, From the Convent to the Fort

Dearest bro.,

How good it would be to sit with a cup of tea and talk to you. Our letters to each other are often more frank discussions than those with others we see daily but to whom we might confide less. Nothing replaces the desire to see your face and hear your voice. It has been more than ten years since I last saw you.

My news this time is concerned with politics and marriages, paintings and music. It seems we may have a new governor of the Canadas by next year. Lord Aylmer proposes a Royal Commission to study the question of the troubled colonies and make recommendations, but he will not oversee its work. In England, the King refuses permission to have an elected executive council because the English would be in a minority when votes are counted. One rumored solution proposes political union between Lower and Upper Canada to make it more balanced. Separations between language groups and religions increase the schisms of our society. Canadian *patriotes* would prefer a small republic rather than be a component of a larger Anglo state. Almost the only certainty is that political loyalties are being questioned and answers differ depending upon who responds.

Our friendship with Governor Alymer and his Lady has been exceptional. We offer Lady Alymer small gifts in token of her many kindnesses, especially toward our students. For several years she has honored the best graduates by presenting the crowns of roses and the Cross of St. Louis that they wear for the remainder of their examination week. Lord and Lady Alymer gifted us with two matched portraits that now hang in the *salle de communauté* to remind us of their friendship and ongoing support. The farewell masses sung by our choir really must soar directly to Heaven because we also pray that their successors will be as kind. In news from the other camp, Mdme. Papineau and her daughter tell me they pose for a portrait painted by Antoine Plamondon who places them within a charming musical setting. You will be amused to know that our French artisans now build organs and harpsichords right here in Quebec. Their keys make delightful chords and the instruments are named Marching Thunder!

I also have been sitting for portraits. Our niece, Emily, who anticipates completion of her novitiate shortly, undertook to paint a portrait of me. Father McGuire transported a miniature to Paris at David's request in thanks for the many contributions to our school and to remind him of his eldest sister whom he has not seen since he was a youth. Although our talented niece has favored me with a smile in this portrait, your restless son might also notice my eagle eye still observes his activities. As you know, our middle-aged brother is finally married. His young wife, not much older than John, is well positioned in society. Her brother inherits the title of Earl of Essex and her Uncle is Viceroy of Ireland, a connection I will not fail to bring to the attention of the new Governor of this colony.

Your daughter's wedding took place at the Military Hall so that Lieutenant Eppes would not be disadvantaged in his career because of religion. They could not marry either in the Roman Catholic faith or the Presbyterian. This evidence of the British bias in favor of the Church of England saddens me, but I assure you that our family was well represented. Some approve of this marital union more than those of other nieces whom I sponsored as Brides of the Holy Father. Cecile Michaud, sister Julie's daughter, professes next year. Honorée's other daughter, Elizabeth, also announces her intention to take the white veil with us so a third niece will join me in religious Sisterhood. It is possible that, in due time, when Eliza sends her daughters to our school they may be taught by their cousins, and even perhaps by their great-aunt. Your son, David, is well named with respect to temperament and should make you proud when he is introduced in Europe. His interests seem less inclined to medicine than engineering. I do my utmost to encourage all my nieces and nephews to visit here and am gratified at their willingness when the city offers so many other temptations.

I wish that you could meet Father McGuire who soon returns to us after two years in Europe. As beloved chaplain to our Order, he is an indefatigable Irish fighter for our interests. He and I have become particular friends. We are bound by cultural heritage, each having a mother who converted to the Faith, our mutual dedication to the Church, shared joy in music. Most importantly, we have conviction that the best elements of French and English society might, in this new continent, build a conjoined future. When you come out on furlough, I anticipate that you both will join me in the parlor to listen to some music. I also will take you to the *chapelle* to view the magnificent paintings of Mr. Bowman, a respected painter who moved to Quebec from Boston because of the troubles there. We have restored the sanctuaries that house the coffins of our Fondatrices and General Montcalm so perhaps you will also kneel before their tombs to glimpse the eternal Holy Spirit that glows within all, more brightly visible in these predecessors than in some others you greet.

The most difficult news I have left until the end of this epistle. Two fires have reminded the Ursuline Sisterhood how fragile are our material efforts and how strong must be our Faith. Fortunately, we had the historic example of Marie de l'Incarnation herself, who without hesitation left the manuscript of her spiritual writings to burn so that she could save more holy objects. This past January, a lighted candle in a shed adjacent to the kitchen ignited combustible material and the fire spread to the roof. We collected our students outdoors and lead them in prayer, just as was done two hundred years previously. The damage to our Convent was much less than during the pioneer days. This time, however, we had the benefit of fire engines, day students, the military and even an offer from the Governor to take refuge in the castle. The fire provided opportunity for us to exemplify the teachings of Mère Marie and to accept in grace many offerings from the citizens of Quebec. The second fire occurred at the House in Boston and was probably arson, set by an anti-Catholic mob. Some of the Sisters will now travel north to reside with us. The only joy I can find in this disaster is that we add to our roster of English-speaking teachers and some of our newly arrived Sisters have wonderful singing voices that strengthen the choir. I have asked God to explain this type of Irish joke to us but He still apparently debates His response. I will ask again, but in a more polite tone. You are not the only McLoughlin with hot blood, dear brother.

By this confession, you will realize, my dear brother, that after these many years your calm sister still has a temper and occasionally finds the actions of men and God beyond belief. I struggle to find answers to my questions but do not doubt my Faith. God bless the Mysteries that manifest such unity and variety in the ways we serve.

My blessings and prayers go with this letter as always,

Mère St. Henri

1835, From Fort Vancouver to the Convent of the Ursuline Sisters

Dearly loved sister,

It seems the great forces of the world produce pressures like cogwheels in machinery. Small and large are interlocked, always in motion and grinding away. There is no rest for either the wicked or the good. Perhaps our tensions result from the pulls between such pressures. Now that I have observed my fiftieth birthday, it is past time to decide where I will settle in retirement. I must come out on furlough but hesitate to leave because the situation fluctuates so much here.

The unanticipated expulsion of my son John from Paris by David is the cause of much so pain, particularly since I have not been informed of all the reasons. I hope Dr. David's marriage was not a contributing reason. The young bride is closer in age to my son than to my brother but differences in social class are not as navigable. As a student, John would be exposed to Bohemian ideas. His personality would be much attracted to the ideas and gaiety of the Boulouge environment. I hope he has completed his studies, a *baccalaureate* is essential for any respectable gentleman who wants to enter at a proper level of an occupation. On him rests my greatest hopes for the future. However, I refuse to advance further monies for John if he cannot engage in some success. His youth is getting behind him and he has had as much or more opportunity than any young man from this country. Perhaps when prodigal John returns to the colonies, you might once again exert an influence.

My other son David apparently is enrolled in the East India Company College at Addiscombe in England but seems unhappy at being so separated from all family. He is more compliant and perhaps fitted for a bourgeois life but I doubt whether the HBC will be more open to these young men who have some mixed blood than in previous years. There are so many of them now, with so many a father's hopes resting on their shoulders. And there are fewer opportunities for any young man to advance from the ranks since the amalgamation and reorganization of the Trade.

Cuthbert Grant has organized his nomadic clan but his appointment as Warden is not equivalent to that of a gentleman of the Company. He spends his inheritance to experiment with his ideas about Metis settlement. I was most disappointed to be informed his mill had washed out again in the Spring floods at Red River because the mill I established at Lac La Pluie still does well. We have built another good one here at Willamette Falls. Since the death of their son, Mr. Simpson and his Lady Frances finally have abandoned efforts to locate her at Fort Garry. Thus, yet another Governor of the HBC withdraws from Red River. Perhaps when established in Montreal among more companionable society, the Simpsons will have additional children. He would therefore join the majority of men who worry about the actions of their chief claim to immortality: their children. Please do extend him an invitation to visit you and my married daughter when he visits Quebec.

Mr. Simpson grows so arrogant in his sorrow, many voyageurs now save money that they might settle and discontinue paddling in his brigades. One of our men became incensed so he let the little man, who must weigh less than the usual load of two fur packs, fall – accidentally of course – into the water. We hear that the location was well chosen so there was no danger of drowning but the Company has gained another new retiree. Now that his address is on the other side of the continent, Governor Simpson contemplates training a Montreal brigade of Iroquois to increase speed across the great traverse. He thinks to send some of these Indians to the Oregon country to trap furs because the local tribes prefer to fish salmon. That mélange would make further problems for me.

Coastal Indian communities are much decimated by the dreadful cholera. I must talk further with David about this epidemic that seems to attack the poor in Quebec, London, and the indigent in Oregon without much discrimination. Our population does not decrease in this territory however. Settlement expands at Champoeg, near the Willamette Falls, in part because of HBC families who do not return across the Rocky Mountains.

We expand most rapidly because of Americans. Mr. Wyeth has returned with a party of land-hungry Americans and brings news that thousands of settlers are on their way. They will bring with them many republican ideals and demands for United States authority, churches and schools. As you know, I encouraged our retirees to petition the Catholic Diocese in Quebec for priests so that the French language and faith may nurture our settlers as they establish farms and a society. Do not hesitate to send a letter to Abbé Provencher to confirm they may travel with the return brigade. Cultivated English ladies do not transplant as well as the Scots highlanders and the French habitant stock, but American missionary wives will work industriously. However, I do not intend a repetition of the harassment and violence that occurred among the various groups at the Red River.

One difference between the settlements that formed twenty years ago on the plains near Lake Winnipeg and Oregon is that I do not support men who live nomadically with their wives' families and I do not tolerate those who encourage dissolute drinking. The industry of HBC men extends lumber and farm produce beyond what the Company requires and can sell to the Orient, so we have supplies to offer incoming settlers. Mr. Simpson informs me that the steamship he has decided we need for the Columbia will arrive next year. How very nice that the Company has such excess of profits it can afford such expensive experimentations. I wish that it would support my request for ministers and educators beyond what I can provide or this greater human need will be met by arriving Americans.

This Oregon country already has its first missionary who comes recommended by Mr. Wyeth. My stepson Thomas McKay approved of the sermon he listened to when they met at the mountain trade rendezvous. Mr. Lee is a Methodist with a faith much like Mr. Ryerson in Toronto and Mr. Wyeth of Boston. He is knowledgeable about the Canadas and seems a good representative, well liked by our diverse populations so he has been supported in his efforts to build a cabin along the Willamette. This news should spur efforts among your seminarians in Quebec should they wish to garner more souls for the Catholic faith. Although I translate the Bible and make a sermon in French, our *Canadien* men listen to Mr. Lee speak directly to their spiritual concerns. He knows the Canadians well having lived among some previously.

We began to be inundated with Americans this Summer, proving that they have the temperament to persist and take this country. The Governor and Committee will want to sustain profits from the Department for as long as possible and have been generous in rewarding my efforts. But in the United States all these positive reports from respectable men and the Protestant missionary zeal to aid poor Indians, plus a push to be first to establish vast farms, turns the trickle into a deluge. More families will arrive soon, weary and hungry from their overland journey. As always I will greet them, asking only that they share their talents while guests in my establishment and try to advise them where they might most harmoniously settle. Those whose presence would be disruptive to our interests and distracting to other settlers receive less support. With this strategy and by the power invested in the HBC monopoly, I hope to maintain order for another few years. This situation requires a hardiness that is too rough-edged for civilized society but it seems to me that civilization might be strengthened if it better tolerated some of the spirited individuals that come here.

The Royal Horticultural Society in London honored me with a medal after Mr. David Douglas published his scientific report subsequent to his visit here. It is yet another tragedy that his young Metis wife drowned because Mr. Douglas was comfortable living in our conditions and she was a favorite of ours. We benefited from his diligent classification of local species, especially the red fir. He has now gone to Honolulu. This past Winter we were also interested in the observations of another naturalist, Mr. Kirk Townsend, who is a United States citizen. He confirms impressions that the Willamette Valley is ideal for expansion and admires the efficient layout of our establishment. I have ordered the new *Encyclopedia of Agriculture* so that the Cowlitz Farm and lands near Nisqually and Vancouver may be harvested with greater skill and economy. Nonetheless, our tenure here will be brief unless we encourage more settlers who are British subjects to farm along the north shore.

By ship, the Spanish Governor of California warned of an overland party who arrived here last year with two hundred Mexican horses that might have been stolen. Their leader, Mr. Young, claimed land south of the river but I refuse to establish a trading relationship until his name is cleared. His young friend, Mr. Kelley, was allowed within the Fort for several months because of illness although few thought his conversation appealing. These young men remind me of my eldest son. All have an energy that wants more freedom than society will absorb.

So, by land and by sea, the world comes to our shores. As for me, I must travel out soon. I do not anticipate the long journey and the impact it will have upon my hip and other joints. I postpone seeing you and my children and our other relatives because of the pressures surrounding my emporium. You will understand these daily demands, I am certain.

Wishing you good health, I close this long letter about a long and busy year.

Your bro.

1836, From the desk of an Ursuline to the desk of a Chief Factor

Dear brother,

Thank you for your gift in honor of my *fête* July 12! It was an historic moment to reflect upon my professed commitment! On the Day of Dedication it was a triple celebration for three women, each at a different stage of life. For the past quarter century, one half of my life, I have been elected to governance responsibilities in our Community. Also celebrating this special Mass was a young convert to our faith, Sarah Ann Holmes, who joined our Sisterhood wearing the white wreath of her First Communion. The third celebrant has been a professed religious for sixty years. Now very elderly and not very mobile, she remembers walking silently as a little girl behind the funeral cortege of Montcalm after the fall of Nouvelle France! Representatives of three generations of professed religious, we sat at the head table in the old refectory with its oak-paneled walls and brick floor. Observing the vivacity and strength of my Community during this anniversary provided particular nourishment for my soul. I listened to the happy voices among the long files of nuns, gaily enjoying these festive hours, and felt the connection to early Christians through a direct link of Love. What a tradition! What an offering! What opportunity to serve God.

Outside the doors of our Community, the shadows of dissent become ever more stormy. The political situation is complicated because language, religion, land grants, and votes are mixed in an unsavory stew that no one wants to swallow. The new Governor, Earl of Gosford, has visited us, bringing news of our Dr. David in Paris. The Governor is an Irishman who is friends with the family of our new sister, Lady Jane. Her uncle is Viceroy of Ireland. However, Governor Gosford's refusal to permit restoration of the volunteer militia has been an unpopular decision. When military guards are posted in the streets, people do not like to see red-coated British soldiers everywhere. Those of us who have French and Irish heritages may be British subjects but dislike being treated as second-class colonists. The rebellious Legislative Assembly continues to refuse to send monies raised by taxes to the British government. We need this revenue here, especially where there is no municipal government to tend to roads, housing and other necessary affairs that arise when towns expand into cities. The legislative session was adjourned early after a brief meeting characterized by shouting and insults.

I do hope the Royal Commission Report on Governance arrives before a public rebellion. Government House might be threatened with destruction similar to what the Boston mobs did. These troubled times necessitate that my religious Community be more open so that those who are not Catholic understand our educational mission. Our Convent applied for aid from the government and received $2,000. These monies were well used to complete renovations to our buildings so that we could handle more of the destitute newcomers. We expanded our curriculum as well. In January we prepared a public reception for all members of the Legislature, who were invited to visit our school and inspect how their monies have been used. *Le Guardien* reported their satisfaction with the sacred drama (*Corialan chasse de Rome*). The specimens of painting and drawing prepared by girls who studied under Mr. Bowman's tutelage were much appreciated. We also exhibited examples of our needlework, good but not as competent as when we had French hands to guide our little girls. Some of the honorable gentlemen, those who are Catholic, heard the music of Mozart in our Masses, an offering that might guide their souls to further and ongoing support. They will be the shepherds of our proposal to establish *une école normale,* for which purpose we require legislative approval. The teachers we train will go to villages and congregations that we cannot serve and that will release the priests for missionary work elsewhere as well as provide more children with a better education.

You might welcome representatives of various Christian faiths at your faraway emporium, my brother, but we face more competition among the fathers of our girls as to where they will direct the feet of their daughters. Thankfully, most of the mothers have been educated within our walls and wish a similar educational opportunity for their children. Your scholarly kindlinesses will be ever remembered in our prayers for you and your families. Father McGuire returned with many gifts of class books and ornaments from Paris, where he consulted with Dr. David, and we will soon have a new musical organ as well. Our new science classroom is adorned with the hemispherical globe, chemistry and physics equipment, botanical specimens, and books that you helped provide. Our girls take avian skeletons into our garden where they are encouraged to think about how science and religion intermingle as they listen to the sweet warbles of sparrows, finches and at least eighteen other species of birds. My brothers greatly assist our efforts with their gifts and support.

In three years, we will observe the two-hundredth anniversary of our presence in Canada and will use the occasion to inaugurate public examinations, along the lines of the Jesuit seminary, as well as prepare a public concert. Surely the spirit of Mère Marie will approve of these adaptations to the times. She was a great innovator of curriculum and even dared to write religious stories that the Indian girls could understand.

Your son John seems to have further need of some strong hand, probably yours. As you will know by now, he returned from Paris as a silly dandy and I can think of no place for him here. Mother is too ill, Uncle Alexander has a too large young family, Uncle Simon is too old. It is a pity that he absorbed the worst of the student world in Paris and did not adjust well to David's marriage. Those doors are also now closed to him. I know his behavior causes you much grief and dismay because your hopes were for him to be accepted in society. Mr. Simpson plans a visit to Quebec and has indicated he will call upon us. I will invite his wife as well. If Governor Simpson is open to a suggestion that John enter the employ of the Company, please think of this solution as an opportunity. I think your face and guidance may be his greatest need at this time. Your son would have you as a model of one who can succeed when maturity arrives. Despite difficult internal debates, I know that you respond magnificently to every test of character. Turbulence tests the soul as well as the mind. John will undoubtedly provide further opportunities for testing you.

Our increased public contact with dignitaries has provided occasion to mention the need for priests in Oregon, as your region is sometimes now called. Your offer to transport them will soon be accepted, I believe. I know that your position does not permit you to declare a Catholic faith such as ours, but be certain that our prayers support you in your work. Perhaps these offerings might pull you all the way across the continent in time for our next celebration. I hope to welcome you in person once again before we observe other less joyous memorials. Our mother and mentors noticeably age. Why should I be surprised when my own body offers evidence of my mortality? Although my sore leg restricts some physical activities, the blessed medal that Fre. McGuire brought from Paris, encircling my neck, comforts my restless mind when I cannot do more. I am somewhat recovered from my illness of last year but it provides a reminder that my mortal corpus is not as eternal as my immortal soul.

In her Te Deum, Marie de l'Incarnation wrote:

Brisant l'aiguillon de la mort, tu as ou vert aux croyants le royaume des cieux. Et nous croyons que tu viendras juger le monde.

(When thou hadst overcome the sharpness of death, thou didst open the kingdom of heaven to all believers. We believe that you shall come to be our judge.)

Come not to judge our efforts, dear brother, but do come. I pray that you might be on furlough and able to visit us on August 1, 1839 because our activities of these past years were but rehearsals for the grand anniversary of two hundred consecutive years of Ursuline Sisters doing God's work in Canada.

Your sister, in Holy Spirit as well as family

1837, From the desk of an admiring brother to the desk of an Ursuline Mother

Dearest sister,

I will depart Fort Vancouver with the Spring Express but go north for the Annual Meeting at York. Afterward I will come for a visit to the Canadas before I sail from New York to London. Perhaps our next conversation will be a *tête à tête* at your gracious tea table off the *Rue de Parloir*. A reunion with Mother and all of our family is long overdue and my business affairs in Québec cannot be ignored any longer. My attendance at the Northern Council Meeting at Hudson's Bay can no longer be neglected, as it is time to determine where I will retire. It is long past time that I appear before the London Governor and Committee to take its pulse and inform the members in person of my views. Our David, as you know, has many connections in London, especially Mr. Ellice. They think my presentation is overdue because the seats among the Committee also change with retirements. Let the gentlemen themselves inspect and question me, rather than permit my interests be represented by others, especially Governor Simpson.

I have been much put out with the presence of a Mr. Beaver, sent from England to be chaplain at Fort Vancouver by Governor Simpson. This chaplain must have been selected more for his spite than for his Christian charity. I took my cane to him after he publicly insulted Marguerite. As a consequence Mr. Beaver will cause more mischief upon his return to England by ship this year. It is necessary that the HBC governing powers understand how the Church of England cannot address all human needs among us and how its representative must be a man with tolerant views if he is not to generate troubles at Fort Vancouver. Perhaps I might also influence the situation in Oregon regarding the boundary by informing the powerbrokers in England of the potential this country has beyond furs. Political turmoils in the Canadas may weaken imperial resolve and interest in this area. It has become very clear that a business monopoly cannot handle the interests of the Empire when republican fires burn ever so much more strongly in the minds of men everywhere. Settlers arrive wanting seeds. Missionaries preach about good civic works. Sailors rebel against captains. Our employees' industrious labor turns away from pressing furs to working as a supply depot. All are indications that increased demands to own land, to vote, and receive broader participation in civic governance cannot long be deferred.

The Willamette settlers have formed an Oregon Temperance Society because Mr. Young, an American horse rancher who has caused trouble ever since his arrival, attempts to set up a distillery business. Whether British subject or American missionary, those settlers with families and a view of a high future do not want to live among the destruction inflicted by whiskey trading. Some of the settlers south of the Columbia River have formed a Cattle Co. because they might import Spanish stock from the south. I have made a donation because there is more chance of a larger herd passing safely through Indian country, and our own herds have prospered in this climate.

Yet another visitor, Lft. Slacum from the US Army, arrived on an inspection tour with some men. Tom McKay rode with him and reports that his eye is trained for military defense more than settlement. They are interested in claiming a good port north of the Columbia River mouth. I am certain Officer Slacum will agitate his government for a boundary line north of the Columbia. His report will arrive in Washington about the same time as a petition made by our settlers to the USA Congress that a provisional government be established soon in this territory. The dominant days of the HBC Department at the mouth of the Columbia River will not be marked off much longer on yearly calendars but my hope is that the greater option of building a good and earnest society be not a lost opportunity. This is a fair place at the edge of the Ocean, better situated than Red River. Like the Metis, our efforts result in visions of a new nation for our descendants.

Settlement does bring with it old disputes. Ugly debates about religious truths find new fertile ground here in Oregon but I hope that some high ideals as well as good sense prevail until the transition to a more broad form of governance is completed. Early deaths that occur in these lands result from living in strenuous physical conditions, from the debauchery of liquor, or the vengeance of infections. It does not seem necessary to add the dangers of civilized discontents to such a festering array of challenges. The local Indian tribes will be quick to sense frictions and to take advantage of any weaknesses. My protective cloak extends to all human beings but even Israel had but twelve tribes – and lost one of them. Mr. Beaver's departure will be a welcome retreat because he insults all who carry Indian blood, including my wife.

I am pleased to have confirmation that the Catholic priests will arrive with the Fall brigade. The arrangement agreed to by Mr. Simpson during his meeting with the Bishop of Quebec was to support some settlement in the Cowlitz Plains on the north side but I think the black robes will wander where they will among settlers and Indians as they always have. In anticipation, our Canadians built a church they name St. Paul's. They wanted it close to their homes so located it on the south side of the river. Your gentle influence in furthering this request is much appreciated by our retirees and their families.

The presence of white American women, wives of Methodist ministers, excited much comment since they arrived overland in a state of near starvation. When women of our culture establish themselves in a new area, always it signals the advance of civilization. These gentle women also remind our men of what they miss and revive rusting social graces. Mrs. Whitman and her friend Mrs. Spaulding do not always much care for the social strata they observe, including practices of slavery among the Indians even though similar arrangements continue in their republic with imported blacks. Mrs. Narcissa Whitman tutors my daughter in her reading and writing and rides during the afternoon with my wife. Such deportment with my wife and daughter as well as that of Mr. Douglas' family bodes well for good future relationships. They plan to establish a farming mission inland but we try to persuade our guests to settle in a less isolated place. These families herald a commitment to building homes, sowing crops, and raising children. Their ambitions will threaten some Indian tribes, especially the Nez Pierces who regard the area as their hunting grounds. Uneasy and sometimes surprised with the version of society they find here, these hardy Methodists are more compatible than the Anglican chaplain Mr. Simpson bestowed. Although our British commercial monopoly is not responsible for the safety of American settlers, our interests will be affected whether it is Indian violence or missionary converts.

Mr. Beaver's wife was kind enough to our Eloisa who soon marries clerk John Glen Rae, a Scot from Edinburgh. They have sewn a lovely wedding gown, quite in fashion with those in London I am informed. Before departing, I will be proud father of the bride at this wedding celebration and ensure their safe departure to Yerba Buena, in the South (which translates as "fine herbs" from Spanish). When I arrive in Quebec, it will be a great joy to see the children of Mrs. Eppes and my wife expects a detailed description of each grandchild. Thus, both my daughters have married well, having benefited from as good an education and preparation as any young women might receive.

My son David continues to do well in his studies in England but I am not much in favor of the plan to send him to the Far East. HBC has not had advantageous dealings with the East Indies Co. so neither the Fraser clan nor his McLoughlin mixed blood will be of value to him there. I rather think he would do better on this Pacific Ocean coast than on the other side of it. John has returned here as a clerk in the Company. After John unwisely joined the Dickson rebels' expedition at Red River, Mr. Simpson offered him a contract and sent him here. Mr. Cuthbert Grant has my gratitude for some personal guidance in this matter because the mistakes of Seven Oaks need not be repeated among this generation of mixed-blood youth. As a consequence of his education, John already is promoted to a post to which his adulated step-brother Thomas McKay could only aspire. I encourage all my sons here, Joseph, Tom, and John, to join the new Temperance Society. You will be relieved to learn that John settled in reasonably well this past Winter at Fort Vancouver. I hope that he may yet realize the promise of a talented and educated young man.

Also arrived – finally – is the steam-powered sawmill that was sent from Aberdeen to Moose Factory in 1814 but not used much in that remote northern post. Twenty years later the Gov'r and co. decided it should come to the Columbia and so it has, shipped back to London then traveling around Cape Horn. It has much potential in our ever-diversifying trade. In this location, we have the large trees and a growing demand for planed lumber, plus ships to carry it to our various markets. Mr. Douglas will oversee this option while I am away. If this rusty, old, and heavy machinery can travel so far in two years without permanent damage and still be useful, than so must I! Another of Gov'r Simpson's enthusiasms, the *Beaver* steamboat, has arrived, consuming much wood and men's time beyond its contribution. This is yet another type of Beaver not suited to the trade for which the HBC was established. Mr. Simpson delights in sending me poor types of Beaver, perhaps he complains equally of our pelts. They at least can function in this place.

In addition to extending HBC commercial interests South and East, we move into greater contact with Russian fur traders in the North. Established in trading forts, we combine to squeeze out American coastal traders who supply Indian trappers with watered liquor. Our produce from Fort Vancouver is now of sufficient quantity that we could provision the Russians with food as well as the exchange of some furs. That indefinable traveler Mr. Simpson will meet with Baron Wrangell of the Russian American Company to effect a long-term lease, but it would be auspicious for me to remind the London Committee that it is my Department which provides the surplus goods.

All these difficulties make a long list that letters cannot fully describe. My busy furlough agenda is set. The stiffness in my hip will abate after a soak in the hot springs near Boat Encampment but the horseback climb over the Athabasca Pass is an obstacle I do not anticipate. After having survived it, I will see you. If not in personal attendance at your anniversary mass celebration, be assured that David and I will remember you in many ways. It will be a charming adventure to make the acquaintance of his wife. And I wonder how my son David has changed. I wish that my family might live at least on the same continent. Since they cannot, I am fortunate to have this much postponed opportunity to visit. My wife is too old to make the arduous return journey so she will remain here while I go to Europe and the British colonies. I must decide where our final home will be. Like the arriving settlers, I travel far in search of fertile soil where my roots might sink most deeply.

Bless us all during such journeys.

John

The restored John McLoughlin house at Fort Vancouver. Source: National Park Service, Fort Vancouver Historic Site.

Current view of the 1836 expansion of the Ursuline Convent School.
Photograph taken by the author.

III: The Final Years, 1838–1846

Within six years of John McLoughlin's return to Fort Vancouver after his successful visit to England and France, his sister died. These years were a sad cycle for both brother and sister with more sorrow than joys. They descended from pinnacles of success into deep valleys of pain. She suffered from ill health and was bedridden. The loss of their beloved mother and the final illness of a favorite sister shadowed her internal world even as external tensions erupted into political rebellions that would result in a new political framework for the Canadas. He lost a son and two sons-in-law who met premature and violent deaths. The crisis resulting from the murder of his favorite, John, provoked the end of his career and resignation as Chief Factor of the Hudson's Bay Company. As more American settlers claimed land in Oregon Territory, the HBC withdrew from the delta of the Columbia River. Fort Vancouver declined in importance and Fort Victoria on Vancouver Island became the new headquarters. In the Willamette Valley, pre-existing property titles were contested by thousands of new settlers. Most newcomers did not know or care about the many kindnesses the Chief Factor had shown the first waves of starving pioneers. They were more interested in obtaining statehood for the territory. Prior claims and rights of the HBC retirees and the Indians were generally ignored, as were Dr. John McLoughlin's contributions to maintaining peace. Amidst these many griefs and disappointments, one solace was his renewed religious faith, and one milestone was his formal marriage to the woman he had lived with for thirty-three years.

John McLoughlin's office at Fort Vancouver.
Source: National Park Service, Fort Vancouver Historic Site.

Interior view of the Ursuline Convent – the Chapel.
Courtesy of le Monastère des Ursulines de Québec.

1838, McL. writes a letter en route from the Columbia to Canada and England

My dearest sister,

I forward this letter from Red River where my son John turns north with our fur produce and the HBC Annual Council meeting. My body does not sit well in York boats so I have stopped for a rest and to extend my visit with John Todd, Cuthbert Grant, and the Sinclairs rather than go further north. My plans are to follow this post shortly to Lower Canada when the express brigade returns from the meeting. My letter should reach you a few weeks before I arrive, thus sound the trumpet that warns of my return. Please prepare the family, especially Mother. If possible arrange that Uncle Alexander's children come meet me at Terrebonne or anywhere near Montreal. Now that their father has died, it is time they meet our Uncle Simon and his son, John Fraser. Family feuds that continue after death dishonor both living and deceased and ultimately the family name. Who will remember the reasons for the quarrel and why should young lives be distorted by past hatreds they did not cause or understand? My time with you all will be brief because I intend to depart from New York on the new steam-powered packet boat, *Great William*, that leaves the end of August for London. I must also detour to Boston if possible to see Billy McKay, Tom's son, and visit some prospective settlers among the American Methodists.

Behind me at the Columbia, three stalwart men guard my responsibilities at Fort Vancouver. Mr. Douglas, Mr. Ogden, and Mr. Black will be a hardy triumvirate while I am away. Mr. Douglas, becoming Justice of the Peace in my absence, agreed to marry Marguerite and I in a civil ceremony before I left. Should anything happen to me en route, my wife will be protected as much as is possible under British law and HBC policies. Others await the arrival of Father Blanchet. My stepson Tom McKay plans a marriage with Isabelle Montour and they will join the other Canadian retirees who settle at the Willamette. Billy, his eldest son by the Indian princess who died, shows scholarly promise having done well in our little classroom last Winter. I had expected that the boy would accompany me to England and then go to Scotland for medical training. However, Dr. Whitman has persuaded Tom the boy might have a better future if he became American in thought and feeling, so he went west with Mr. Lee who promised to ensure he is enrolled in a proper school. Mrs. Whitman has taken Tom's daughter under her wing at their new Methodist mission. Thus these missionaries foster Tom's children as if they were truly family. However, en route to New York, I plan to visit Billy and if the youth is not happy I will insist he join me when I sail. I will also use the opportunity to recruit good people to settle south of the Columbia just as I encourage the Sinclairs to come overland from Red River and establish farms north of the river where they will be sponsored by the HBC Puget Sound Co.

My son John was much impressed with our traverse through the snowy Athabasca Pass in mid-winter. This type of physical challenge is an overdue test that proves his manhood and he responded to it well. I do not permit him to return to visit his errant friends in Red River but have sent him, under the guidance of Mr. Douglas, on with the furs to Norway House. They return together to Fort Vancouver and I trust his recent responsible behaviors will persist in my absence. John has been warned to impress Mr. Simpson with his new maturity and to respond well to any questions about our establishment. Govn'r Simpson would have preferred that I returned to London by Cape Horn but I am more than his obedient servant and prefer the comfort of a steam-powered packet boat to a ship that sails around Cape Horn in stormy weather. As well, I wish to see so many of the faces I have missed and to hear your voices. All of us become more vulnerable when in the latter stages of life, even Mr. Simpson who has fewer family members to care for.

My furlough will be spent responding well to questions posed by the London Directors. They are prompted by Mr. Simpson's conviction that the Columbia Department would show more profit in furs if I operated our coastal fur trade from visiting ships rather than land posts around which Indians gather. For my part, I must convince the directors that settlement on either side of the Columbia River mouth is inevitable and immediate, therefore it is necessary to attract the type of pioneers who want to purchase our goods and services, not steal them. In the American Midwest, families have been driven to the Great Salt Lake area because of their Mormon religious convictions. In some of the instant towns that pop up on the Great Plains, no law or order prevails unless enforced by guns and fists. In Oregon we must avoid that lawlessness. It is in HBC interests to encourage farms that produce surpluses which we could sell not only to the British navy, but to Russians, Spanish, and even Cantonese. If I were such a poor business manager of my establishment, it would not be necessary to have three younger men carry out my responsibilities whilst I absent myself to meet with the directors.

The longer the boundary line dispute is sustained, the more likely it is that Americans will push into all of the Columbia drainage basin and claim it for themselves. The triangle between the 49th parallel and the northern shore of the Columbia River has good bays in which ships might safely anchor to lumber out the great forests and obtain fresh supplies. Once the fertile southern shore of our river is settled, it will be difficult to prevent the push northward. Therefore, I intend to convince the HBC Directors that if they cannot send settlers from England, they must support those who come from elsewhere and add to the diversification of our prosperous trade.

As you know from the rebellions in the Canadas, everywhere men agitate for greater personal freedom and more independence in how they earn a living. The United States of America are clustered along the Eastern seaboard of the Atlantic and reach into the bowels of the continent but are not yet established along the Pacific shores. The Charter of the HBC established a great monopoly on this continent that extends to Europe and touches Asia. Under that protective umbrella I hold the peace among diverse Indian tribes as well as amongst whomever sails up the mouth of the Columbia River, but my greatest challenges are those who come overland. Individually they cannot compete for long against the wealth of such a great company. Collectively, men who consider themselves free, including employees who retire from our Trade, generate a political momentum that cannot be resisted for long. You and I know that revolutions spawn excessive violence and terror among innocent people. My dream is that this vast emporium I administrate may be guided into peaceable political evolution. My preference would be that in this outlying region we form an independent State such as has been done in Texas and is proposed in California. Perhaps this point of view makes me as radical as my sons and joins me with the unfortunate rebels in Quebec and Red River. Political right does not always generate might. However, the rights of common men will not be respected when their gatherings are chaotic. Some authority is necessary if order is to prevail. Perhaps power is best exercised when a new settlement is agreed about how to live together and that common link may be as binding as family blood or as noble as your Christian vision. Most frequently, men work co-operatively not so much because of ideals but because prospects of immediate profit bind them in shared goals.

Beyond these business and political issues, I have family to visit in Rivière de Loup, grandchildren and a son-in-law to greet in Quebec, even a sister to admire in all her authority as *Mère Supérieure*. Dr. David will require a good accounting when we sit at his table in Paris together with his gracious wife.

A bientôt.

With some haste and much anticipation.

Affectionately,

John McL.

1838, Thank you from Sr. St. Henri

My dear John,

This brief letter flies down the roads to New York with the desire that you will receive it prior to departing for London. I send it with a priest who travels directly to that city whereas you plan a detour to Boston. May your presentation to the American Board of Commissioners for Foreign Missions convince them that conditions in the Oregon Country will improve if they support your efforts. Dr. Whitman's letter of introduction will be of value in this respect.

Thank you very much for arranging affairs at the seigneuries in Rivière du Loup. My mind is much eased now that our mother and sister have sufficient cash income to manage the farms. As two widows, they remain vulnerable to many troubles but money now will not be part of their difficulties. I also offer you my thankful prayers for the amount you gifted our Ursuline House, in advance of our two-hundredth anniversary celebrations. You heard our gratitude in person when you visited us but please be reassured that you are daily mentioned during our Masses. When I walk around the garden reciting my novena, you stroll beside me in Spirit.

Most of all, thank you for insisting that I sit with Mr. Bowman so he may paint me. Who would have thought a nun would be so vain! God forgive me this indulgence! Our restful time together is filled with delightful conversation, an added pleasure to the sin of stolen time from other duties. To avoid too much waste, I arranged that each day a young pupil read to us while he paints and I sit. Such enjoyment should be extended to others in our Community and they would benefit from the practice of speaking English.

My dear brother, I beg of you another gift. When you meet with my other brother, in Paris, would the two of you please arrange for miniature portraits that I could study? I would then have you both in my presence at the same time although we might be continents apart. Pray agree to the request of your elder sister.

May God watch over you during your absence from our continent. I am certain He blesses the joyous reunion between you and David as much as He did when you and I met during our brief recent visit.

Your sister,

M. L. McL. (Sr. St. Henri)

1839, Letter from McL. in Europe

Dear Mère Marie,

Rest assured that your McLoughlin brothers do not ignore your *Anniversaire* and our wives join us in wishing you future good health. May your Community continue to benefit from your talents, and your students will undoubtedly demonstrate the effects of your guidance. Your classrooms should be filled with many delighted pupils examining items we plan to send to enhance their studies. I tour the shops to add to your list of articles.

As always the sights and sounds of Great Britain and France are a marketplace of ideas and adventures that a gentlemen more habituated to wilderness can only sample before he becomes overwhelmed by the array. Our Dr. David and his Lady, quite the cosmopolitan couple, guide me through the delights of Parisian salons. I become a bourgeois republican sampling epicurean delicacies whereas in England I am a British subject, shareholder in a vast mercantile enterprise. I inhabit the lounge chairs of men's clubs in London and discuss the temperature at which water boils in mountainous terrains compared to that at coastal levels. In my heart, I am ready to return to my distant hearth where waits my quiet wife and the comforts of home life.

Along the Champs Elysees two new monuments are installed. Both are reminders of how brief are the *grandeurs* of Empire. Napoleon will not see his completed *Arc de Triomphe*. It was modeled after the Arch of Constantine in Rome. Where are the Empires of France and Rome today? The other remarkable *objet* is a four-sided stone pillar, an obelisk brought from Egypt. It is marked by hieroglyphics, some inscription from a lost ancient civilization. Who knows what it records. You are correct, *chère soeur*, the Kingdom in which you serve is a more eternal one than any of the commemorative glories built by men. As for me, I sip excellent wine at magnificent tables and appreciate the *gaîtée* of sparkling *repartée*. The misery of revolution seems to have sharpened French appreciation for how much life must be savored – today!

In England, I visited many personal landmarks. I have toured estates of the Duke of Kent, paused at Seven Oaks and General Wolfe's birthplace before visiting my stepdaughter and her daughters in Woolrich near Chatham, Kent. They live not far from the great shipyards that build naval boats to carry British men into every part of the globe. It is from this same county that my son-in-law William Randolph Eppes emerged to eventually take the hand of my daughter you know so much better than I ever will. As we journey through the winding village streets, I try to imagine how experiments such as street lamps and railways will change the lives of the inhabitants. Sons will not follow their fathers – perhaps that is as well because space limits expansion. But as they crowd into cities or travel to the colonies, they pack only part of their heritage. What they treasure and what they discard establishes the new cultures we sponsor. When Ambassador to France, Thomas Jefferson acquired a deeper perspective about democracy from viewing his new Republic from a distance, as if through a telescope he said, "All, regardless of birth, have the capacity to enjoy liberty and happiness to the extent that each becomes self-governing and lives in a nation that is a collectivity of self-governing states." However, I think the poverty easily observed on the streets of great European cities leads in another direction, reducing many below the level of animals to sustain their existence.

David prepares his manuscripts on bodily paralysis caused by damaged nerves and I urge him to report his thoughts about cholera. He has taken me to the great lecture hall of the Sorbonne to listen to presentations about human anatomy. They leave no doubt in my mind that circulation of blood in the body is like the waterways our traders follow – each is a carrier of death as often as they are transports of goods that nurture. A hardy lineage increases the possibilities of one's success but even mustard seeds need fallow soil if they are to thrive. Thus, I look to my children and grandchildren as the monuments that will outlast my life.

Probably you regard your students with much the same aspirations.

My presentations to the Governor and Directors of the Company went well, I am pleased to report. They seemed to grasp some of the vision that could turn the Company from a trade dominated by furs to the potential of more diverse commodities. Company ships could carry produce and supplies to our islands in the mid-Pacific and China as well as outfitting the Russians and bartering with the Spanish. This dream I inherited from Alexander MacKenzie and many explorers before him. Generations of British Kings and Queens, Lords and Ladies have listened to merchants and adventurers make the argument that the undeveloped continent of North America has more unexploited riches than the easy spoils of the Far East. I hope to have persuaded the Directors that the HBC profits might eventually surpass the East India Company if British access to the Pacific Ocean is assured. The British government has agreed to extend the HBC Charter for another twenty-one years so we retain our trading monopoly. Less explicit is the issue of where the boundary between British and American governance will be drawn. The fertile triangle between the north shore of the Columbia and the 49th parallel is a particular concern to us who live there but seems a small piece of land to those who control a global empire. The boundary line is not yet a settled dispute because the British government has many other boiling pots on the stove, but the Americans become more determined Westward expansionists.

I go to London in February to hear the opening of the parliamentary debate about Lord Durham's report on amalgamating the Canadas into one colony with a more representative government. While in wait, I plan a trip to Hyde Park to watch the young new Queen Victoria canter past. She is about the age of my daughter Eloisa who also loves to ride horses but in the Indian fashion of straddling a horse. I will also attend my son David's graduation from Addiscombe but think to dissuade him from joining the East India Company, a venerable company but in decline. He could do as well in the Columbia among family as he might in some further outpost of Empire to which I have already lost one son-in-law, husband of my stepdaughter Catherine.

My furlough concludes with an increased bonus because our Department produces a profit and the stability provided by my governance in the region is consonant with the aims of the British government. The only other NWC partner who prospers since the amalgamation with HBC nearly twenty years ago is Mr. Ellice, my London ally. Like our David, he married well and thus is well positioned in high society as well as in financial fortune. Mr. Simpson's power over the entire geography of the HBC consolidates. In addition to the Montreal Department, he is now Governor-in-Chief of Rupert's Land, which is the new title for the amalgamated Northern and Southern Departments. HBC Deputy Governor, Lord Colville, Mr. Simpson's mentor, anticipates the British government's decision to join Lower and Upper Canada by consolidating the older trading areas. The Columbia Department is still in the Indian Territories, far removed from the Canadian colonies and the twenty-eight American states.

For a while longer, I have the freedom of distance and exercise some independence in my governance. I sustain a certain measure of influence at our London merchants' court and will continue sending annual reports directly to the HBC Gov. & Committee Directors by ship, as well as sending reports to Mr. Simpson in Montreal by the Columbia overland express. Mr. Simpson and I prosper because of these powerful men who sit at London tables making decisions that influence the lives of hundreds, as well as the direction of the British governmental policy in North America itself. No wonder so many men cry out for more local representation and self-governance. But how many can truly handle those rights and responsibilities? Revolution is too sudden a birth, too filled with pain for too many men and women.

President Thomas Jefferson was correct. He understood that a graduated release into more freedom and liberty through persuasion, practice and perseverance results in a better harvest, both when gardening and when governing. In North America we have opportunity for a crop greater than that in Europe if we but selectively cultivate. In the next few years before I retire, I hope to become more a gardener of men and crops than a trader of furs. In these declining years of the fur trade, I have permission to develop two leased Russian forts situated in the northern coast and will experiment with a new post in California. We desire to attract industrious and virtuous settlers who will help retain the triangle of land between the north shore of the Columbia River but below the 49th parallel. We watch the struggles for independence in Texas and California. But an evolution into self-governance must be led by honest men who cultivate peaceful settlement. They seek opportunities to make good homes for their families and fair advancement for their children. Traders, Indians and settlers can live together if there is an orderly transition period. God grant me success in my ambitions to foster such a situation along the west coast of the Pacific Ocean.

I think I have made my last visit to Europe and doubt I will return permanently to the shores of the St. Lawrence River. Other gentlemen have made good marriages in these societies but those who have served me well settle in Oregon. My good wife who is sixty-four years of age remains more drawn to the Protestant faith than the Catholic. She is unlikely to venture beyond the Red River or Columbia River regions where most of her grandchildren will grow up. Far from civilization, we will settle in a comfortable location somewhere in those vast territories among friends and family.

Weather permitting I will stop over for a brief visit but must, as you know, catch the York Factory brigade at Red River when it leaves for the Columbia River. I hope to be at Fort Vancouver by my birthday in October. Now that I have viewed other imposing HBC establishments along the route, I am convinced that none is so fine as mine.

With enduring affection,

John

PS. Enclosed is a letter from David's wife who is a charming English flower but fragile.

1840, Letter from Quebec to the Columbia

Cher Frère,

Although a disappointment that you could not remain for the exact day of our two-hundredth *Anniversaire*, August 1, I offer God thank yous for the time we did share before you returned to your duties in the Columbia Department. The changing of the seasons wait for no man and the annual business cycle dominates the seasons of your life. You were absent from Fort Vancouver for more than a year and could not linger longer from your wife and duties there. The furlough in Europe made an obvious impression because you now comport an outward distinction that I shall carry for a long time in my heart. I ask the family to bring the small portraits of you and David with them on visiting days to keep your faces vivid in my mind as well as heart. Although our hearts will be forever linked, it seems unlikely we shall meet again in person here on Earth. I pray we meet each other in Heaven one day.

Do not be distressed to be informed that I was recently administered the last sacrament. It does not seem that my painful leg will recover enough for me to enjoy moving about the Convent as I once did and the condition progresses. If I depart this life sooner than I would wish, it is simply to prepare a way for greeting all those I love when it is your turn to arrive at the Holy Gate. We know not when we might meet God face-to-face but He does. I pray to God that He delay His summons for me until after He has called our mother to Heaven. As you know well from your recent visit, she is quite aged now and we all are fortunate that our widowed sister Julia is so attentive. The future cannot be revealed to mortals such as we, or we would lack the strength to face our trials. Therefore, the present must be endured with as much Grace as one can muster.

Let me turn quickly from illness and aging to describe a more joyous event. You saw many of the beloved accouterments we have gathered to express our joy in serving God for two centuries in this colony. Our sanctuary lamp has burned continuously since 1719 and we always will guard it zealously. The walls of our chapel are decorated with fine paintings from France salvaged when more than 300 convents were destroyed during the tornadoes of revolution. Because of supporters such as you and David, we now have a glorious organ to supplement the offerings of our choir.

On the great day of the anniversary, our altar was decorated with flowers from our gardens and many banners made by our pupils. We even had colored sunlight because the windows were covered with decorated transparent tissues. Flags from all the regiments and other religious orders bestowed their blessings. Perhaps the climax of the Mass, other than the consecration, was the singing. Sixty clergy formed one choir and forty-two nuns sang Mozart's music and chanted a *Te Deum* composed by Marie de l'Incarnation. The pipes of our new organ, thank you once again, swelled to the fullest possible note. Our Chaplain reminded us of the many challenges that have darkened lives during the past years, especially the cholera and the political rebellions. He indicated our Ursuline Convent of Quebec was a sanctuary of the Holy Light itself that illumined the community, even during its darkest times. I am so blessed to have been a witness to this continuous service to the city and to God. May this sanctuary forever light the souls and minds of our pupils.

Outside the convent walls, political winds swirl about the cloaks of all who stomp the streets. We await the outcome of Lord Durham's report about whether the colonies in Canada shall be governed from one or two legislatures. I hope that he did not learn about one act of our charity during the rebellion. It was your birthday! We provided sanctuary for Mssrs. Dodge and Theller, two *Canadien* rebels hunted by British soldiers. As the refugees hid in our supply room, I informed the officers, quite innocently, that if we caught a glimpse of these men we would report it and then we left the room unlocked and went to evening prayers. We did not, of course, see the rebels again. Our guests left without saying adieu, *je ne sais quoi*. That was my birthday gift to you dearest radical. If the fugitives had participated in any violence that resulted in death or destruction we could not have shielded them. But they were guilty of no more than advocating increased freedom of speech and of religion, sentiments with which we are in accord. *Pax de paix dans la province*! These men need amnesty and their leaders are escaped to far away places. Mr. and Mrs. Papineau will undoubtedly meet Dr. David among the exiles in Paris because his wife carries a letter of introduction from me.

We also are informed that the Red River population totals about 5,000 people, and you have persuaded some to settle in your Columbia paradise. May they have a safe journey. Surely adding to the contingent of French souls along your Columbia River will help insulate your society from the political dangers to which you are so exposed. They will contribute to the work of the Church in your region as well.

With great gaiety in my heart and enforced patience because of my poor health, I send blessings and some mementos of our *Anniversaire Messe.*

You will forever have my affection,

Mary

1841, Letter from McL. to St. Henri about the harvest

Dear sister,

This year's letter is a story about extending our roots and the growth of our various endeavors. I enjoy the immediate harvests of my efforts. Perhaps in two hundred years, this enterprise will become as substantive as your Convent. In areas proxemic to the Columbia River, farms and a village appears. In more remote regions our trade prospers. At Fort Vancouver my home is filled with busy ambitious people. My children all do well in their various endeavors, thereby honoring their mother and me. When the newly knighted "Sir" George Simpson arrives next year, he will observe how productive this Department can be when properly supported, and I hope he approves of my governance. We have a better chance of prospering here than in Lord Selkirk's utopian colony because the settlers' amalgam is infused with deep understandings about personal ownership and responsibilities. There are no foreign soldiers to keep order but there now are priests and missionaries who inspire good conduct.

Around Willamette Falls the number of farms has doubled since my return. While I was in England, Mr. Lee recruited several hundred mission families in New England where land is mostly claimed. After seven months at sea, about thirty of them arrived in June and the others who travel overland are expected next Spring. HBC Canadian retirees who farm there include my son Joseph and stepson Tom McKay. This group is approximately equal in number to the American newcomers and the total is about 500 settlers. Although the international boundary is expected to be established on the north side of the Columbia River, I have built a little store and some houses to supply new settlers who stake claims south of Fort Vancouver and to maintain a semblance of community among them. Thus far, I am pleased by their industry. Their efforts do not upset local Indians because each has separate areas in which to follow their respective ways.

However, they are not so far apart that they cannot learn from each other and observe each other's customs.

The fur trade moves to the far North where beaver pelts and sea otters are more plentiful and the pelts are of a better quality because the weather is more cold. For these remote areas where frost-free days are few and men preoccupied with trapping, we supply goods and produce from the abundance of our establishment at Fort Vancouver. Like jewels, my children have been moved into this string of trading forts. Returning from Fort Stikine, my daughter, Eloisa Rae, was delivered of her first child aboard the *Beaver* steamship. After recuperating with us, she will depart with her infant daughter, named after my wife, to join her husband. John Rae is in charge of our new post, Yerba Buena, California, which is known to be the best harbor along this coast. He will explore trading options with the Spanish and expects to link our diversifying trade to China. So after more than twenty years, Mr. Bethune's forecasts about a prosperous market in the Far East begin to be realized. Captain Cook and Alexander MacKenzie would be proud that we maintain their dreams.

My son John is left in charge of Fort Stikine and has an able and seasoned assistant, Mr. Roderick Finlayson. John has taken an Indian wife and so is more settled himself, very removed from past temptations. David has become involved in the clerical work at Fort Vancouver, preoccupied with all the arrivals and departures. I brought my wife's marriageable granddaughter with me from Red River to replace my daughter at Marguerite's side. Young Catherine Sinclair has provided a useful pair of additional hands as they ease newcomer women and children into pioneering conditions. Catherine, named after her aunt in England, was known as the prettiest maiden in Fort Garry so I have not refused Francois Ermingter's offer of marriage, although he is twenty years her senior. I hope she has a life somewhat like my daughter Eliza Eppes, busy with children fathered by a husband double her age. Perhaps these seasoned men are also more settled when surrounded by young families who spur them on to greater endeavors. Members of the Sinclair family will lead a group of immigrants from Red River in the Spring. These settlers we encourage to farm north of the river to consolidate the British claim in that disputed triangle of land. However, I think they might abandon their grants to claim land closer to the mill, stores and church near the Willamette Falls.

For my part, I am content to discuss the successes of our family with my wife whose nine years seniority still proves advantageous. I come roaring into our quarters about some stupidity that has occurred, but she calms this aging lion so that he may lie down among the sheep, so that he tends and does not scatter his flock among the winds of chance. Most evenings, with my wife on my arm, I tour the fort carrying the gold-topped cane I brought back from Europe. It eases my hip so I limp less and an effective poke produces action as much as words.

You will be pleased to hear that behind my desk is a picture of a ladder made by Father Blanchet to explain how Christians might ascend to Heaven. It reminds me of the inspiring vision you tell your students. How does it go? Centuries ago, your founder Ste. Angela was a pious young Italian maiden when she dreamed of a great ladder reaching to Heaven from Earth. On each step was a Virgin, guided by an Angel. And, she heard a voice telling her that she was to found an order of Virgins. We all have dreams of ascension do we not, *chère Soeur*. In Medieval times, Angela Brescia named her religious order after a fifth-century martyr, Ste. Ursula. In your turn, you have lead the celebrations of two hundred years in the New World colony, on a continent not even dreamt of by your patrons.

Sir George Simpson is much puffed up about his new title that he received at the hand of Queen Victoria herself. He tells everyone how he knelt in front of Her Majesty at her new residence, Buckingham Palace. It was renovated after her marriage last year to Prince Albert of Germany and provides gracious evidence of British supremacy, according to all reports. We were most astounded to hear news about an assassination attempt on the life of the young pregnant Queen. Her calm deportment during the attack has much endeared her to everyone, including her new knight, Sir George. To bestow further honor upon her reign, he determines to be the first man to circumnavigate the globe, forever traveling within sight of the Union Jack flag. It is a like a lap dog squirting out the boundaries of his territory. Governor George Simpson has become ever more vain since he negotiated the profitable agreement with Baron Wrangell in St. Petersburg, Russia, two years ago. To remind him of his lusty past mortality as he strives for eternal immortality, the HBC Factors and Chief Traders present him with a great sterling silver cup, carved with beavers that run away from him and naked ladies that dance toward him. He is now past fifty, another aging man with a younger wife but few legitimate children to carry on his legacy. He has been quite indifferent to the education of his "bits of brown" who grow into men and women with little support from their father. His treatment of his two young Scottish cousins, both youths now dead at an untimely age, was not worthy of a gentleman in the Trade nor as a foster father. Mr. Simpson has made many pockets heavier but very few hearts happier.

My kingdom here on Earth was a happy, busy, and beautiful place to be this year. This bountiful land becomes ever more fruitful by applying modern methods of science and organization. My position is sufficient to provide those dearest to me with gifts that honor their efforts and achievements. My children thrive, each in their respective spheres, as do the settlers. We are guided by men of God who remind us that due and diligent attention to character might win a place in a greater Kingdom. I grow ever more fond of this one however and do not wish to leave it soon.

If this year is a harbinger of the harvest of my lifetime, then I am a settled man. I may not ever kneel at the feet of an English Queen nor dine among members of the Royal Court. But as I toast their health in public, I honor you, a leader in your cloister, privately in my heart and am content. The head of my table in Fort Vancouver is a satisfying place to sit.

May God and the good works of your Sisters reduce your physical pain. I know your suffering will be an offering that God will cherish at His own table.

With brotherly regard and enduring affection!

Chief Factor, J. McL.

1842, Letter from Sister St. Henri, who is very ill

Dear John,

My news this year is about the inevitable decline toward death, the promise of new life, and gratitude for honors that we receive for a lifetime of effort.

It seems that God has decided to enclose my life within a mantle of illness. It provides further opportunity to earn blessings by offering my suffering to God in the same spirit that Christ offered his life. Of course, I am not so holy a vessel as Christ, therefore my sacrifice is not such a perfect gift. I study His example of how to taste the bitter cup of physical mortification with infinite grace and love. The priests have administered the last sacrament several times, and my companions have offered prayers that I be spared more pain. This collective appeal has been of sufficient quality to restore some vigor. Thus I continue to make a contribution in this world, rather than in the more ethereal spheres. God seems unwilling to take my immediate offerings so I still have time to polish and perfect my gift of life.

The physicians inform me that this tug for my body and soul might go on for some time. Whatever is causing the wound in my leg to suppurate rather than heal is an infestation for which there is no cure, and, therefore, no recovery. My Community is concerned about my changed appearance and limited abilities to be physically active. I seek to redirect whatever energy I have in directions that exemplify the message of Christian charity.

I chafe at becoming a burden for my busy Sisters. My abilities to participate in the Orders of the day are so restricted I cannot visit the Chapel. Although I might walk in the Garden of Gethsemane more frequently in my agony, my tours in the lovely gardens at the back of our Convent House are ended. It is not proper to ask others to leave their work and tow me. When the weather is warm, my open window invites all the familiar sounds and smells to visit. That must do. My long tenure as administrator is ended, but I pray that other talents emerge so our service may continue unabated. My time as *Mère Supérieure* is over, although I listen and offer advice when the incumbent visits my room.

Do you remember the story of Martha and Mary, each eager to show how much she loved God? Whenever Christ visited their home in Bethany, which was often, they demonstrated their willingness to serve Him in different ways. Pious Mary would sit at Jesus' feet and listen to his teachings, perhaps to transmit them to children as we strive to do. Martha would provide for His needs, laboring in the kitchen and washing his linens. Which sister made the greater offering to God? Would He value one more than the other when the time arrived to assess their service? In our Convent, we have two types of avocation. The choir Sister has the privilege of chanting the Daily Office and teaching our youthful charges. The lay Sister attends to the daily wants of the household. Both types of professed religious labor in the spirit of peace, seeking in all we do to please God. The duties of both are intermingled. When a lay Sister has prepared the meal, the choir Sister serves her. While the lay Sister knits, the choir Sister reads the daily meditation.

In the time I have left to me, my challenge is to maintain a balance between my Mary and Martha offerings so that I sustain my vows and offer service to God but also do not become a further burden to my Community. When a Mary, I review the applications of those girls who feel the Call and express a desire to join our Order. It is my task to redirect those who do not have strength to sustain such a disciplined life and to nurture those who seem to have sufficient qualities to walk this path, which is not always a route without temptation, I confess. Many times when I was younger, I longed to attend one of those dances you also missed so much, dear brother. I listen now to the troubles of the incumbent *Mère Supérieure*, then I gratefully draw upon my administrative experiences to advise. When a Martha, I knit garments for the poor who always feel the cold so acutely or I mend corners in novitiate garments worn down because of youthful zealous energy. As a Mary, I have more time to offer prayers on behalf of those more distracted by worldly responsibilities. As a Martha, I devote time to the little tasks that always need doing, such as polishing silver sacramental vessels and correcting lessons. Thus, I try to make myself useful to my Community while at the same time be of service to God.

My Ursuline Sisterhood extends a charity beyond any that I could ever return. Our aged mother is also very ill. She is beloved to my Sisters, often having visited when I was more able and active and bringing us gifts from the farm. They consider her a model of virtue and kindness. The story of her life, and her fidelity to the Catholic faith, is well-known and frequently repeated because as the number of non-French Sisters increases they suffer family schisms between the Protestant and Catholic manifestations of Christian faith. Our mother now resides with us in the Convent for what will be the final few months of her life. This rare invitation to admit a layperson into the innermost corridors of the life of our Community is the greatest honor I could be bestowed. You and David, through your regular gifts and letters, share in this accord. Thus, our mother prepares herself among us for the final passage, and my Ursuline Sisters demonstrate our Faith to the larger community. I hope the *Ville de Quebec* understands that this private act of charity is a more perfect example of the goodness of our Order than our public celebration of the two-hundredth *Anniversaire* of the establishment of our House. In my confinement, I have a living example of a pure soul, our own mother. At eighty-three, she offers to God a life in which numerous travails were met with transcendent grace.

All of her children benefit from her excellent lesson as we prepare for our final passages, which I hope will be a long time yet for you, our brother David, and other sisters. That request is sent daily as a prayer to God and it seems He must hear some part of the message because both of you are at the apex of your careers. May the glory of your public lives be matched in the illumined depths of your private soul.

You may have heard from David or the HBC Directors that his long awaited *Légion d'Honneur* is finally to be presented August 15. He is the first non-French person to be so recognized. The tribute is not only for his work to establish a military hospital while a prisoner of Napoleon but also for his recent pamphlet, *Consultation médico-légale sur quelques signes de la paralysie vraie et la valeur relative*. This publication should attract more prestigious clientele. I hope also that you and your wife have been informed that your daughter Eliza Eppes and her active family do well. She has made an application to send her eldest daughter to our school. It makes the fifth generation of women in our family to enroll – although great-grandmother attended classes for only several months.

And now, my beloved brother, this letter is closed with a kiss and prayer that you remain well. By the time it rests in your hand, our mother will have departed this Earth, but I expect I will remain here awaiting your next post.

Be blessed by God as you go about your daily work in good health.

Your sister,

Mary

1842, From McL. – in crisis

Dear sister,

The letter goes out as usual on the Columbia Express with a sad message, a burden much heavier than any of my previous epistles. I hope it will be placed in your living hands although I am relieved that our mother's death spares her this further grief. Where do I begin to explain my anguish? First, the news itself: my son John is dead. He was murdered by his men at Fort Stikine shortly after Sir George Simpson visited there. Governor Simpson has not reviewed the incident as a violation of British law nor has he treated my dead son's body and reputation with the respect that a gentleman customarily receives. And thus I am bereft, shattered by the betrayal of ambition, the denial of British justice so vaunted throughout the globe, and the great loss of my beloved son upon whom so many of my hopes rested. Let me try to explain the circumstances.

As expected, Mr. Simpson arrived in August with the Columbia Express intending to tour the Alaska Forts and continue through Russia back to London on his global tour. He remained only a week at Fort Vancouver but has left havoc everywhere in my Department. Swollen with pride, Sir George even had a writer with him to record their adventures en route so that his record of circumnavigating the world might be clearly verified to all and for posterity. Mr. Simpson does not care for comfort when traveling and thinks all HBC employees should live without most accouterments of civilization wherever they are located. Therefore he did not much approve of our country estate, rural and removed as it is from the centers of power. I think he also has some jealousy of Chief Factor Douglas' and the other gentlemen's contentment in our mixed-blood families. Our daughters would grace many sitting rooms anywhere in North America and would be admired for their deportment in most salons of Europe. At the same time, they can ride a horse and repair clothing as well as most Indian princesses. Our sons prove themselves competent within the ranks of the HBC as far as is permitted or demonstrate they can independently manage their own goods and property.

But I think Sir Simpson's greatest reservation is directed toward me, my governance of the Columbia Department, and family connections. When we came overland to establish the Columbia Department in 1824, we united in common purposes to develop a more peaceable and prosperous trading zone in what had been the most uninhabited and violent region of North America. We were confident that within ten years we could profit ourselves, secure British rights to areas largely unsettled and unexplored, and bring a modicum of civilization to local tribes through our presence even though our territorial political boundaries were not confirmed. In those early days even when uncertain of earning a profit in our risky ventures, Mr. Simpson and I ordered rations for spirituous liquors, and we did not indulge in consuming even the fresh beef that was produced on the Vancouver farm but sent it for trade. Our profitable accounts, the population growth among all settler groups here, loss of men and equipment from vagaries of nature but rarely from human violence all testify to our success. But material success breeds covetous desires for more gain, and intrinsic qualities of character become less flexible, hardening with time.

Sir George Simpson has genius in envisioning and planning the output of a great Company. He is wealthy, and now titled, considerable recognition for an illegitimate son of a Scottish governess. He owes such successes to his own innate talents, his indefatigable temperament, and his English mentors. Of the gentlemen under his command he demands not only hard work and obedience, but often an unbecoming servility. Of Indians he is concerned more with expediency than respect. Of his children, he is distant and isolated, rarely relaxing at home and worse, indifferent to their futures. His wife, their three daughters, and one son reside in London where he occasionally visits. His mixed-blood children are scattered throughout our depots. He spends monies on some but does not invest time with any. Thomas, one of the two nephews he sponsored, was murdered two Summers ago at Grand Forks while returning from an exploration of the Arctic. Simpson hushed up the investigation because he thought any negative report might harm the Company's reputation. At the time it had applied to extend its Charter and the Council had nominated him for knighthood. Last Spring the young man's body was brought to Fort Garry where it rests in an unmarked grave near St. John's Church, but the circumstances were never properly investigated nor his name cleared. Sir Simpson is a man increasingly dedicated to no other God than that of Mammon and his only church is the HBC, which Mr. Ogden calls "Here Before God" meaning greed is a more elemental force than spiritual. Our Governor-in-Chief forgets to love and he cheapens British justice. This is the gentleman who was one of the last to sup with my son John and was one of the first to step over his remains.

The final week in August that Gov. Simpson spent in Fort Vancouver with me was stormy, perhaps an overture to what would occur when he traveled to visit our northern posts. He and Chief Factor Rowand from Fort Edmonton journeyed together. In October, Mr. Simpson removed Rod Finlayson, John's assistant at Fort Stikine, to Fort Simpson and continued to Sitka for consultations with the Russians. When Gov'r Simpson returned south to Fort Vancouver, he announced that all northern posts except the one named after his nephew were to be closed. One post is to be constructed on the southern tip of Vancouver's Island to connect with Fort Langley and reinforce the boundary line should the Puget Sound triangle be lost to the Americans. Whatever remains of the fur trade will be conducted by sea. Competition from Russian and American traders in these territories has been abandoned because in England silk supplied by China replaces the demand for beaver. In making this decision Mr. Simpson has consulted all my gentlemen officers along his travels but ignored my opinions.

After Christmas, Sir Geo. and I traveled to California to take Eloisa to her husband at Yerba Buena and go south on our way to Oahu. After altercation with Mexican customs officials at Monterey and discussion with Ermingter just arrived with our overland California brigade, he decided also to close Yerba Buena. As a consequence, he orders the expansion of the fort on Vancouver's Island and sends Mr. Douglas to command it. Some employees at the other posts are to be relocated there. My arguments with Mr. Simpson continued throughout our sojourn in Hawaii with much rancor but little resolution. When I departed in March, I informed him that our private correspondence must in future cease. We would communicate only about business matters. The man has become a dictator, not a leader, of other men.

Heading to Siberia to continue his overland trip, Mr. Simpson stopped at Fort Stikine. He arrived to find the flag flying at half mast. During the morning of April 21, John had been shot. Mr. Simpson took depositions from those who were present, and transported one guilty man to authorities at Sitka because the murder occurred on territory leased from the Russians. It was the least he could do. In June I received two letters from him, penned April 27. One was a private message and the other a public dispatch which will be reviewed by anyone who can read. It demeans John's leadership and character at every level. Since the dead young man could not defend himself, it has been left to his father to do so.

A man can survive amputations, but not having his heart lacerated. Chief Factor Douglas has gone up the coast to close Taku, Fort McLoughlin, and Fort Stikine and to establish the new site named after Queen Victoria. I have spent the Summer reviewing the depositions that Simpson took. In his hurry, he didn't even cross-examine these employees who certainly were not predisposed to implicate themselves although evidence of premeditation is clear. In my capacity as Justice of the Peace, I also held a formal hearing in the presence of Chief Factor Douglas and other witnesses, including Reverend Jason Lee, with one of those men present at the murder. John's men were angry because he did not permit them access to liquor stores and nor could they steal gifts for their women. His business accounts were in order and up-to-date. The mistake John made was to enforce discipline among disreputable hires when he had no back-up. The men told Mr. Simpson that John mismanaged HBC affairs because they knew he was predisposed to hear that story. My grief increases because I wonder whether my recent disputes with Mr. Simpson influenced conditions. Everyone knew I was not pleased about the dismembering of my Department. Did some of these employees take action knowing that the Columbia Department was to be reduced to a skeleton and they might become excess? Mr. Simpson arrived at Fort Stikine to find John "hurried into eternity," to use the words he wrote in his public letter. How did my actions assist in this tragedy? Is John a victim of his father's ambitions?

My beloved sister, confessor who hears my weaknesses and sins, to what extent am I responsible for the dismemberment of nearly everything I hold dear? Has my famous temper once again betrayed me to my enemies? Should I have kept my son by my side longer or cut him off from support earlier? More than any of my other children, I saw myself in him. Perhaps he should have gone to Edinburgh rather than Paris for his education. He might have returned with a more sober countenance. Did you know that he nearly drowned in Lake Erie not far from where I had my canoe accident when I was a young man? Both of us were engaged in ill-fated expeditions to assist less fortunate men. Those narrow escapes were each an unforgettable baptism into maturation for my son and me. John's greatest sin was that he was educated and elevated to the status of gentleman during years when the definition of gentleman has shrunk to fit a small man.

No father ever expects to bury a son but even more anguished is that man who might be guilty of contributing to his son's death. It is an unbearable burden. I have come down from the Mountain to the Valley of Death and there is no one who can comfort me although many try. I truly know now about the desolation of Christ's forty days in the wilderness. I have lived in the territories for nearly forty years, always believing that the good in men is a weightier currency than the bad. But now I am bankrupt in spirit and can scarcely carry on with any duties.

Dear Mary, if you live to read these words, please offer a prayer for the soul of my son John. Hasten a response to this bereft father. My usual source of consolation, Marguerite, is as desolate as I am. It is the first child she has lost to death, not distance, and she had him at her side for such a brief period of his brief lifetime.

Your forlorn brother,

John

1843, Letter from Sister St. Henri: in response to his crisis

Dearest brother,

How very saddening to receive the tragic news in your last letter. Be assured, God tests but he does not sent travails that are beyond our capacity to transcend. Life is a gift but the living of it involves trials that challenge the worth of every soul. Like gold that is purified, some become more humane while others barter their way into eternal penance. We pray for your son who was maturing, and in the last bloom of his youth demonstrating his manly possibilities. We are grateful that John's time on Earth was of sufficient duration to be returned to his own father's care. Like the prodigal son, he was welcomed and earned forgiveness. We share your sorrow and that of your wife and family. Be assured we say Masses for John McLoughlin Junior, his father and mother as well.

Though you walk through the Valley of the Shadow of Death, you do not walk alone. The rod and the staff of God comfort you, even if you cannot see Him. That is part of the Mystery of religion. We have Faith that the application of reason will reveal an order to events we cannot understand with the hope that one day more will be revealed to us. It is not magic; it is phenomena that might be understood. Think about our brother who uses the scientific method to publish his observations of patients. His minute and careful notes identify an order, a pattern in the symptoms that reveal the nature of a disease. One day the cause may be better diagnosed and the disease treated more successfully. Is this not a guided tour – what was once unknown becomes manifest through a disciplined application of reason and reflection. You have made this argument to me, as have others. In this orderly progression is not the hand of God gradually being revealed? But the hand of God moves in mysterious ways always beyond the ken of human comprehension. One only needs to regard the stars to be humbled by human limitations.

The Royal Chartered Company of which you are a partner is one of the greatest in the world. Its corporate activities and ambitions push the boundaries of the British Empire itself. By living in an outpost as you do, exemplifying civilization as best as is possible, you realize more than most the limitations of such material power. When young men die and older men ignore their extreme sacrifice, what becomes the true message? Individuals form a community to augment their respective interests, but who truly is served? A healthy society serves all citizens, perhaps not equitably, but fairly. A society is diseased to the extent that those at the top of the hierarchy benefit without regard for those less fortunate. If too great an imbalance, there is rebellion. Civic diseases may not be too much different than physical ones. Who will be the diagnostic physician? The proper study of mankind is man but every mirror distorts when held close to that which it reflects. Thus, hold your mirror to your face to study your own heart better, but also to look to the stars so that you might heal your pain. As you do so, you will have greater clarity about what is just and proper future action. You are a human, not God, and therefore vulnerable to weaknesses as much as any other.

When men forget to look at the stars, they obsess with their own glory. Although they fly high with desires, eventually they will fall further than a star that shoots along the heavenly firmament because it does not know of Hell. There is more in Heaven and Earth than we will ever know. When we turn to the depths of our hearts, shadows and light will ever distort reason. For certain, our trials test our Faith in all that we hold dear. Therefore, at the end of life, we have only love: of ourselves, of those we hold close, of that which we don't understand, of God. As you struggle in your solitude with the temptations of revenge and bitterness, seek to love and strive to set hatred aside. I pray that your spirit will arrive at an oasis of comfort.

My family news contains the usual mix of sorrow and happiness. I regret to add to your cup of sorrow, but pass on the news that Uncle Simon has died at Terrebonne. He joins Uncle Alexander and our mother and I trust they will guard the spirit of your son John, if possible. You will be pleased to learn that your efforts to mitigate hostilities among these brothers were successful. The introduction of Simon's son John to his cousin Elizabeth has resulted in a solid marriage between them. We were pleased to receive a visit from Eliza Eppes and children who all are well. There is talk of your daughter's family going to Jamaica. He may be posted there if the coming election in these colonies finally settles the unrest here. My own health continues to restrict mobility and God provides ample opportunity to earn more purity by never releasing me very long from pain, even at night. When I cannot sleep, I gaze out my window into the deep blue searching among the brilliance of the stars. You often are in my thoughts. Although distanced, you are not nearly so far as you might be one day. May you find religious sustenance as you prepare for that journey, dear brother.

May God's blessing be upon all members of your family. We pray for the soul of your son John.

With deep love,

Sr. St. Henri

1843, Letter from McL.: via America

Dear elder sister,

I write a quick letter that might overlap with any that you have forwarded because it goes out with some Americans this Spring before I have opportunity to receive yours when the brigade arrives. After these friends reach Boston or New York, they will have it forwarded. At least, I live with the expectation that I will receive my regular letter this Summer. Should an Athabasca brigade ever arrive without a letter from you, I would be desolate. Its absence would have a fearful significance – that your soft voice of wisdom would never guide my thoughts again.

Throughout these many years, your advice has been an indispensable source of comfort to the many lonely places in my heart and ignorant parts of my head. At crucial times when tempted to falter in my humanity, I have thought about our annual dialogue and have been loath to admit to behaviors that would disappoint you. Throughout many terrific turbulences, we have remained steadfast, maintaining love and loyalty to each other and our family members. This connection has provided a calm anchor during so many storms of my life. Because I know that you suffer a disability that impacts your general health but not your heart or head, I send this news with Faith that you will be well enough to read it. Perhaps my message will be as healing to you as it has been to me.

For many years, I have believed that men need regular moral lessons or their character will be forever stunted. But a life in the wilderness has made me much removed from the various disputes that inhabit Christian religions and provoked some curiosity about the Indian belief that all sentient beings possess a natural Spirit.

The Roman Catholic Church is a grand establishment, as powerful in its sphere as British Kingdom is in politics and the HBC is as a commercial enterprise. Despite human fallibilities, these organizations have dominated for centuries. Inspired as much by nationalism as by religious sentiments, England sanctions an established state religion, favored by Crown and Houses of Government, but this patronage has not stopped men from expressing and following dissenting beliefs. The Church of England makes even Royalty bow but the Crown governs a commonwealth of diverse peoples and faiths. In France it is practically a religion to honor individuality yet most people subscribe to the universal Roman Catholic faith. The political spirit that motivates men and the religious one that illuminates them seem rarely aligned.

Mr. Thomas Jefferson's "philosophy of Jesus" is a reading that has much merit. He has compiled a list of Biblical statements attributed directly to Christ in an attempt to comprehend how Jesus understood God and the Holy Spirit. American citizens make freedom of religion a core component of their Republican values. In the British colonial Canadas, the Catholic Church retains a supremacy in Canada East but there is no state-sponsored church. Followers of dissenting faiths influence the schools, and therefore the minds of youth and the future of their societies. This public display is more about status than about the truest method of saving souls, but at least young people are exposed to higher human values.

At the heart of religious dispute is the issue of whether an individual might commune directly with His God or whether a skilled intercessor is required. In my position as Chief Factor, I have found it expedient to encourage men who respect God's words because of the positive influence upon employees, settlers, and their families, as well as upon demoralized Indians. Thus, I have remained open to the exhortations of wandering Catholic priests, pioneering Methodist ministers and their wives, as well as joining in the reflective smoking of pipes among circles of Pagans. In the absence of priests and pastors, I have led services myself, reading Biblical passages and telling inspirational stories. Some exposure to good works produces improvements in good conduct and, in the absence of government, churches and schools, has been as much of a blessing as could be expected. Nevertheless, even a powerful Chief Factor needs spiritual guidance at times.

Grief over John's murder pushed me into a crisis of my soul from which I never thought to emerge. My enjoyment of well-prepared food vanished, my pride in my establishment diminished, my family found me listless, unwilling to plan activities, my friends thought me embittered and obsessive. Simpson, the little Napoleon, had commanded that I dismantle my domain and reduced my stature. Therefore, I decided upon a Retreat. After I toured Fort Nisqually last Fall I remained a while. For a period seeking some seclusion, I wanted to be more alone in my loneliness, to find some solace in my solitude. Perhaps it is no coincidence that this fruitful time in the wilderness struggling with Devilish temptations took place in late October, about the date of my birthday. I was in need of a rebirth.

During the period of my reflections, reading *The End of Religious Controversy*, a book that was published in 1830, comforted me. It comprised a friendly correspondence between a religious society of the Protestant Faith and a Roman Catholic divine. A series of letters was exchanged between Dr. Carey, L.L.D., Church of England, and other English rational dissenters, including Quakers, Socialist Presbyters and various Methodist sects, with the Right Reverend John Milner, D.D.V., of the Catholic Academy of Rome. The first of their letters were revised in 1803 and the ongoing debate not made public for a further fifteen years. In other words, their exchanges paralleled my own life from the time I entered the Trade until the deadly canoeing incident in which I nearly forfeited it, then to this last phase when I would have given my rescued life if I could have saved my son.

During this past year of profound anguish I truly have been a lost soul, consumed with anger, despair and grief. However, the dialogue among the clerics in this book remained in a sphere of rational exchanges, not emotional arguments, an application of scientific methods in the attempt to comprehend more of God's Mysteries. Such a disciplined approach to religion is not unlike the spiritual universe you have inhabited all this time. I have visited these spheres occasionally but not lingered within.

There is no need to recount all points that each side raised. You will be familiar with all the arguments and perhaps even have read the book. I had not heretofore thought much about religion through the lens of science. Suffice it to say that now, after all these years of indecision, I have professed the Roman Catholic faith.

As you know, I was baptized in the Church shortly after birth. But my news is more recent. The Vicar General, Father Blanchet, heard my confession November 18, 1842 and on the same day he blessed Marguerite and me in marriage. During the four weeks of Advent I fasted and took my first communion at Fort Vancouver at midnight Mass on Christmas Eve. The little chapel was nicely decorated and candlelit. It was full of people, both white and Indian, with a large number of servants of the Hudson's Bay Company. Two choirs of men and women sang the Canticles of Nöel in French and Chinook. Since that profession of Faith, and the comforting rituals that now cloak my chilled soul, I have known more inner peace and am prepared to address the next chapters of my life.

My struggle to mitigate injustices surrounding John's untimely death continues. The battle has become a legal review that will take some time and expense. Sir George's shallow application of British justice resulted in interviews with only six of twenty-two men present at the murder, and no review of any documents on site. There is a long history of Company officers, including Simpson's nephew, providing arms, ammunition, and spirituous liquor to Indians in this area, despite HBC standing orders, orders that are followed elsewhere in this Department. In my capacity as Justice of the Peace in the Columbia Department, I ordered a full investigation. As a consequence of all the testimonials and a closer examination of the accounts and stores at Fort Stikine, it became obvious that my son had not been drinking, had tried to enforce discipline for infractions of policy and had kept accurate accounts of all trading transactions. His greatest error was to apply too much physicality in his discipline, given he had no other officer on site for support. To clear John's name, and mine, I paid from my own pocket to have the witnesses sent to Norway House in anticipation of a fair trial and sentence in England. In these actions I replicate the scenario of my own youth in which we who were the accused were transported out of the Indian Territories for trial by judge.

It is time the Governor and Committee are reminded once again that unless British law is applied fairly in these Territories, no

HBC supplies or depots, and officers, are safe from harm. If British justice is not carried out and enforced when a British subject is murdered, it will not be respected. Thus I express my concerns to them not only as a grieving father, or an enforcer of British justice, but as a HBC stockholder and Factor in charge of a productive Department. Since the massacre of the Tonquin in 1811 until my son's murder in 1842, I have been the most successful officer in maintaining order in this region and we have prospered.

We have more American citizens arriving each year. This past May the newly arrived settlers met to form a provisional government. They have made a petition to join the twenty-eight States of the American Union and that document is signed by some of the HBC retirees, including my sons Joseph and Tom. I have greeted scouts of the US Army who also travel down to California. When they make their report, undoubtedly the trickle of settlers will become a flood of pioneers, all ready to stake a claim to this fair place. This is no time to set a poor example of British law and order. Oregon will likely become an American state because the new republic purports that all citizens have equality, even when it does not deliver that promise.

With time, the truth about John's death will become known, because truth has its own force. The End of My Own Religious Controversy is but one example of how it cannot be suppressed for long. Meanwhile, I must be custodian of this place and of these uneasy lands as well as guardian of my newly professed Faith. I anticipate that Sir George will influence the London Committee but John's name will be cleared because they cannot hide the public evidence, nor should they ignore Sir George's culpability in this tragedy.

This epistle is now ended, a much longer document than was promised. However, I hope the content fills your soul with joy and alleviates your bodily suffering as much as is possible. Your steadfast example and lifetime of prayers undoubtedly influenced my public declaration of allegiance to the Roman Catholic religion.

In Faith,

Jean Baptiste McLoughlin

1844, Letter from Sister St. Henri: with great joy

My brother in Faith as well as family,

Your American letter was an unexpected gift from God. My Community has offered a celebratory Mass with the hope that our voices pleased Heavenly ears as much as your choirs did on Christmas Eve. Do you remember so long ago in 1798, that I was confirmed on the same day as I took the veil that made me a Bride of Christ? Now, I learn that you were confessed, thereby filled with the Holy Spirit, and then married in the Faith during the same day. It is a small, strong link in love that joins us as brother and sister in the Catholic Faith as well as blood. Your declaration doctored my soul as well as you have doctored so many suffering bodies.

My heart is so very full of thanksgiving and praise that you have space in your heart for more than revenge. When a man has exercised as much power over other people and has as much responsibility for financial transactions and management of a great Company as you have enjoyed, it can be difficult to cultivate spiritual wealth. Your good wife must have reminded you with her sewing how difficult it is for a rich man to pass through the eye of a needle. But if you had not an innate nobility to quest for God's truth, it would not have been revealed to your soul.

What a gracious and public profession of faith you described. The sacraments of the Holy Roman Catholic Church have evolved over many centuries and provide a clearly marked path, revealing more of God's grace if we will but follow in Jesus' steps. God must have been very pleased with this Witness, especially now that the Earth resounds with the raucous cacophony of religious dissent more than religious discourse. God's seasons are eternal and their passage is a much greater cycle than any creatures understand. Whatever their Faith, men and women need to cultivate their spirituality, to believe that more Mysteries someday will be revealed to us. To earn a deeper understanding of these truths each must exercise some spiritual discipline, whether Protestant or Catholic, Pagan or Heathen, scientist or illiterate.

The seasons that rotate through a human society are more brief, however long they seem. At times their patterns may be understood. Others will be forever beyond comprehension to me, at least. Let me provide an example. Mr. Joseph Papineau recently returned from exile in France, having been granted amnesty for his part in the '37 Rebellion. He lives quietly among family and visiting friends, but his time on center stage of the public drama is over. Nevertheless, his contributions to French Canada, for that is the name which has most currency now, will not be forgotten. This distinct society in North America is a necessary part of Canada. Those who are British or from elsewhere in the world could learn about cultural survival from us, even how to adapt and thrive.

When Mr. Papineau left Quebec, I never thought to see his wife and daughters again. But they have reappeared and remember me, even though we cannot sit at tea as once we did because of my illness. The ideas of more representation and self-governance that Papineau espoused will outlive him as they are but the latest manifestation of something eternal in the human spirit. To learn more about how to govern ourselves in civilized societies, individuals must manifest more self-governance. After a lifetime of living in Community, I know how difficult it can be to attain such an ideal balance. The two types of development are intermingled. If individuals are too indolent with respect to their own behaviors and toward other citizens, society will constrain the excess. If a society becomes too restrictive, its members become restless. When either an individual or a culture is too controlling or too lax, some natural dynamic is activated. Depending upon the extent of the resistance, the release can be great. You have discovered spiritual freedom by submitting to the discipline of our Catholic religion. A revolutionary mob may destroy more than the desired cleansing of a stagnant culture. One never knows what will be the force of Spring thaw, but one may count both on the cycle of Spring and the resultant thaw.

I do not expect to see you face to face again, dearest brother, because individual life cycles are even more brief than God or society. But though our bodies will rest on opposite shores of a vast continent and our brother remains in Europe, we will meet in Spirit, through thoughts and gifts, in prayers and petitions, and in those whom we have mentored. During our lifetimes, our sparks of spiritual life maintain the soul fire by which humanity is warmed and fed. When our bodies return to the Earth from whence they came, our souls return to God from whence they came. Whether Heaven dwells in the skies or in another sphere on Earth is a Mystery, but eternal life is not. It is a promise made to all peoples in all places, however they interpret it.

To relieve my aching body, my dear Sisters have made a sling of leather straps so that I might lie more comfortably. However, I think that further comfort for my aching body is not a condition of this life. God has been gracious in that He provides me with daily opportunity of how to exhibit grace when under duress. It is not an easy lesson for any member of our family to learn. He does not send heavier trials than we can bear, dear brother. Do not forget this truth, even when you struggle with injustices meted out by men. Like Jesus, we may wish our trials reduced, but we decide whether to bend or break by our responses to them. God has given us free will and the right to seek His support during our distresses.

What to say about Governor George Simpson! I am certain that when he arrives at Fort Vancouver and visits your comfortable establishment, he recognizes the coldness of his flying canoes is not just a problem of nature but one of nurture. When he observes your steady wife and lively grandchildren, he realizes what he has been denied, even though he has a family in far off England. As he listens to the bell ring at Fort Vancouver and watches your men step to their daily chores, he must acknowledge these noisy quotidian routines are more lively than the quiet pulse of a head office. When he saw the increased maturity of your eldest son, he would need to acknowledge that you are a master of men while he is but a master of time or space. If you can conquer your fiery temper, truly your greatest challenge, then although you never become a Knight of the British Empire, you will be a Knight who serves at God's table. You are a good father to the residents of Oregon and to your sons and daughters. Choose the greater example, that of our Father who resides in Heaven, as your mentor and forgive Sir George his sins.

Let Shakespeare's King Lear speak the final words:

> The weight of this sad time we must obey,
> Speak what we feel, not what we ought to say.
> The oldest hath borne most; we that are young
> Shall never see so much nor live so long.

Until we meet again, may love of Faith and family encircle you.

Farewell,

Sister St. Henri, Marie McLoughlin

1845, Letter from McL.: in resignation

Dear sister,

I have had much need of your thoughtful words this past year and therefore your letter is nearly worn through at the folds. It is my intention to have it copied so that I might consult your wisdom without worrying the words might disappear. Do I begin by sharing with you the most tragic or the most tortured decisions I have made since my previous communication? Let me share family news and then proceed to a statement of my new status. You will read first whatever parts of my life history most interest you, and if you cannot, I trust your good Sisters will do so.

At the end of January the sad news arrived from Yerba Buena that William Glen Rae suicided January 19, four days after the birth of his fourth child who is also now deceased. I will not go into details about my son-in-law's death except to say he advanced Company credit to Mexican political rebels who failed in their cause. There is no hope of repayment and in any event Sir George Simpson had ordered closure of this California post as part of the HBC retreat from the Pacific. Mr. Rae was very depressed about the reversal of fortunes and blamed himself excessively. My daughter attempted to stop him from using his pistol but he would not be deterred from his tragic action. The stress prompted her delivery of a baby boy who lived but another four days. They are buried in California. David leaves soon to escort Eloisa and the three older children back to live with us.

John's body has been returned to Fort Vancouver and is buried outside the fort near St. John's Catholic Church. My deputations regarding his murder have been reviewed by the Governor and Committee in London, and I do believe have had some effect. At least, they do not any longer think my son was negligent in his duties at Stikine nor was he dissipated in his behavior. His name is now somewhat restored to respectability by the Governor's report. However, the legal situation is complicated. Although the event occurred on land HBC leased from the Russians, they did not want to try the murderers and returned them to our jurisdiction. I had them sent to Norway House. The Factor there thought about sending some of the accused men to Montreal where my agent resides but this gang of liars are not all British subjects and their premeditated actions did not occur in Canada. Therefore the murder was outside of colonial jurisprudence, just as the Seven Oaks murders were so many years ago. I would need to pay from my own pocket and my fortune is considerably less than that of Lord Selkirk or the McGillivray bros. who all bankrupted. If these eleven men were to be sent to England, the costs would be more than $10,000. As Sir George was quick to recognize, the HBC Governors would not welcome such publicity in London itself. It seems I have done as much as is possible to obtain some justice in this matter. Nothing can restore John to life, but his name has been cleared and I will ensure everyone in the HBC knows that he was innocent of the insults to his character.

It would seem that the Honorable Company retreats not just from its ideals of gentlemanly justice with respect to young John McLoughlin but also to me, the father. On the ship that carried the sad news about the Rae family was a letter from the Governor and Committee in London informing me that my bonus is to be stopped because the major depot for the Columbia Department is now shifted to Fort Victoria on Vancouver Island. My visit to that harbor last Summer revealed it is a fair place but it signals the retreat of the British from the mouth of the Columbia River and adjoining coastline.

The excuse is that the boundary is probably to be extended to the 49th parallel, excepting the tip of Vancouver Island and some of the nearby smaller San Juan Islands. The HBC does not want to invest in a land-based proposition it might lose and the British government does not want a war with American cotton planters. Therefore the Company takes final advantage of the declining trade in furs while assisting the empire to ensure the international boundary is not established any further north than the 49th parallel.

All the Columbia Department's increasing trade in animal tallow and hides, agricultural produce, and lumber is to be held in check until the political situation is clarified. Further, the promises of support made to the Metis settlers who came from Red River are to be denied them if they move south of the river instead of clearing land on Puget Sound. Finally at long last, the policy now is to conserve the beaver population in this region rather than trap it out. The number of HBC retirees escalates. Would that the Company conserve its men as well! It is very late in the day for me and I sense Simpson's hand at the inkpot and ledgers.

Sir George Simpson has been active also in controlling decisions at the annual HBC Rupert's land council meeting at Norway House. Fort Vancouver, in spite of its prosperity, is permanently delegated to a lesser outpost. Once again there is a triumvirate of rulers at this establishment. This time I am reduced to one of them. In the short term, Mr. Ogden, Mr. Douglas, and I will manage the decline in its affairs but I am recalled east of the mountains. James Douglas must go to Victoria because he is in mid-career just as I was when I first came to this coast, but I think that Ogden will retire here. As for me, my soul belongs to God, my heart to this Columbia region, and my body will rest here in Oregon. The Governors and Council will receive my resignation shortly after you read this letter.

American settlers continue to flood into the Columbia delta and claim land. More than 3,000 arrived this Summer, most very needy and requiring assistance in basic supplies if they were to survive the Winter. These goods they have received on credit, a courtesy that places my accounts in an unfavorable balance this year. These newcomers are of a mixed character and not all are well disposed to view previous claims with respect. Some helped push Mormons from their Missouri land claims and think to do the same acquisition at this edge of the continent. Thus, they antagonize our retirees, deny my rights to claims staked when I first arrived in the Willamette Valley, and the newcomers crowd out the Indians from their traditional grounds. There are now so many, more than 6,000 in total, any attempt to guide peaceable settlement is almost futile. Although they derive from differing states of the American Union and carry diverse perspectives about religion, slavery, and governance, they are united with one cry: "All Oregon." I think that London must hear this raucous chorus as clearly as when the shouts arose in Boston harbor.

My sister, I am past sixty years. My son lies buried outside the doors of the establishment that thrived because of my efforts, near the church I have sponsored. My wife is seventy and will not be parted easily from the daughter and grandchildren she loves. Another widowed daughter and her children have claims to the farms in Quebec. A third widow receiving assistance is my stepdaughter in England who has two girls to raise on her own. Young David must be set up in business since he is here by my persuasion. But more than all these family obligations, I do not wish to live any longer under an English jurisdiction so influenced by Sir George Simpson. With these powers aligned against me, my cup of bitterness fills to the brim. Mr. George Shelley understood the folly of great ambitions when he wrote:

> "My name is Ozymandias, king of kings:
> Look on my works, ye Mighty, and despair!"
> Nothing beside remains. Round the decay
> Of that colossal wreck, boundless and bare
> The lone and level sands stretch far away.

The lone and level sands of the British Empire in retreat will stretch far away, as happens with all the great empires of ambitious men. Does anyone know of King Ozymandias? Who will recall the names of Sir George Simpson, the Hudson's Bay Company Governing Council, and Chief Factor John McLoughlin a hundred years from now?

In the maelstrom that envelops us here, I turn my nose to the wind. The freshest breeze seems to come from Jefferson's mind. "We hold these truths to be self evident, that all men are created equal, that they are endowed by their creator with certain inalienable rights; that among these are life, liberty, and the pursuit of happiness." I have seen too much of the world and observed enough of American behavior at the edges of society to presume that his ideals will be realized during my remaining years. But with the help of God, I might assist in preparing foundations of a new State in which my grandchildren and their descendants will thrive. And, therefore, I have resigned from the Hudson's Bay Company and will apply to become a citizen of the United States of America. God Bless Us All.

With great affection,

Yr brother, John McLoughlin

1846, Letter from Ursuline Convent: with regret

Dr. McLoughlin,

It is my sad duty to inform you that Mother Mary McLoughlin of St. Henri was released from her earthly pain and suffering July 3 about 11 P.M. She was surrounded by members of our Community, in particular your nieces, our OSV Sisters Josephine Michaud, Marie Talbot, and Emilie Deschene. On July 2, she received the Last Sacrament and from that time until her final breath, she was filled with so much calm and joy that, in our grief, we celebrated. We hope that you and your family will feel some of the joy that accompanied this sad passage and mourn our mutual loss of Mère Marie's guidance.

During her last week, she continued to knit and even to write letters. Her concern was not for herself but for your sister, Madame Julie Michaud, who was very ill at her home in Rivière du Loup. As you may have been informed, Mdme Michaud followed her elder sister twelve hours later. We pray that the souls of these two admirable sisters are as close in Heaven as they were on Earth.

Be assured that in our loss we have not forgotten to honor our venerable Sister. It is our custom to write a *nécrologie* for any deceased member of our Community and we have now completed one for Mère St. Henri. Most such commemorations are five or six pages. Hers is thirty-one pages long! Even so, we have not done justice. Her contributions to our daily lives and the growth of our Convent and Religious Order in Canada were so impressive. The oil painting, which you and your brother David requested, is now one of our most cherished possessions. It will serve always to remind us of her piety, charity, and talents.

You will be pleased to learn that next January all our pupils will be required to wear a tartan jumper as their school uniform, thus a little bit of her Scottish heritage will be visible. The girls will be guided by a curriculum that Mother St. Henri dedicated many hours to composing. We have added her story to the narratives they read. As the girls learn about her life and thoughts, some may be inspired, just as we have been. Your grandchildren, the daughters of Mrs. Eliza Eppes, are now enrolled in our school so your unbroken McLoughlin tradition continues with the next generation of girls in your family to be educated by our Community.

Masses have been sung in remembrance of Mère St. Henri. So many from the larger community attended her funeral Mass that the Chapel was very crowded. The *Quebec Gazette* published an obituary in English that said in part:

> During the long period of forty-six years of religious profession, she filled at various times the office of Superior of the community with that rare talent, prudence, and justice which merited for her the highest confidence and esteem. She will be long and deeply regretted, not only by the citizens of Quebec, of every class and nationality, who have so often rendered homage to her virtues and fine qualities, but also by all those strangers who have had occasion to visit that estimable institution, none of whom ever went away without expressing the highest admiration for the noble manners and the interesting conversation of this amiable lady.

Our Ursuline Community has been informed that the Treaty of Oregon was signed June 15, 1846. It seems that your establishment is now located within the boundaries of the United States of America. We hope that the region benefits from as much peace and prosperity that it enjoyed during the years you guided the development of the HBC Columbia District. We pray that you and our family that remain on the Pacific coast have continued good health and fortune.

God be with you,

Mother Isabella McDonell of St. Andrew

Order of the *Soeurs Ursuline*

Epilogue

John McLoughlin's correspondence with family members in London, Quebec, and Red River continued until his death, September 3, 1857. The last twelve years of his life included several sad events because two sons died (Joseph by accident and Tom McKay of tuberculosis). Conflicts regarding his land claims in Oregon were not settled until years after his death and his HBC accounts were not concluded until 1868.

His daughter Eloisa remarried in 1850 and her husband, Daniel Harvey, eventually became administrator of the McLoughlin estate; they had three children. Eloisa Harvey and family moved to Portland in 1867 and husband Daniel died the following year. Her daughter, Mary Louisa Rae, his favorite granddaughter, often acted as scribe when Dr. McLoughlin's arthritic hands became too stiff to write letters himself. His daughter in Quebec, widowed Eliza Eppes, who had title to the three family farms near Rivière du Loup, sold them to a cousin and moved to England, according to some sources.

Marguerite McLoughlin survived her husband by three years. Initially she was not buried beside him because of her Indian background but civic permission eventually was granted. As she was dying in the family home, several nuns came to sit with her; however, she sent them away. In her final hours, she asked that they return, saying she did not want to die alone. Grandson Dr. W. (Billy) McKay boarded with the McLoughlins after his return from medical school in the New England States and eventually became a well-known doctor on the Umatilla Indian reservation. Granddaughter Catherine Ermingter returned to Canada, although she did not always live with her husband Francis. The three McKay daughters who did not go to the Columbia all had children. Nancy McCargo remained in the Sault Ste. Marie area; Mary Sinclair lived in the Red River Metis community, and Catherine O'Gorman's civil records were recently located in Gravesend, England. John

McLoughlin supported his stepdaughter, Catherine, and her two daughters in Kent, England until his death.

Fort Vancouver, Washington, was restored in 1954. It was declared a National Historic Site and is the location of the largest archeological site in the Pacific Northwest region. McLoughlin House, Oregon City, is a museum at which personal artifacts such as his gold-headed cane and silver tea service are displayed. In 1970, the graves of John and Margaret McLoughlin were moved to the grounds and tombstones erected. Many authors have written about various aspects of McLoughlin's life, including several bibliographies, but no authoritative biography of Sir George Simpson has been published.

The Cayuse Indian Wars began in 1847 and continued inter-mittently for thirty years. McLoughlin's testimony after the Whitman massacre was considered too pro-Indian by some, but he clearly intervened several times toward the end of his career and in retirement to reduce tensions. By the time Oregon was declared an American Territory and USA governance established, the HBC Western headquarters depot at Fort Vancouver was closed and moved to Victoria. Some early settlers never repaid their financial obligations to him, while others never forgot his assistance. New settlers knew McLoughlin only as a businessman who operated the French store, the grist, and saw mills, and who had been the first mayor of Oregon City. Many charitable acts are recorded. He finally became a full citizen of the USA on September 5, 1851.

In the 150 years since his death, his contributions have been recognized in many ways. In 1925 the United States government issued a silver half-dollar with McLoughlin's bust on one side, the only doctor of medicine shown on a US coin. In 1953, McLoughlin was one of two Oregon citizens to be honored with a statue in Washington DC. Many local place names carry the McLoughlin family names. In 1946, a group of Canadian and American citizens officiated at the unveiling of a plaque and stone monument in Rivière du Loup that honored him at his birthplace. In that town and at Malbaie, some historical references to the Fraser family may be found, but the McLoughlin name is relatively unknown.

Mother Mary Louise McLoughlin of St. Henri is buried among her Ursuline sisters in Quebec City. The convent is still in the same location, but the Ursuline School for girls is now a private day school with a male principal. Although the religious community is quite small and the nuns quite elderly, they cherish the Bowman painting of their predecessor. *Mère Marie* is still considered one of the best emulators of founder Marie de l'Incarnation's vision. In the convent museum, some of the gifts sent by Drs. John and David McLoughlin are on display. Outside in the narrow winding cobblestone street, the Quebec government recently erected a statue of a woman's hand holding a quill pen in honor of early women educators in Quebec. The Ursuline Sisterhood is honored at the top of the list.

Dr. David McLoughlin and his wife returned to London after the Parisian court of Louis-Phillipe was ousted in 1848. Lady Jane Capel died shortly after. Their names are listed in Burke's Peerage & Baronetage. Dr. David McLoughlin published a number of articles about the symptoms of cholera. He was named to the Royal Societies of Medicine in both England and Ireland. He died in Victorian England, quite elderly, leaving a very small estate of £200. The section of London where he had an office was heavily bombed during WWII; his Parisian address is still one of the desirable neighborhoods in the city. Very few people remember his name.

In the weeks before his final flight, the "White-Haired Eagle," retired HBC Factor Dr. John McLoughlin, told a young visitor, USA Congressman Grover, "I might have been better shot forty years ago (when he was on trial for treason as a consequence of the Seven Oaks Massacre) than to have lived here and tried to build up a family and an estate in this government." Fifty years after his death, the Oregon Legislature named him "Father of Oregon." McLoughlin was never knighted by the Queen of England but he was made a Knight of St. Gregory by the Catholic Church in 1847 and received a piece of the true cross from Pope Gregory XVI, carried back to Oregon by Mgr. Blanchet. At his deathbed, Dr. Deschene, a nephew from Quebec whom McLoughlin had mentored, asked "*Comment allez-vous?*" and the old man's last words were "*À Dieu*."

John McLoughlin is remembered for his many kindnesses and visionary ideals about peaceable settlement. He was a good man, a flawed human being, whose life story captivates many because of the internal struggles about appropriate moral action and his resistances to societal injustices. Given the challenges, what would we have done in his place?

Exterior view of Fort Vancouver. Source: National Park Service, Fort Vancouver Historic Site.

Exterior view of the Ursuline Convent, Québec City, present day. Courtesy of le Monastère des Ursulines de Québec.

Annotated glossary of French words and phrases

This list is organized alphabetically. The primary resources for definitions were drawn from references listed in the bibliography. They include: *Dictionnaire Québecois D'aujourd'hui,* Larousse, and some willing Francophone friends. Errors, are of course, the author's unfortunate contributions.

Anniversaire Messe: Anniversary mass. This religious service would be held to celebrate the day the person took vows.

Au façon du pays: "According to the style of this country." It means a "country marriage," a relationship not sanctified by a priest or minister but a recognized public union from which children would result and be acknowledged by the father as his to protect and raise. Implied is an artisan or craft approach to shaping or making something. In the "auld" Scottish tradition, such alliances were common among Highland clans. It includes mutual consent expressed in front of witnesses and considered legal because no greater authority was available i.e. a judge or priest.

Blessés: A light cut of the skin that would mark the individual. Usually located on a shoulder, it was a signal of brotherhood.

Bois brulées: Literally "burned wood," the term was used to describe mixed blood people. It was used mostly during the *coureur de bois* period because the metaphor is so obviously connected; trails often were marked with burned slashes on a tree trunk. The term chosen by mixed-blood people for themselves is Metis.

Bon mot: Pun or witty phrase or saying.

Bourgeois: The HBC title "Chief Factor" meant superintendent of the factory (although the fur trade in Canada was very different from any factory in England, excepting the production of beaver hats). This emergent class was not as distinguished as nobles or priests but had a higher social status than those who labored with their hands as artisans or apprentices. They were respected merchant families made wealthy by the industrialization of society and expanded trading opportunities. Eventually they successfully challenged the governing power of nobles and kings, sometimes overthrowing them, always directly or indirectly shaping national policies. Subsequent to the emergence of labor unions, the working environments they established were criticized but that dynamic occurred after the time period in which these people lived.

Calèche: An open stagecoach with wheels or sleigh runners, it was pulled by oxen or horses and colorfully decorated with bells and ribbons.

Canot du Nord: This type of canoe was smaller than the freight canoes, *canot de maître*, but larger than recreation canoes used today. It was the preferred mode of transportation between the end of the Great Lakes and Lake Winnipeg. It was twenty-five feet, could be paddled by six to eight men and carried more than a ton of furs.

Chansons:
These songs were like a chant, with strong rhythms and simple refrains. They were often love songs or mimicked birds or repetitive action. *Voyageur* songs are among the great folksong repertoires of the world. They helped paddlers to maintain a steady pace and reduced tedium during long hours in a canoe.

Chapelle:
The consecrated part of a church where the altar is maintained. The Ursuline chapel is very famous because of the decor, rare paintings and embroidery are displayed, wonderful music has been created, and the ambiance is very holy. Visitors are admitted for restricted periods.

"Consultation medico-legale sur quelques signes de la paralysie vraie et la valeu relative":
"The relative value of medical-legal consultations on symptoms of true paralysis." Copies of this paper, and other publications of Dr. David McLoughlin, are filed in the Wellcome Medical Library, London.

Coureur de bois:
"Runners of the woods." These men roamed the forests outside the environs of New France, the colony. They trapped, hunted, canoed, sometimes lived with Indian families, and were often away for a year or more. Their interaction with various First Peoples

contributed to the peaceful settlement of Canada because they didn't settle or farm and they interpreted traditions and customs to French and English colonial powers.

Dépositaire: This title is similar to that of treasurer but would include financial planning as well as recording all transactions. The person who guards the *dépôt* (the financial resources and holdings) of an organization.

Deputés: The word has more significance in French than in English. In France, it is the title of elected representatives to the National Assembly. An approximate English equivalent would be Member of Parliament. The French word also connotes the republican ideals of men who have liberty, equality and freedom, who have ultimate authority for their behavior and attitudes, who are individuals designated by other citizens of equal status.

En écorcé: Lace ruffles used to decorate gowns and waistcoats during the 1800s, placed as if they were an outer cover of the garment, especially at the neck.

Engagées: Laborers who served a limited-term contract. Often the men would sign again for another period of service but the obligation to continue was understood by both the employer and the men that the commitment was less than that of a clerk or partner.

En songe: A powerful dreaming state. The youthful vision of Marie de l'Incarnation that inspired her to become a missionary in Nouvelle France is well known. It is still honored at the Ursuline Convent House and in the small museum house visitors may view many interpretations, including murals. Other artifacts from the early colonial period that demonstrate her success are on display.

Entrepôt: A place where merchandise is stored after it has been produced and before it is sold. It could be a warehouse but also a link in the transporting of merchandise. It is related to entrepreneur, who is the middle person involved in a business.

Fête de Ste Anne: July 26: A day reserved to celebrate the life of this saint, the mother of Mary. Any day designated as a Saint's Day provides occasion for a solemn religious celebration as well as a party.

Fête: A designated day during which celebrations, both religious and social, occur. Saint's days, birthdays, and statutory holidays belong to this category.

Finale: The final component in a series. For example, the last syllable of a word, the last act of a play, the final game of a tournament.

Foule de peines: A cluster or grouping of pain and expenses.

Frére: A brother, not just in a familial sense but someone who is as close as a blood relation. Used by a nun, it connotes a religious bond.

Gaîtée:	Someone who loves life, having good humor and disposition.
Gâteau aux bleuets du Lac St. Jean:	Blueberry cake made from berries near a large lake in the Saguenay region, in which Murray Bay *(Malbaie)* is located. Sometimes these berries are called "saskatoons" in Western Canada, "june berries" in the USA.
Garçonnière:	European French, the term defines a small apartment owned or rented by a single man. A bachelor pad, in North American contemporary slang.
Gentil:	A person who is enjoyable, pleasant and charming, with good manners and a graceful style.
Glitterae:	People who were known to the public, famous because of talent, family, money, or social connections.
Habitants:	During the colonial French period, colonists who worked land parcels administered by the government or its delegates *(seigneurs)*. Later, the term was used to denote small farmers and sometimes the phrase was used derogatively to indicate a rustic demeanor.
Hivernants:	Men who spent the Winter in the high country woods of the Indian Territories. Not used for the gentlemen of the Trade.
Incendie:	Fire was a great threat during the colonial period because most buildings were constructed of wood and heated by wood fires. Little could be done if a building caught fire because it would go up in flames very rapidly.

241

Isle aux érables:	Island near Sault Ste. Marie, Ontario. Probably had maple trees that served as a landmark from the water.
Je me souviens:	"I will remember." This phrase expresses the signature value of Quebec. It invokes the rich cultural heritage, especially French language and culture.
Jeunes gens:	Young people, youth. Someone no longer a child but one who lacks mature experience.
Je suis preste:	"I am ready to serve." The phrase implies an alertness, a virtuous quality of commitment. The Fraser motto, like many Scots clans, was in French. The Scots had a close relationship with France because Bonnie Prince Charles, Mary Queen of Scots, and other royal leaders were supported in exile. Sons and daughters of clan chieftains often studied or served with French nobles. Eventually, Scotland was drawn into the British Empire. When Scots Highlanders fought as British soldiers on the Plains of Abraham, they insisted on wearing kilts, illegal attire at home, but evidence of their distinctiveness.
Je ne sais en quoi:	"I don't know why!" An ironic expression implying that the person does have a good idea.
Jolie:	Very enjoyable, giving pleasure. For example, it could be a costume, a song, a garnished plate of food.
Lac la Pluie:	Known as Rainy Lake in English, the post was strategically located between

East and West depots of the fur trade during the contested years of NWC and HBC rivalry. After the 1821 amalgamation, it became less important because most furs were shipped from Hudson's Bay. When George Simpson brought his young bride to Red River, the name was changed to Fort Frances in her honor and that is how it is known today.

La majesté: Something or someone imposing, grand, with allure.

Légion d' Honneur: Napoleon created this award in 1802 to recognize outstanding individual military and civil service to France.

Les paroles des anciens chants du Quebec: The words of the old songs of Quebec, particularly the French colonial period. Many of these folk songs are now performed by *l'Ensemble Nouvelle France* and available on CDs.

Levées: Dikes built to raise the banks of a river to prevent flooding, especially in tidal areas, and provide fortifications.

Le vrai galant: A man who likes women and makes pleasantries or actions, regardless of his age or hers, i.e. compliments, pulling out a chair. "A gay spark."

Malbaie: Murray Bay. A village located on the north shore of the St. Lawrence River at the mouth of the Saguenay River.

Mère Supérieure: Mother Superior. The highest office to which a nun could be elected having responsibilities for the entire Community.

Metis:	Mixed-blood people, usually of French or Scots origin; "half breed" was used for those with English blood but it is a more derogatory term. The Cree called these people "*oteepaymsoowuyk,*" meaning "in charge of themselves" because these families belonged to no established colonial or Indian grouping. Their language, music, and dance is a fusion of all cultures they represent: Scots, Gaelic, Irish, French, and Indian. Their dress was colorful but practical. They built distinctive carts. At first it was a fluid nomadic culture, moving together during the Summer season and fanning out in Winter. But the annual cycle was back to the Red River region for the buffalo hunt and for making dried pemmican that was sold to fur traders traveling rapidly in brigades or to settlers short of food. When the buffalo became extinct, many moved into northern Saskatchewan and Alberta. These people are enjoying a renaissance of their traditions and increasingly are a powerful political lobby. They are the first true Canadians!
Nécrologie:	An obituary, a biographical summary about the life of a recently deceased person.
Objet:	An object. When in artistic form, it represents a concrete manifestation of an ideal or value. These abstract values may also be written as aims or goals.
Outré:	Rakish, somewhat beyond the boundaries of acceptable behavior or dress but not necessarily offensive or violent.

O.s.u.:	Acronym for the Sisters professed to the Ursuline Order of Service to Christ. It is appended after an individual name, and serves a similar function to academic titles such as M.A., Ph.D.
Parisiens:	Not only residents of the great city but people who embody its culture: urbane, sophisticated, valuing creativity more than social conventions.
Pax de paix dans la province:	This phrase combines Latin and French and means "A peace treaty in the province."
Pays d'en haut:	"High Country." This phrase was used during both the French and English colonial periods in reference to any land beyond that claimed by colonial powers and originally included all territory beyond the Great Lakes and Mississippi River. Boundaries were vague and shifting. The term had less to do with geography than with governance or cultural ambiance. It meant going into unknown, inland trapping areas accessed only by rivers and lakes and the resultant lifestyle.
Pays de Maria Chapdelaine:	Refers not only to the remote region on the far south shore of the St. Lawrence, but also to the habitant culture and ambiance during the English colonial period.
Philosophes:	Intellectuals or articulate thinkers. The Age of Enlightenment (eighteenth century) was a high point in French philosophy. These writers were appreciated for their balanced arguments, moral reasoning, and wise essays.

Que Dieu me vienne en aide: "To God who will give me help," a prayer.

Régales: These were festive occasions characterized by good food, vigorous music, and lively dancing. Like country fairs, they could continue for days and include sports and contests. They were important social events that relieved tedium and boredom. Sometimes they were rewards for good behavior, an abundant season, or celebrations of a special event.

Religieuses professes: A person (nun) who vows to make a career within a religion. After an initiate period of several years, a woman who felt she was called to serve God in a full-time religious capacity could join one of the many organizations within the Roman Catholic Church. These women still cannot become priests, but they increasingly serve a more public role during Mass. As a Bride of Christ, a nun dedicates her life to serving Him with vows of charity, poverty, and chastity. Upon "taking the veil," most of the professed would also historically assume a new name and dress according to the habit of the Order in which she was accepted as a Sister. These identifying practices now have been discontinued in many parts of the world, and some other religions also have avowed women's Orders. A religious vocation is usually expressed through nursing, teaching, or missionary work, depending upon the purpose of the Community.

Repartée:	Quick-witted responses and conversations, with a good dose of pointed humor.
Rue de Parloir:	Parlour Street. The old village of Quebec City is walled and within is a charming small winding cobblestone street. The Ursuline property has been situated here for centuries. The school, Community residence, and enclosed grounds are private but the public may visit the museum and has access to the chapel during designated time periods.
Salle de communauté:	The private room in which members of the Community gather to relax; a living room or a family room. These paintings still hang in the Convent, in a room used as a library and archive for the Ursuline Sisters. In a time period before photographic technology, miniatures and paintings were the most common way of remembering people. It was an honor to have a portrait done, also an occasion. It was expensive, therefore only the elite were painted and usually only once during a lifetime. It was like a formal photo session except that it took longer but people prepared for it by dressing in their best clothes and wearing jewelry. Often they allowed favorite possessions to be used or included a dog or horse.
Sauvage:	The term refers to people who were indigenous but not necessarily savage. It is defined as "that which lives in liberty in nature." The term was used in contrast to "civilized" by which was meant "European." It was a classification, but

247

not necessarily a diminutive put down. It could be racist but didn't necessarily infer a person was uncouth or unintelligent. The *bon sauvage* was a humane state, uncorrupted. However the term could also mean naïve, rude, and brutal.

Seigneurie:

(Sometimes spelled as "seigneury" or "seignory"): A feudal system of land management introduced during the French colonial period in Quebec. Land was granted as a reward for service with the expectation that the man in charge (the seigneur) would develop it by organizing colonists to farm various smaller parcels. Property allotment was long and narrow with river access, because roads were difficult to maintain. The owner usually had a large house, agrarian income, and farm workers (*habitants*) paid a tithe in produce, labor, and money to the seigneur in exchange for protection and services. Common interests resulted in the development of religious, social and political communities with strong bonds. Over time, because of inheritances, the land became subdivided to the point where the system was not sustainable. Friction occurred in outlying areas such as Red River and Oregon because it contrasted with the British quarter system of land allocation. The title "seigneur" is an honorific, still used by the Roman Catholic Church. The English equivalent would be "esquire" or "sir."

Soirée(s):

An after-dinner social evening of entertainment at which music, dancing, recitals, and stories are enjoyed. Both men and women participated. In the 1800s it was a more common form of entertainment in France than in most European societies.

Tête à tête: "Head to head." A private chat between two friends, usually face to face. Agreement about the topic content is implied, but not necessarily agreement regarding the topic itself.

Une école normale: Normal School. Teachers were usually trained at normal schools until the profession evolved into a university-level qualification. "Normal" in this context meant "standards" that teachers needed to learn before assuming responsibility for a classroom.

Une ère d'agitation: A time of unrest. Both colonies, Lower Canada and Upper Canada, had political parties that advocated more responsible government during the 1830s. Both movements resulted in some violence, including death, and the result was the Act of Union, 1840. The leader of the *"Insurrection des Patriotes,"* Louis-Joseph Papineau, was exiled to the United States in 1838 and the family subsequently went to France. They returned to Quebec in 1850 to live at Montebello.

Un homme du Nord: An honorific title the voyagers gave to a man who had lived away from civilization for at least one Winter season. It meant he was tough, had survived cold weather, scarce food supplies, and dark lonely days and nights. Most men entered country marriages so the vow they took upon receiving their title was a variation of that of a medieval knight. They were to serve their God, their king, and respect other men's wives. The tradition died out after the HBC gained control of the Trade but most of the older traders and trappers remained loyal to obligations they had vowed to respect.

Bibliography

These letters are fictional documents. However, the people were real and the facts included within this book have been extracted from either unpublished or published sources and verified as much as possible. Summary notes for each section indicate sources but specific page references are not provided.

PRINT DOCUMENTS

Deciding how to organize the reference sections was difficult. Details regarding specific facts, however unknown, would have made the book bulky and too academic. Providing no resources seemed too superficial. Therefore, an alphabetical list of secondary print documents evolved, followed by a summary of reference sites for unpublished primary resources and a list of relevant CDs/videos. Websites and URL addresses have been inserted very sparsely because the quality of information is so variable and the life of some sites so temporary. If anyone wants more information about the contents of this book, please contact the author for a further discussion (edonalds@ucalgary.ca).

Adam J. (2001) *Old Square-Toes and His Lady; the Life of James and Amelia Douglas*. Victoria: Horsdal & Schubart Publishers Ltd.

Akrigg G.P.V. & H. B. (1975) *British Columbia Chronicle (1778-1846)*. Vancouver: Discovery Press

Alvarez J. (1996*) Living in Paris*. Paris: Flammerion

Andrews A. (1981) *The Scottish Canadians*. New York: Van Nostrand Reinhold Ltd.

Barker Brown B. (1959) *The McLoughlin Empire and its Rulers*. Cleveland: The Arthur H. Clark Company

Barker Brown B. (1949) (Ed.) *The Financial Papers of Dr. John McLoughlin*. Portland, OR: Oregon Historical Society. reprint

Barker Brown B. (1948) (Ed.) *Letters of Dr. John McLoughlin, Written at Fort Vancouver 1829–1832*. Portland, OR: Binfords & Mort, Oregon Historical Society

Beattie J. H. & H. Buss (2003) *Undelivered Letters to Hudson's Bay Company Men on the Northwest Coast of America, 1830–57*. Vancouver: UBC Press

Biographie de la Rev. Mère St. Henri. 22ième Supérieure du Monastère, (morte en juillet, 1846). Ursuline Convent Archives 32 pp.: unpublished

Bland J. (2000) *Sainte Anne de Bellevue Heritage Town: An Architect's Perspective*. Ste. Anne de Bellevue, PQ: Shoreline

Brooks W. H. (1970) "British Wesleyan Methodist Missionary activities in the Hudson's Bay Company, 1840–1854". *The Canadian Catholic Historical Association Study Session Proceedings*. Winnipeg, Manitoba, pp.21–33

Brown R. S. (2000) "A Canadien Bishop in the Ecclesiastical Province of Oregon". *Canadian Catholic Historical Association, Historical Studies, #66*, pp.34–55

Boulanger J-C. (1993) (Ed.) *Dictionnaire Québécois d'Aujourd'hui*. St. Laurent, PQ: Dicorobert Inc.

Boulton M. (1994) *Just a minute: Glimpses of our great Canadian Heritage*. Toronto: Little, Brown and Company (Canada) Limited

Bowley A. L. (1909) *Macaulay's History of England*, Chapter III. Oxford: Clarendon Press

Bowman B. (1973) *Dateline: Canada*. Toronto: Holt, Rinehart and Winston of Canada, Limited

Brown J. S. H. (1980) *Strangers in Blood*. Vancouver: British Columbia Press

Bruns R. (1986) *Thomas Jefferson*. New York: Chelsea House Publication

Campbell M. W. (1974) *The Nor'Westers, the Fight for the Fur Trade*. Toronto: Macmillan of Canada

Cannon J. & R. Griffiths (1988) *Oxford Illustrated History of the British Monarchy*. Oxford: Oxford University Press

Carey J. (1987) (Ed.) *Eye-witness to History*. Cambridge: Harvard University Press

Carl, G. C. (1963) *Guide to Marine Life of British Columbia*. Victoria: British Columbia Provincial Museum, Department of Recreation and Conservation

Clarke S. A. (1905) *Pioneer days of Oregon history*. Cleveland: The Arthur Clark Company. Vol. I–II

Clark R. (1997) *River of the west: A chronicle of the Columbia*. New York: Picador

Codignola L. (1988) "Conflict or Consensus? Catholics in Canada and in the United States, 1780-1820", *The Canadian Catholic Historical Association*. Ottawa: Historia Ecclesiae Catholicae Canadensis Publications. Inc., pp.43–59

Coel M. (2000) *The Spirit Woman*. New York: Berkeley Prime Crime

Cole J. (2001) (ed.) *This Blessed Wilderness: Archibald's letters from the Columbia 1822–44*. Vancouver: UBC Press

Creighton D. (1957) *Dominion of the North: A History of Canada*. Toronto; Macmillan Company of Canada Limited

Crowther M. O. (1932) *The Book of Letters: What Letter to Write for Every Purpose, Business and Social. The Etiquette of Correspondence*. New York: Doubleday, Doran & Co., Inc.

Cunningham Noble E. Jr. (2000) *Jefferson vs. Hamilton: Confrontations that Shaped a Nation*. Boston, MA: Bedford/St. Martin's

Darnton Robert (1984) *The Great Cat Massacre*. New York: Basic Books Inc.

Davis N. Z. (1995) *Women in the margins: Three Seventeenth Century Lives*. Cambridge, MA: Harvard University Press

Dictionnaire biographique du Canada, Vol. IX, Quebec: Les Presses de l'Université Laval

Dobbs C. C. (1975) *Men of Champoeg*. Cottage Grove, Oregon: Emerald Valley Craftsmen

Dobbs K. & M. Harris (1984) *Historic Canada*. Toronto: Discovery Books

Dubé P. (1990) *Charlevoix, Two Centuries at Murray Bay*. Montreal: McGill-Queen's University Press

Dumont M. (2001) *Découvrir la Mémoire des Femmes*. Montreal: les éditions du remue-ménage

Dye E. (1926) *McLoughlin and Old Oregon, A chronicle*. New York: Doubleday, Page & Co.

Easterbrook W. T. & H. G. Aitken. (1965) *Canadian Economic History*. Toronto: Macmillan Company of Canada Limited

Eaton D. & S. Urbanek (1996) *Paul Kane's Great Nor-West*. Vancouver: UBC Press

Eccles W. J. (1967) *The Ordeal of New France*. Toronto: CBC

Egerton H. (1923) *A Historical Geography of the British Dominions: Canada. Volume V*. Oxford: Clarendon Press

Finley G. E. (1979) *George Heriot, 1759-1839*. Ottawa: National Gallery of Canada

Fogdall A. B. *(1978) Royal Family of the Columbia: Dr. J. McLoughlin and his Family*. Fairfield, WA: Ye Galleon Press

Fox C. (1992) (ed.) *London – World City 1800–1840*. New Haven: Yale University Press & Museum of London

Franchere G. (1968) *A Voyage to the Northwest Coast of America*. New York: Citadel Press. (M. Quife ed.)

Gulland S. (1998) *Tales of Passion, Tales of Woe*. Toronto: HarperCollins

Harper J. R. (1976) *William G. R. Hind, 1833–1889*. Ottawa: National Gallery of Canada

Herbert R. (1988) *Impressionism, Art, Leisure & Parisian Society*. New Haven, USA: Yale University Press

Herman A. (2001) *How the Scots Invented the Modern World: The True Story of how Western Europe's Poorest Nation Created our World & Everything In It*. New York: Three Rivers Press

Hopkins J. C. (1901*) Histoire Populaire du Canada: Quatre Cents ans des Annuales de à Moitié d'un Continen*t. Toronto: publisher not stated. (trans. B. Sulte)

Huck B. (2000) *Exploring the Fur Trade Routes of North America*. Winnipeg: Heartland Associates of Canada

Isherwood J. (1972*) A Historical Walking Tour of Sainte-Anne de Bellevue*. Ste. Anne de Bellevue PQ: Shoreline pamphlet

Jennings J., Hodgins B. W. & D. Small (1999) (Eds*.) The Canoe in Canadian Culture*: Ottawa; The Canada Council for the Arts. Natural Heritage Books

Jones C. (1994) *Cambridge Illustrated History: France*. Cambridge, UK: University of Cambridge

Jones N. (1968) *Marcus Whitman: The Great Command*. Portland, OR: Binfords & Mort, Publishers

Keith H. L. (2001) "'Shameful mismanagement, wasteful extravagance and the most unfortunate dissension,' George Simpson's Misconceptions of the North West Company." *Oregon Historical Quarterly* 102:4, pp.434–454

Lebel J-M. & B. Ostiguy. (1999) *Saint Anne de Beaupré: An Inspiration*. Québec: Les Éditions de Chien Rouge

Lemieux L. (1970) "Mgr. Provencher et la Pastorale Missionaire des Évêques de Québec" *The Canadian Catholic Historical Association Study Session Proceedings*. Winnipeg, Manitoba, pp.31–49

Levesque R. (1988) *Légendes de la Rivière du Loup*. Rivière du Loup: Sylvain Dionne Communications

Lloyd-Evans B. (1989) (Ed.) *The Batsford Book of English Poetry*. London: B. T. Batsford Ltd.

MacKay D. (1966) *The Honorable Company*. Toronto: McClelland and Stewart Ltd.

Maclennan H. (1977) *Seven Rivers of Canada*. Toronto: Macmillan of Canada

Margetson S. (1971) *Regency London*. London: Cassell

Marie de l'Incarnation (1963). *Formulaire de Prières a Usage des Élèves des Ursulines*. Québec: Ursuline Convent

Mackie R. S. (1997*) Trading Beyond the Mountains: The British Fur Trade on the Pacific 1793–1843*. Vancouver: UBC Press

Matthews G. (1992) *The Rise of Public Woman: Women's Power and Women's Place in the United States, 1630–1970*. Oxford: Oxford University Press

McLoughlin J. (1971) "The Indians from Fort William to Lake of the Woods," *Amphore VIII*, Spring/Summer 5–16. Introduction by Richard Dillon. MacGill University Mss. #2364

McMillan A. D. & E. Yellowhorn (2004) *First Peoples in Canada.* Vancouver: Douglas & McIntyre

Merk F. (1995) *Manifest Destiny and Mission in American History.* Cambridge: Harvard University Press

Merk F. (1978) *History of the Westward Movement.* New York: Alfred A. Knopf

Merk F. (1967) *The Oregon Question: Essays in Anglo-American Diplomacy & Politics.* Cambridge, MA: Harvard University Press

Merk F. (1966) *The Monroe Doctrine and American Expansionism, 1843–1849.* New York: Alfred A. Knopf

Merk F. (1968) *Fur Trade and Empire, Geo. Simpson's Journal.* Cambridge, Mass; Harvard University Press

Morris, J. (1973) *Heaven's Command, an Imperial Progress*. New York: Bantam Books

Morris J. (1979) *Farewell the trumpets: An imperial retreat.* London: Penguin Books

Morris J. (1979) *Pax Britannica: The Climax of an Empire*. London: Penguin Books

Morrison D. N. (1999) *Outpost, John McLoughlin and the Far Northwest.* Portland, OR: Oregon Historical Society

Morrison, J. (2001) *Superior Rendezvous Place.* Toronto: Natural Heritage Books

Morrison, J. (2003) (Ed.) *Lake Superior to Rainy Lake.* Thunder Bay, ON: Thunder Bay Historical Society

Murray J. (1817*) Statement Respecting the Earl of Selkirk's Settlement Upon the Red River in North America.* Toronto: Coles Publishing Co. reprint 1974

Newman P. C. (1987) *Caesars of the Wilderness*. Markham, ON: Penguin Books Canada Ltd.

Newman P. C. (1985) *Company of Adventurers*. Markham, ON: Penguin Books Canada Ltd.

Nisbet J. (1994) *Sources of the River: Tracking David Thompson across Western North America*. Seattle: Susquatch Books

Palmer R. R. & J. Colton (1965) *A History of the Modern World*. Toronto: Random House Canada, Ltd.

Pannekoek F. (1991) *A Snug Little Flock: The Social Origins of the Riel Resistance, 1869–70*. Winnipeg, MA: Watson & Dwyer Publishing

Paterson Merrill D. (1970) *Thomas Jefferson & the New Nation*. New York: Oxford University Press

Pearsall J & B. Trumble (2002) (Eds.) *Oxford English Reference Dictionary*. Oxford: Oxford University Press

Pearse T. (1968) *Birds of the Early Explorers in the Northern Pacific* Comox, BC: "The Close," Centennial of Canadian Confederation Project

Percival Smith R. (2001) *Captain McNeill and his wife, the Nishga chief*. Surrey, BC: Hancock House Publishers Ltd.

Peterson Merrill D. (1962) *The Jefferson image in the American Mind*. New York: Oxford University Press

Reid D. (1999) *Kriegoff: Images of Canada*. Toronto: Douglas & McIntyre & Art Galley of Ontario

Rich E. E. (1968) *The Letters of John McLoughlin from Fort Vancouver to the Governor and Committee; First Series 1825–38*. Nendeln, Liechenstein: Kraus Reprint Ltd.

Rich E. E. (1968) *The letters of John McLoughlin from Fort Vancouver to the Governor and Committee; second series 1839-44*. Nendeln, Liechenstein: Kraus Reprint Ltd.

Rich E. E. (1967) *The Fur Trade and the Northwest to 1857*. Toronto: McClelland and Stewart Ltd.

Roberts K. G. & P. Shackleton (1983) *The Canoe*. Toronto: Macmilllan of Canada

Ross A. (1972) *The Red River Settlement.* Edmonton: Hurtig Publishers (reprint)

Rumilly R. (1980) *La compagnie du Nord-Ouest: une Épopée Montrealaise*, tomes 1 & 2. Montreal: Fides

Saum L. O. (1965) *The Fur Trader and the Indian.* Seattle: University of Washington Press

Searle A. (2003) "A beautiful friendship: British and French artists of the 19th century constantly fed off each other. The results were tempests, wars, carnage and madness," reprint from the *Guardian.* www.guardian.co.uk/arts/features/story

Seigel J. (1986) *Bohemian Paris, Culture, Politics, and the Boundaries of Bourgeois Life,* 1830–1930. New York: Viking Books

Shakespeare W. (1987) *The complete works of William Shakespeare.* New York: Chathan River Press

Silver A. (1991) *Where the Ghost Horse Runs.* New York: Ballantine Books

Silver A. (1990*) Lord of the Plains.* New York: Ballantine Books

Silver A. (1988) *Red River Story.* New York; Ballantine Books

Slacum W. (1972) *Memorial of William A. Slacum Praying for Compensation for his Services in Obtaining Information in Relation to the Settlements on the Oregon River.* Fairfield WA: Ye Galleon Press (reprint)

Smyth E. (1998) "Women Religious and their Work of History in Canada, 1639–1978: A Starting Point for Analysis". *Canadian Catholic Historical Association Historical Studies #64*, pp.135–150

Soeur Sainte-Marie (1961*) Sous le Signe de l'Esprit, la Pédagogie de Marie de l'Incarnation.* Montreal: Le Messager Canadien

Stellamaris Mission (1972) *Catholic Church Records of the Pacific Northwest, Vol. I & II and Stellamaris Mission.* St. Paul, OR: French Prairie Press. (trans. M. de Lores Wormell Warner.)

Stenson F. (2000) *The Trade.* Vancouver: Douglas & McIntyre

Time-Life Books (1977) *The Canadians.* Alexandria, Virginia

Turgeon C. (2002*) Le fil de l'art: Les broderies des Ursulines de Quebec.* Quebec: Musee du Quebec & Musee de Quebec

Ursulines de Québec (1995*) Repertoire Numerique Detaille de la Series 1/k éducation (1639–1995.)* Québec: Les Archives des Ursulines de Québec

Ursulines de Québec. (1989) *Les Ursulines de Québec 1639–1989.* Québec: L'ecole des Ursulines de Québec

Ursulines de Québec. (1989*) 350 Ans au Coin du Four.* Québec: Ursulines de Québec. Author

Ursulines of Québec. *(1897) Glimpses of the Monastery: Ursulines of Quebec During Two Hundred Years, 1639–1839.* Québec: L. J. Demers & Frère. By a member of the order

Van Kirk (1980) *Many Tender Ties: Women in Fur Trade Society in Western Canada, 1670-1870.* Winnipeg: Watson and Dwyer

Vibert E. (1997) *Traders' Tales: Narratives of Cultural Encounters in the Columbia Plateau.* Norman, OK: University of Oklahoma Press

Villeneuve R. (1998) *Quebec Silver.* Ottawa: National Gallery of Canada

Webber B. (1994) (Ed*.) Dr. J. McLoughlin, Master of Fort Vancouver, Father of Oregon.* Mefford, OR: Webb Research Group Publisher

Wilson B. G. (1988) *Colonial Identities, Canada from 1760 to 1815.* Ottawa: National Archives of Canada

Woodley E. C. (1949) *Untold Tales of Old Quebec.* Toronto: J. M. Dent & Sons (Canada) Ltd.

Woodham-Smith C. (1972) *Queen Victoria.* New York: Dell Publishing

Wright R. (2001) *Clara Callan.* Toronto: Harper Perennial Canada

Xydes G. (1992). *Alexander Mackenzie and the Explorers of Canada.* New York: Chelsea House Publications

UNPUBLISHED AND GENERIC DOCUMENTS

Many archives and public records have reference materials or family documents. Those that were consulted during the preparation of this book include the following:

John McLoughlin: Oregon Historical Society (Portland), John

McLoughlin House (Oregon City), Fort Vancouver National Historic Site (Washington State), University of Washington (Seattle), HBC Archives and Record Society (Winnipeg), Glenbow Museum Archives (Calgary), Soc. d'Histoire Rivière-du-Loup (Québec), Fort Frances Museum (Ontario), Thunder Bay Library (Ontario), Province of Quebec Archives, Laval University (Quebec City), Chatham Library on Riverside (Kent, England).

David McLoughlin: Wellcome Library for the History and Understanding of Medicine (London), Guildhall Library (London), Royal College of Physicians and Surgeons Library (London), British Library Manuscript Collections (London).

Sr. St. Henri: Ursuline Convent Archives (Quebec City).

Generic: Fraser Fonds, National Archives of Canada (Ottawa), Archives Nationales du Québec (Laval) (Québec City), McGill University Library Rare Books and Special Collections (Montreal), McCord Museum (Montreal), University of British Columbia Archives and Rare Book Collection (Vancouver), British Columbia Provincial Archives (Victoria), Terrebonne Municipal Library (Quebec), Library and Archives Canada (Ottawa), Kent Country Records (England), Robarts Library, University of Toronto (Ontario), City of Toronto Archives (Ontario), Public Library Board of Toronto (Ontario), Canadian Institute for Historical Microreproductions (Ottawa), Burke's Peerage (London), Vancouver Island Regional Library (British Columbia).

SITE SPECIFIC

The Banff Centre in the Rocky Mountains was an inspirational setting for the genesis of this book. The writing programme is an excellent cradle for emergent writers and Fred Stenson was a mentor who rocked the cradle as this book was formulated. Athena Press ensured the manuscript matured. Thank you.

CDS AND VIDEOS

Benedictine Monks of St. Michaels. (1998) *Gregorian Chants.* Santa Monica, CA: Delta Music Laserlight. Two discs

Brown R. and the Northern Roots Band. (2004) *The Big Lonely* Thunder Bay, ON: Starsilk Records, with information pamphlet

Filmwest Production (1991*) Metis Nation. My Partners, My People.* Kelowna: author. Video, 24 minutes

L'Ensemble Nouvelle-France. (1999) *L'Epopee Mystique. Marie Guyart de l'Incarnation. Les Ursuline et Augustines.* Québec: Musée de l'Amérique Française, with information pamphlet

L'Ensemble Nouvelle-France. (1997) *Femmes, corps et âme.* Québec: Musée de L'amérique Française, with information pamphlet. Louise Courville, direction

L'Ensemble Nouvelle-France. (1997) *Musique du Québec, L'Epoque de Julie Papineau (1975-1862).* Québec: Musée de L'Amérique Française, with information pamphlet

L'Ensemble Stadaconé. (2002) *L'Aventure en Nouvelle-France.* Québec: Disques Lyres Records

McGill Symphony Orchestra. (1988) *Three Metis Songs from Saskatchewan.* Sung by Maureen Forrester. Montreal: McGill Records

Pays de Bretagne. (1998) *L'Esprit Celte, Musiques et Chants de Bretagne.* France: Editions Freeway

Rocky Mountain Trench Discovery Center Society. (1995) *Spirit of Discovery.* Golden, BC: Golden and District Chamber of Commerce

Warner M. (1972) *Catholic Church Records of the Pacific Northwest* St. Paul, Oregon: French Prairie Press

Wilson N. (1999) *John McLoughlin, "Master of the Oregon Country."* Oregon City: Rose City Radio Corp. McLoughlin House

Printed in the United States
103867LV00001B/4-36/A

9 781844 017492